# THE OTHER

*The Other*

ANTHEM PRESS
An imprint of Wimbledon Publishing Company Limited (WPC)
First published in the United Kingdom in 2016 by
ANTHEM PRESS
75–76 Blackfriars Road
London SE1 8HA

www.anthempress.com

Original title: *Oteki*

Originally published in Turkey by Dogan Book


A CIP record for this book is available from the British Library.

ISBN 978-1-78308-452-4

This title is also available as an ebook.

# THE OTHER

Ece Vahapoğlu

ANTHEM PRESS

"Have you ever kissed a woman?"

Kubra was startled. This was a question she had not expected. They often sparred in conversation and she was used to Esin's curiosity about the religious life and the turban,[1] but she wasn't ready to have such a subject spoken of out loud.

"N... no," she managed to say.

Esin averted her gaze shyly, with a slightly flirtatious air and looked up at the ceiling. She gently tossed back her blonde hair.

"Hmmm. I've never tried it either. I wonder what it's like to kiss someone of the same sex."

What was Esin trying to say?

Kübra felt uncomfortably hot. Her own emotions frightened her, probably for the first time in her life. She felt guilty and ashamed. She longed to sense Esin's skin, feel her breath and lie down beside her.

She wanted her.

She couldn't sleep for several nights. She had crossed the line; she felt attracted to a woman. She had always wanted to love innocently. She didn't want anyone to know. She didn't even want Esin to know. She was ashamed.

---

[1] A scarf worn over a bonnet to veil the hair for religious reasons is called a "turban" in Turkey. A bonnet of rougher material is worn underneath to flatten the hair and prevent the silky scarf from slipping. The veiled costume is usually completed by a raincoat or other light, long coat. – Trans.

Kübra enjoyed being with a woman who'd married for love. She enjoyed Esin's company more than that of the boy she was being forced to marry. Her fiancé did not excite her at all. Maybe deep down, she envied Esin, who could tell? Esin felt a secret bond with this girl, although Kübra came from a world she knew nothing about. Through Kübra's eyes she saw herself differently. Without her, she might never have discovered the woman she now saw in herself: a woman who could love the *other* without prejudice, welcome her into her life; a different sort of woman, one who didn't shun religion; a person not all that different from Esin but someone she hadn't known existed until now.

They were both experiencing feelings they'd never had before. They couldn't figure each other out but were growing closer and enjoyed the time they spent together. They seemed to fill each other's unfinished spaces.

This was a moment they would never forget, one that might even hold a bit of happiness they would not be able to measure. The electricity between them filled the room. Would what seemed inevitable be realized?

That tiny moment seemed to last for hours. They felt so strange they could not even look one another in the eye and smile. This was something rare, a chance not everyone had. A girl engaged to be married, a married woman; one veiled, one not. What was this? What kind of pull was this? Was it love? Mutual attraction? Curiosity? A quest for new experiences? Did they want to *be* with each other? Learn something? Or was it a game?

They had run into each other a few months earlier at an award ceremony, and that insignificant coincidence took them to a place they'd never expected to be.

Six Months Earlier

She looked into the bright spot lit mirror one last time. Her make-up was right, bringing out her straight blonde hair and big blue eyes. In a few moments, she would walk out to face a select audience of five hundred.

She was a young woman who preferred to make her own destiny. She took orders from no one, was rarely intimidated, and did not get lost in the crowd. She was not the sort to live according to the expectations of others; she did not let herself go with the flow. You could say she was a bit of a narcissist. She'd obeyed her parents as a child but did not let her lovers lead her around when she grew up, and she wasn't dominated by her husband now. And if she had children someday, she was not going to be restricted by that either.

In her country, unions between women, "free" by Western standards, and Eastern-style men, offered some hope, though they might not go smoothly. Turkey's role as a bridge between East and West had become confusing for everyone by now, foreign or Turk. One lived a modern life in all senses while respecting tradition. This was a society nurtured on differences. Some were lucky enough to make a synthesis of it all but others did not know who they were.

Like other girls educated abroad by their Westernized families, Esin had a comfortable life compared to the general run of society. She'd had lovers before she married, did as she liked and traveled; she had a broad social life and work that put her before the public. True, girls from conservative backgrounds too were having freer relationships these days and trying to choose their own professions.

After studying in the States, she had returned to Istanbul and done public relations and marketing for several companies. While working in the international news section of a TV station, she'd taken lessons in diction and begun hosting evening business events, award ceremonies and select gatherings. She liked being out front; she liked her work.

Once again, she was hosting an award ceremony, this one for "The Most Successful Personalities of the Year" chosen by a financial magazine. Although the winners were supposed to have been selected by the magazine's readers, it was clear at a glance that, that was not really the case.

The awards had been given in line with the loyalties of the conservative publishing group that put out the magazine.

True, the "Businessman of the Year" and "Businesswoman of the Year" were prominent, modern personalities but the other award winners represented a "certain" social sector.

The name of the "Entrepreneur of the Year," Hikmet Akansan, seemed familiar to her. He was often mentioned in the press but she knew the name in another connection.

For now, she had to focus and put such thoughts aside. She was about to go onstage and give the presentation.

Esin Ulucan Aksoy had taken part in a continuous string of such events during the last few years and this one did not unnerve her. She impressed people with her speech, her fine diction, her lively tone and emphasis; her presentations were a success. It was the pleasant thrill of being out in front of people that made her heart beat faster for a few seconds. When she first started doing this work, she had not been able to control her nerves. She used to have to press her hands on her breast and take a few deep breaths before she could walk out to the podium. And when she did go out on stage, she felt completely naked before the crowd. Only after she began reading out the text in her hand, did her self-confidence return, and the sense of being naked in public pass.

The lights went down in the large, air-conditioned hall. The music started, the spotlight fell on Esin, and she walked out onto the stage. The wireless microphone attached around the back of her head to her ears clashed a bit with the classic style of her beige suit but it was the most comfortable sort of microphone for this kind of work. She looked out toward the audience, glanced imperceptibly at her notes, and began. As she uttered the word "welcome," the hall exploded with applause. She introduced the first speaker. Then one by one, she called the award winners and award presenters to the stage.

The Minister of Finance was presenting The "Entrepreneur of the Year" award to Hikmet Akansan. Esin's attention was drawn to a slight stirring in the front rows of the audience. She saw a familiar face in a seat just behind the protocol row but couldn't make out who it was. A young woman with her head veiled was clapping enthusiastically. "She's probably a relative of Akansan," Esin thought.

In recent years, she'd begun to see more turbaned women at these sorts of events. The change taking place in the protocol row was arresting. It was a tableau reflecting the change in the country, and it was engraved on Esin's consciousness.

As the flash of the cameras exploded and pictures were taken, Esin was thinking, "Who was that girl?"

The award winners overdid their expressions of gratitude at the microphone and the ceremony ended later than it should have. By the time she came down off the stage, she noticed that her high heels were killing her. She took a seat in the audience once the crowd had gradually begun to disperse. Just as she was thinking, "If only everyone would leave, so I can get out of these high heels and put on my Babettes," the girl in the turban she'd seen a little while before, came up to her. "You were great, it was a lovely ceremony. Congratulations," she said nervously. "I got a bit excited when my father received an award." She paused and continued: "Actually, I wanted to say something else. I think we went to the same school. I'm Kübra ..."

Esin was thinking it couldn't be in lycée, because her lycée here in Istanbul didn't allow girls to wear the turban. So it must have been a college in the States, in New York.

Kübra had apparently got over her reticence, for she was speaking in a friendlier tone.

"We never talked to each other at school but I remember you. You've changed your hair color."

"Yes, I'm a blonde now," Esin said a bit haughtily. "I don't remember your hair. How could I, since I never saw it ..." She stopped. Was this any time to say something like that? If only she could control that tongue of hers! What was it to her if the girl's head was covered? Especially, here ... And her father was one of the award winners.

Kübra frowned, realizing what Esin meant. She remembered how wearing a veil had served her as a shield in the crazy rush of New York City. She found peace of mind in being veiled. She withdrew into her own world and the madness of the world outside didn't bother her.

Now there was tension, even if not a lot. Esin sat there uncomfortably, not knowing how to restart the conversation. She knew it wouldn't help to say something flattering. Just then, Kübra's father Hikmet Bey came up to them.

"So, you know each other?"

"Yes, Papa, we went to school together in the States. She was in her last year when I started," said Kubra.

Surprised Kübra would have known that, Esin turned to her father and held out her hand. "Congratulations on your award." Hikmet Akansan did not like to shake women's hands but in recent years, he had had to get used to such civil behavior because of his rising position. He shook Esin's hand.

Hikmet Bey's presence warmed things up a bit. Esin turned to Kübra, wanting to repair the blunder she'd made: "Can you give me your telephone number or business card?"

Kübra smiled. "I've just started working in my father's company, and I don't have a business card yet but I can give you my cell phone number."

Esin noticed how sweet and pretty her face was when she smiled. The scarf and long coat she wore concealed her beauty. Esin had involuntarily focused on her dress and paid no attention to anything else. How that smile changed her whole appearance!

Father and daughter said goodbye and left.

Esin left the hall soon after. To avoid the parking ordeal, she had chosen not to come in her car. She jumped into a taxi and fished around in her purse for her cell phone. She looked at the time; it was almost nine. Alp had asked her to call when she was finished with work. Maybe they would meet out somewhere.

Sometimes, happiness is crossing off something on your to-do list. You feel better when you get things done.

Esin was full of adrenaline after a successful job and never wanted to go home and put up her feet or sleep, no matter how tired she was. She'd rather relax by going to see friends and chat.

For her, the point of working was to be able to create a style of life which pleased her. She believed she would be happy in her private life if she was successful at work. Her husband felt the same way. They didn't see being male or female as superior; they thought they completed one another.

Alp's voice was warm on the phone: "Did my baby finish her job?" he asked as soon as he picked up. There were other voices in the background, so he must be out somewhere. "Yes, darling, I've left the hotel. Where are you?"

"The weather was so nice, Volkan and I came up to Bebek. We're at Lucca. Come and join us."

It was perfect. She would enjoy sharing the sweetly tired thrill of work well done while her adrenaline was at its peak.

In fine weather, Istanbul traffic was always like rush hour. Though the taxi driver leaned on his horn, trying to pass, he wasn't having much success making progress down the shore road.

As they approached Bebek, she thought how much the sweet little shore village looked like Sausalito. She'd heard so much about that seaside town. She'd visited it while traveling around the States two years ago. The moment she got there, she thought: "It's the image of Bebek!"

After some delay, she arrived at the latest Turkish Sausalito hot spot – the Lucca Cafe. She wanted to be in a crowd but was glad it wasn't the meat market it usually was. She wanted to kiss her handsome young husband as soon as possible, not make her way across the room, stopping to greet everyone she knew.

Alp and Volkan were talking stocks as usual. Maybe they just did that when she was around, putting on a workaholic air, who knew. She was sure they talked about women when she wasn't there. Volkan worked in advertising but played the market as well. He knew which stocks had peaked, which were on the rise, and which were expected to fall. He didn't like to call it "playing the market"; he "invested."

However good it was for a man to be successful, it was boring for him to go on and on about it when he was with his wife or lover. Sometimes, Alp and Volkan so overdid their stock talk, it would have been more exciting if they talked about the eternal rivalry between the soccer teams, Galatasaray and Fenerbahçe. Esin still couldn't fathom why these two good friends suddenly became enemies when the subject turned to soccer. One day, Alp had said: "When you're passionate about something, it goes beyond logic. The *other* is a stranger, your enemy. A Fenerbahçe supporter isn't likely to put up with a Galatasaray fan."

Esin realized they'd been on stocks for half an hour. "Enough, boys, I can't breathe. Isn't there something else to talk about?" She didn't mean to scold them but like every woman when she's out with her man, she wanted to be the center of attention. She'd been married to Alp for six months and wanted his feelings for her to always stay fresh. Passion shouldn't cool in a few months. Though many women in the world of finance had been in love with Alp before they'd married, he now belonged to her. His mind should be on his beautiful young wife.

Ah! Sometimes, it made life unbearable to always be expecting things. If only she could really "love without expectations"... Fat chance. Just one more thing she knew she should do but couldn't!

# Kübra's Days
## (Family)

She was sitting with her father in the back seat of the black Mercedes their bearded chauffeur Cenan Efendi drove. The car was new, thanks to Hikmet Bey's increasing success in the past few years. They must have been suffering their share of Istanbul's traffic fate, for the car only managed to inch across the Bosphorus Bridge. Kübra and her father, Hikmet Bey, talked little as they drove to their home in Ümraniye district. There was always a certain distance between them. They were not quite intimate, nor were they cold to one another. Hikmet Bey did not have a male heir and had decided to groom his middle daughter, Kübra, to take over the business when the time came.

He was an enterprising man. He was cool-headed by nature. He used his composure as a shield. He was the sort of person who seized victory silently; he knew how to get things done. It could even be said that he had amassed a fortune in the last few years. His marriage to Nadide Hanım was arranged when he was very young and they had three children. Their eldest daughter married and had children early. She led the life of a housewife. The youngest was still in school.

Their middle daughter, Kübra, was the boldest of the three. She had studied hard and wanted to work hard and be a success. She was not the sort of young woman to be interested in marriage. Her father realized this about her, and although his peers did not look kindly upon career women, he'd made a place for her by his side and begun to teach her the business.

New Istanbul suburbs like Ümraniye began as settlements built by conservative migrants from the countryside, and although Ümraniye, on the Anatolian side of the Bosphorus, was the most swiftly urbanizing of these districts and its population was increasing rapidly, it was exemplary in preserving its conservative character. Hikmet Bey had moved there as a youth. It formed a striking mosaic of neighborhoods rich and poor which reflected the country's most recent era of development with its own up-to-date modern high society as well as secluded networks of families insulated from urban life.

The Akansan family had migrated from the central Anatolian town of Kayseri. Hikmet Bey and Nadide Hanım were both born there. With his native talent for business, Hikmet Akansan was like most Kayserians: hard-working, clever, and charitable. The people of Kayseri drove a hard bargain and knew the value of money but did not hesitate to share their wealth when it came to good works. Hikmet Bey was that sort of person. He loved money but knew how to spend it for the good of his community. In short, he was a typical Kayseri man. Once he'd set himself up in business in Istanbul, he returned to Kayseri to find a proper wife.

His relatives had suggested Nadide Hanım. In no time at all, they were married and moved to Istanbul immediately. While the children grew up, Nadide Hanım's life was in the home, and her neighbors made up her circle of friends.

Now, thanks to the success Hikmet Akansan had achieved through his enterprise, wit and the network of relationships he established, their home was filled with expensive furnishings. There were two huge plasma television screens in the house, one in the guest salon and the other in the family living room. The floors were covered with thick carpets and fine flat-weave Kayseri kilims bordered with flower and vine motifs. Crystal gewgaws decorated every corner of the house. But Nadide Hanım wanted to move. She had her eye on the beautiful villas of Çavuşbaşı, also on Istanbul's Asian shore. Her eldest daughter, Müberra, was living in a large, airy villa in Florya on the European side and could not praise the peace and quiet and her rich neighbors enough. But once a person got used to one side of the Bosphorus, it was not easy to move to the other side.

The black Mercedes drew up in front of the house and parked. Hikmet Bey got out hurriedly without waiting for his daughter, went up to the door and rang the bell. Kübra followed after her father, a bit cowed. She had got used to walking silently behind men when she was small. This was a custom widespread in male-dominated society and religious circles in particular. Power was in the hands of men. They earned more money, and in most homes, the man was the sole bread-winner.

Hikmet Bey took off his lace-up leather shoes, so highly polished that their sheen could be seen from a hundred meters away, uttered the "Bismillah" and stepped into the house, right foot first. Nadide Hanım noticed Cenan Efendi standing in the doorway and put on the headscarf she always kept ready in the coat cupboard. She bent over and placed her husband's slippers before him. She wished Cenan Efendi a good evening and closed the front door. She took off her scarf and rearranged her hair. Kübra took off the high-heeled shoes she had worn for the award ceremony and stepped into her soft slippers.

As Hikmet Bey wished his wife a good evening and headed for the salon, Nadide called out behind him, "How did it go, Bey? Let me have a look at your award."

He proudly handed over the heavy, cheap glass trophy. "Oh, well, my dear, they have to give these things out to someone," he said, as if receiving awards were something that happened to him every day.

Kübra went upstairs to her room. She put down her handbag and went into the bathroom to wash her hands and take off her turban. First, she removed the silk scarf and then the bonnet underneath which prevented the material of the outer layer from slipping.

She had white skin and blue eyes. She was a beautiful young woman. When she met her own eyes in the mirror, she found a sad expression there. She gave it no further thought and left the bathroom to take off her dress and put on something more comfortable. Her father, TV remote in hand, was channel-surfing. Kübra went to the other end of the salon to help her mother set the table.

The maid they employed looked after the general cleaning and tidying up. But as the lady of the house, Nadide Hanım set the table, especially if Bey was eating. No matter how tired she might be, Nadide Hanım never left that task to anyone else. Her mother had been the same way. In fact, her mother had never had a maid. Nadide Hanım was a skilled and efficient housewife. She watched over the day maids, and if she didn't like their work, she did it over herself. She was an expert seamstress and did fine embroidery in lace. She regularly embroidered border patterns into her own and her daughters' headscarves.

The youngest member of the family, Büşra, was supposedly doing her homework in her room. But Kübra was certain her little sister was sitting in front of her computer, reading the latest gossip about pop stars on the internet. She called out to Büşra to come help set the table.

Hikmet Bey liked the whole family to be present at dinner. Büşra had secretly been eating potato chips in her room, since she didn't know when her father would be back from the award ceremony. She didn't care if she put on weight. She kept getting fatter around the waist, and new adolescent pimples kept sprouting on her face but she loved the taste of potato chips.

At last, the four of them were seated at the table. First, there was a special Kayseri soup made with flour called "*böraaşı*," then pilaf and green beans. Büşra must have overdone the potato chips because she was full after the soup. As she played with the food on her plate, her mother reproached her, "Have you been stuffing yourself before dinner again? How many days has it been since you had a proper meal, my girl?"

Hikmet Bey's mind was still on his work. He'd chatted at the ceremony with the director of a bank from which he planned to seek credit. For religious reasons, he preferred not to have his money earn interest with CDs but had to keep an interest-bearing account at the bank in order to obtain credit or letters of indemnity. He used the interest he earned to pay taxes to the government or interest he was forced to pay elsewhere. In a globalizing world, a businessman had no choice but to conform to generally accepted practices. Hikmet Bey was not the sort of person to withdraw into his shell and make do with what he had. The state of the market was not bright and interest on credit had risen. But he was not about to wait for rates to fall while the political and economic climate of the country remained uncertain. He was excited about his projects and wanted to see them realized right away. He was going to invest heavily in new technology.

Suddenly, it occurred to him that he was at home with his family and should show an interest in his youngest daughter. It would make him feel good and anyway, that was how it should be. If he didn't, his Nadide would say, "He never takes an interest in his family."

Hikmet Bey asked Büşra the classic father question: "How is school?"

Büşra described each of her lycée classes in detail and at length, as if she'd been waiting for this moment. She was hoping to convince her father that she was worthy of studying abroad like her big sister, Kübra. She had in mind an American college in Dubai, just a couple of hours away by plane. She wouldn't be able to attend university in Turkey anyway, because she wore the turban. She'd only recently begun to cover her head but had known about the difficulties it would bring from watching what was happening around her since she was small. As her older sisters had done, Büşra wore her turban as far as the school gate and took it off before going inside. She wore one costume in school and another the rest of the time.

Kübra was distracted all through dinner and didn't speak at all. She was reviewing her way of life. She was not the sort of girl to accept things as they were without question.

When they'd finished eating, Hikmet Bey got up from the table with the formula: "My God, thanks are to You, my God."

Kübra helped to clear the table and withdrew to her room. She felt that something was missing from her life, though she didn't know what. She had felt that way for years. She thought she would be happy if only she could fill that void.

Her family's situation was good, thank God. They were comfortably well off, their ties to their relatives were strong, and they had no quarrel with anyone. She had studied at good schools and was well-educated. She had a perfectly good fiancé, though she felt no love for him. She'd heard enough stories during her school years to keep her distance from the male sex.

Her life was bound by the rules set by her father and the religious community. She could not do whatever she wanted to. The problem was not that she wore the turban; it was something else that bothered her. She herself felt the need to be veiled, nothing had been forced on her. That's what she had seen around her as she was growing up, and she couldn't imagine any other way of life. But an unknowing, a listlessness had gotten into her blood and she was imprisoned by it.

# Esin's Days
## (Alp)

Esin left the cafe with her husband at midnight. Alp was dark-skinned and broad-shouldered, a strong, handsome man. He had perfectly straight white teeth, a noble profile, and thick lips. He always looked at her lovingly, deeply.

Once again, all eyes were on them as they left the cafe. Alp paid his wife a great deal of attention in public as well as in private, putting his arms around her and kissing her. Their relationship was passionate and they loved playing little games of pleasure.

Alp's close friend, Volkan noticed some friends inside and decided to stay a bit longer. Maybe he'd find a girl to spend the night with. He was unattached in any case. He did not intend to get married yet. If things began to get serious with a girl, he had his excuse ready: "If I marry one girl, it won't be fair to the *others*." Besides, tonight that hunting instinct, special to men, was aroused and his libido was high. He got excited when he "went hunting." To choose a target and try to reach it was a great pleasure. But most of the girls around him were easy targets and once he'd had them, the thrill was gone. His way of relating to women had come to resemble chewing gum. Most of the women he slept with were like the gum he spat out when the sugar was gone. Or as the latest slang had it: they were like taxis; they gave it up to every paying customer.

When they got into the car, fatigue settled over Esin. She had managed so far on the adrenaline of the stage. The crowd in the café and having to talk above the noise, had used up all the energy she had left.

When they got home to their apartment in Etiler, all Esin wanted was to wash her face, brush her teeth, and collapse into bed.

She thought of how it used to be when she lived with her family... She'd get home after midnight, exhausted as she was now and find her retired officer father watching television in the salon. Or pretending to. Whenever she or her sister, Elif, arrived home late at night, they were sure to find him sitting in front of the TV. Coincidence or not, a few moments after they'd gone to bed, the TV would go off and their father would retire to his room. Their mother would already be asleep. He was a gentler father than he'd been during his years in the military but martial law could still be declared in the house now and then. As Esin got older, she understood that her father's authoritarian ways, like those of every parent, stemmed from his protective instinct regarding his children. And that's how it was in Turkey: fathers were controlling in all sectors of society.

Esin sighed softly and headed for the bedroom. She never went to bed without taking off her make-up. She'd wash her face and put on her creams. There were no visible lines on her face yet but she was taking preventative measures. Well, she did have very fine crow's feet around the eyes.

She hummed with pleasure because the ceremony had gone well. Then she gazed at her husband lying in bed, looking at her with desire.

She felt guilty that all she wanted to do was sleep. Her husband obviously wanted to make love to her. He laughed mischievously and groped around as if he didn't know what to do with his hands, nibbling at her. Was going to sleep without making love a sign that they had begun to be a classic married couple? She kissed her husband on the cheek and said "Good night," as if she didn't know he was waiting in anticipation. But not so long ago, she had wanted to spend every minute of her life with him. Crazy in love, they'd always been dying to touch one another.

About a year and a half ago, Esin had been to a high society cocktail party. Prominent business people were there. She always noted down dates and business meetings on her Blackberry but for some reason, she had forgotten this event at the Swiss Hotel. If her best friend, Sevim, had not called to say she'd just left the beauty parlor and would get to the party after stopping at home to change, Esin would never have remembered it was a cocktail party introducing a new product. She'd had so much on her mind lately that she'd begun to mistake one person for another. She'd had her hair set and blow-dried the day before, so there was no need to go to the beauty parlor. She stopped at home to get dressed, said hello to her parents as she passed them by and went straight to her room to choose something to wear. She didn't want to wear anything colorful. The weather was cold and a colorful outfit had to be planned well in advance. She did her hair, make-up, fingernails, and chose her jewelry accordingly.

She took her "always to the rescue" black dress out of the wardrobe. She put on her thick black mousse stockings and black high-heeled shoes and took a look in the full-length mirror. The necklace with a jeweled E, which her mother had given her one birthday and she never took off, was around her neck. If she put on a little more make-up, she'd be ready for the evening.

She'd gotten good at this when she started going out constantly in the evenings. She'd become an expert on what to wear, on what purse was appropriate for which occasion. She gauged the tone of her make-up according to the nature of the gathering. She put on her drop earrings and left, calling out to her parents, "Bye-bye, I'm out for the evening."

She slid into her little car. She'd gotten her license as soon as she was eighteen. It especially pleased her that she'd paid for the "sweet" car all by herself.

She picked up Sevim, who lived nearby in Ulus and drove down to the shore. They took Dolmabahçe Avenue, decked out on both sides with old-fashioned black-and-white pictures of Ataturk and lined with grand old trees. Esin loved this road. Driving along the Bosphorus between the magnificent trees gave her a feeling of blue melting into green.

When they got to the hotel, the guests had already moved into the ballroom. She saw him from afar as they were going down the escalator. Her heart started to beat faster. Suddenly, she had butterflies in her stomach. This wasn't just any young man; he was truly attractive and had a profound effect on Esin.

That was the first time she saw Alp.

She loved having experiences that were like scenes from a film. The handsome young man was looking at her too, standing there, wine glass in hand as she glided down the escalator. She'd always found a man in a suit attractive. The dark grey suit the tall young man was wearing obviously fit him well, and he seemed to shine in the crowded hall.

Esin was just about to say something to Sevim but stopped. "Damn, if only I'd worn something more attractive," she thought. Sevim was almost dragging her into the salon, unaware what was going on in her mind. But Esin was in no hurry; pretty boy was behind them, talking to some people.

People were finishing up their cocktails and filing into the salon for the formal introduction of the product. Sevim was already diving inside, she'd had seats saved for them. "Let's stay here a bit longer; we can go in later," Esin was saying. Men didn't easily impress her but when one did, it was as if she were struck by lightning. She couldn't get pretty boy out of her mind and was determined to meet him one way or another.

If only she knew someone in the group of people he was talking to. She'd use the excuse to go up and say hello, and after that, she'd find a way to her target. Esin always knew who was who, why they were there and what they did but lo and behold, this time she didn't know anyone in the group.

The bell to go in sounded and Esin was forced to enter the salon. She sat down next to Sevim, her mind still on the young man outside.

The lights went down and the product film began playing on the giant screen. A few moments later, someone sat down in the empty seat to her right. Although she wasn't interested in the film, she paid no attention and kept on watching.

When it was over and the lights came up, she looked around involuntarily, and Oh, my God! Pretty boy was sitting in the seat beside her.

Her heart began thudding. Instead of saying something to the man who might be the love of her life, she turned to Sevim and started talking about the film. Sevim was saying, "Uh-huh but there's nothing new; no one can come up with anything different," and Esin did not know what she was going to do. Her hands were sweating. Could he hear her heart beating?

She screwed up her courage and glanced in his direction. She wanted to see his face up close, and she wanted to get his attention. Just then, pretty boy said: "Where do I know you from?"

It took her by surprise. She was wondering whether to make a joke or feign indifference. "Maybe from the stage. I don't know..."

Pretty boy smiled. "And you're so modest. I thought maybe we'd met at some vacation spot."

Esin's mind was listening to him but her attention was on his beautiful white teeth. She paused for a few seconds and then, touching him lightly on the shoulder, said, "Let's talk later," and turned toward the stage as if she were going to miss something important. It was a smart-ass thing to do. It was as if she were staring into a great big emptiness, not watching what was going on onstage. She blushed bright red and was sure he noticed.

Finally, the product introduction was over. It was the sort of presentation that consisted of confusing technical information, a few boring announcements, and a host who added nothing interesting. Why didn't the organizations that paid for such things come up with something more watchable and enjoyable? But this was no time to think about that. There was someone she should take an interest in, or appear not to.

Accompanying her friend Esin, Sevim stood up. Clearly, she was bored too but like a typical guest, pretended not to be. As she was about to say, "C'mon, let's go," she noticed that Esin's attention was elsewhere. Esin was usually the first to be out of the salon at such events and Sevim didn't understand why she was lagging.

Aha! Was that pretty boy next to her the reason?

Esin turned to the young man. "Excuse me, what were you saying? We couldn't talk while the presentation was going on."

"No, it's not important. So we haven't met. Your face seemed familiar; maybe it's as you said."

He finished his sentence coolly and was about to get up. Esin was thinking, "Oh my God, he's getting away! What can I do to make him stay a little longer?" when Sevim came to the rescue.

"You're having a conversation, let me go and get us some drinks," Sevim said, and left them alone.

Pretty boy sat back down. "So what is your name, then?"

Esin was not expecting such a swift move and only said, "Esin." And that with a slightly irritated smart-ass air.

"I'm Alp."

Esin looked at the hand he extended to shake hers, thinking, "His hands aren't bad either, maybe his fingers are a little fat but that's okay." She put out her hand too and touched him for the first time.

Yes, their hands had touched. Was she still in lycée? She was trembling inside from his touch.

They smiled at each other. Anyone watching would have seen right away they were attracted to each other.

Alp asked about her work, asked her to explain what she meant by being on stage. Once Esin got started, she kept on talking. When she was attracted to someone, either she talked a lot or not at all. Today was a talking day. At one point, she paused for a breath and asked him what he did.

"I take it easy; well, not really, I mean... I'm a stockbroker. I spend the day running down stocks."

Esin was thinking: "If he's a stockbroker, then he's untouchable part of the day but he gets off early."

"So do you follow the New York and Tokyo exchanges too?"

She was hoping his work didn't keep him very busy. Alp smiled. "Not that much. I usually take it pretty easy." That made Esin feel better.

Telephone numbers were exchanged. Neither called the other for a few days, and at last, Alp punched in Esin's number to ask how she was. The next week Esin sent him an SMS, and instead of writing back, Alp called her and said that he was leaving the next day for two weeks' vacation in South Africa. He was going to spend New Year's Eve there.

The days would not pass for Esin, and she had a quiet New Year's. When Alp returned, she played hard to get, didn't pick up the phone when he called, and when they did talk, she turned down his suggestions of going out on a date, saying her work was keeping her too busy.

Alp wanted to find a way because he was really interested. And so Alp did. One Friday, he asked if she'd like to have dinner and go to a movie. He'd worked hard all week and his head was aching from the market. He wanted a quiet evening away from crowds. He'd be really happy if Esin would spend it with him.

Esin couldn't hold out any longer and accepted at last. There wasn't anything good on at the movies, mostly fantasy films for kids. Esin said she missed Paris and favored a French film. Thank God, it was something fun. It didn't have long scenes of some sad man staring out of a window or a distracted woman without make-up puffing on a cigarette!

They met a few times that way and then started "dating." They had their first kiss in Alp's car. They had parked some distance from Esin's parents' house and were saying goodnight. That goodnight kiss went on for half an hour, long, soft and passionate. A first kiss is very important, Esin thought. For her, it meant the beginning of a relationship and much more. She'd never forgotten the line from a youth film she'd seen years before: "A kiss is a promise."

The relationship that began with a lovely kiss became a marriage six months later. Now they'd been married for a year. She'd found a man just right for her, who didn't cause problems with former girlfriends and was self-confident but not too macho. She admired him more as time went on. He didn't try to hold her back as she went from success to success but pushed her to do even better. Although Esin took marriage seriously, they made a game of it sometimes. Once, as they were leaving the house, she'd lifted a strand of hair from the shoulder of the chic three button-sleeved jacket he wore over his French-cuffed shirt and said: "Alp, you know what I like most about being married? Lifting a strand of hair from your jacket. It makes me feel like we are a real couple. I feel like you are really mine. It makes me feel secure to run my hand over your jacket."

It was candid and deeply sincere. Alp made a gentle joke out of it: "It arouses me when you do that." Esin thought about these things now. It was the third night this week she hadn't wanted to make love but only because she was tired. That was okay; a woman had a right to be selfish too. To sleep without being touched was the thing she most wanted right now. Deep, lovely sleep…

# Kübra's Days
## (The Matchmaking Visit)

She stirred cold water into the coffee in the long-stemmed copper pot and set it on the fire. When it came just to the point of boiling and foam appeared on top, she poured the coffee into tiny cups, taking care to reserve the foam and distribute it equally until only a little flat coffee was left in the pot. She re-heated that to get an extra bit of foam, then filled the cups to the brim and turned off the stove.

There were long-stemmed coffee pots of various sizes on the kitchen counter. Kübra had to use both large and small pots to make enough coffee for the crowd of guests seated in the salon.

She made a last coffee for one in a small pot and poured it into a delicately painted porcelain cup. The foam came out nice and thick. She and the faithful family housekeeper, Auntie Kadriye, arranged all but one of the cups on a tray. Kübra wanted to put the single coffee on a separate tray. It was for the special guest – although that young man in the salon was not special to her because he did not make her happy. She lingered in the kitchen with a strange mixture of feeling: tense, excited, a bit despairing, a bit curious. She could not quite brave the salon. For the "offer" seemed serious this time.

Kübra was wearing her light-colored turban with a floral design and a matching violet blouse and long skirt. She'd applied a light layer of eyeliner and mascara, rouge and a barely visible pastel lipstick.

She felt even more uncomfortable when Auntie Kadriye said, "All right now Kübra, stop dawdling and take in the coffee."

All eyes would be on her when she carried in the huge tray. Her hands would start trembling violently, everything on the tray would spill, and she'd make a disgrace of herself. Maybe she'd run crying out of the salon.

With all this going through her mind, she turned to Auntie Kadriye and said in a tone somewhere between request and command: "You bring in the big tray first, then I'll come in with the little one."

When they'd come for her older sister, female guests had sat upstairs and men downstairs, in old-fashioned *harem-selamlık* style. Her sister had served coffee only to her mother and future mother-in-law, far from the eyes of the men.

Auntie Kadriye served the coffee. Kübra's mother Nadide Hanım was angry when she saw Kadriye instead of her daughter.

The aroma of the coffee on the tray had made itself felt before it was served to the guests in the salon. Turkish coffee made from beans, first brought to Istanbul from the province of Yemen during the reign of Sultan Suleyman the Lawgiver, had derived its name from the method of preparation special to the Turks.

The visitors had brought Turkish Delight as a gift, which was passed around before the coffee arrived. When all had received their coffee and were setting their empty cups down on side tables, Kübra dove furtively inside and got the single coffee on the small tray to serve to her future fiancé, husband, or whatever that young man was to be to her.

Another family had come to ask for Kübra. They'd seen her from afar, found out where she was from and called Nadide Hanım: "We wish to visit you at your convenience for a felicitous occasion." Nadide Hanım had said she would accept a visit. On the day the visitors were to arrive, she'd said to Kübra: "So, are we to give you away? You've only just come back from America. But get yourself ready anyway, nothing too fancy." Kübra met the visitors at the door, put the flowers they brought into a vase, made the coffee and sat with them in the salon. The guests included the prospective son-in-law, his mother, his older sister and a friend of the mother's. Kubra sat with them for a while and then left the room. She'd not been nervous because she assumed nothing would come of it anyway. The mother, representing her son, had told Nadide Hanım: "We like Kübra; she's lady-like. If you are agreeable, the two young people may meet." And she had gone on and on, praising her son. Then they'd left like any other guests. That evening at a family meeting, Nadide Hanım asked Kübra what she had to say and asked her husband what answer they should give. Kübra said: "I don't know him. If he is someone appropriate for our family, let me meet him. If I don't like him, we won't marry. But if we already know he is not appropriate, I'd rather not meet him." It was understood that she wasn't much inclined; she'd just graduated from college and come home. So her inclination was followed and the offer rejected.

But now Kübra was nervous. Her mother had already met the young man's mother. The meeting had been positive, and it was deemed appropriate for the groom's side to come for a visit. The presence of the groom's family seemed to make it more serious. The groom's mother was a plump lady with a bright face in a prayer veil. They were clearly as religious as the Akansans and perhaps more so. They lived in the Istanbul district of Fatih. They were welloff but socially conservative and did not approve of mixing between men and women.

They had come in a larger group because Kübra's father was acquainted with the groom's family. This was serious. That was why Kübra felt so uncomfortable serving coffee to Samet, her prospective husband.

Samet was tall and slim and appeared to have a gentle nature. He wore a dark well-ironed suit. The tie around his neck seemed so tight that he was almost unable to breathe.

Samet seemed to have character. He was well educated but wasn't the sort to show off in such a setting. He spoke little and well. It was clear from his mannerism that he was respectful of custom and tradition. He kissed the hands of his elders, visited only on holy days, and never failed to show respect. His plans for life were simple; he would get a good education, choose a well-mannered veiled wife, they would have children, work, be successful and live happily ever after. He had no big dreams. He did not have the spirit for excitement and thrills. And so, at the appropriate time, he would marry a presentable girl his family approved of.

Samet's father, Memduh Bey, thought very highly of Hikmet Bey. He had observed Hikmet Bey's rise in recent years. The fact that his middle daughter Kübra had returned to her country after studying in America, strengthened her status as a prospective daughter-in-law. His son Samet was a bright young man, well educated, well-mannered, and able to carry on the family business. He promised a bright future. He'd gone to middle school lycée at an Imam and Preacher's school in Konya, the city of his ancestors. He finished his university education in Istanbul, and now, he was going to have a direction in life. A marriage between the two young people was deemed appropriate by the elders. Samet had also seen Kübra from afar and liked her.

Kübra kept her eyes averted as she served coffee to the prospective groom. Samet set his cup down on the side table next to him. He lifted it again, right away, to take a sip, so as not to sit there nervously doing nothing and burned his tongue. Kübra had forgotten to set a glass of water next to the coffee and ran to the kitchen to get it. She had failed to follow the script and now looked silly. But the small incident pleased Samet. He thought it made for closeness between them. The prospective bride had run for water because the prospective groom had burned his tongue!

But that was not what Kübra was thinking. She was thinking that this old-fashioned matchmaking attempt would lead to nothing. She was nervous. She was going through this for the first time and not because sparks flew at her first sight of Samet. She didn't feel ready to get married yet. Maybe it was time but she wanted to have some success in her work life first, she wanted to prove herself. She wished to marry someone she would love, later, in her own time. Once and for all. She had no particular man in mind. She had just gotten back from America. She'd had two offers but she was content for now to stay at her mother's knee and work for her father.

She set down the glass of water and left the room. She sat with her sister, Büşra, and they listened from the hall to what was being said in the salon.

After the coffee, Samet's father formally requested Kübra in marriage, "By the command of God, by the word of the Prophet." Hikmet Bey declared he would respect the young people's decision and gave his permission for his daughter to marry. Kübra hated her father at that moment. He was acting as if she and Samet had talked it over and decided to marry.

The family elders kept on talking, acting as if everything had already been decided. Kübra was distraught. She was desperate to speak with her mother and tell her to put a stop to what was happening. As the men went on to talk about the engagement ceremony and a home for the young couple to live in, Kübra's head began to spin and everything went black before her eyes. Just then, Hikmet Bey paused, realizing he should give his daughter the right to speak as well, even if only as a formality and called out to her.

Kübra came into the salon with her eyes on the floor and sat in the first place she found empty. She felt she was being pushed into a corner. Either she would assent by silence or gather her courage and say she did not want to marry.

She swallowed, blushing and sweating until the words finally poured out of her mouth.

"You have been sitting and talking, and I mean no disrespect but the truth is I am frightened. I feel anxious, I feel there are things I want to do, things I haven't yet been able to finish. With your permission, I ... I ..."

She took a deep breath, met Samet's blankly staring eyes and said more loudly and firmly, "I do not want to get married."

With this final sentence, which seemed to echo throughout the salon, a silence fell. The guests stared at one another in shock.

At first, they just sat there not knowing what to do, realizing how much more uncomfortable their hosts must be. At last, Hikmet Bey, with his authority as father of the prospective bride, broke the silence.

"I cannot say that I am not surprised by this decision of my daughter's but neither can I force her. I am considering another solution."

Just as Kübra was feeling relieved, her fears were redoubled. It was her life at stake but at that moment her fate was between her father's lips.

"Since Kübra is not yet ready, let us wait until she is. Our son Samet plans to do a higher degree anyway; so let him take that degree and complete his military service. In the interim, our daughter will work for me and accustom herself to the idea of setting up a home of her own."

Nadide Hanım joined in: "What will we tell friends and family, Hikmet Bey? Let's at least make our promises, and we can have an engagement later. They can remain engaged for a while. Why not?"

The matchmaking ceremony was over and done with, plans had been made, and the guests had left. Nadide Hanım, Hikmet Bey and Kübra all felt like they had been run over by a train. Everyone was exhausted. Nadide Hanım's blood pressure fell and her head was spinning. She lay down in her bedroom. Auntie Kadriye made salted yogurt for her to drink. Kübra, wanting to clear the air, came to her mother's side and said imperiously: "Neither salted yogurt nor garlic have any effect on blood pressure. All you need to do is lie down and rest."

Her mother was thinking: "How is this girl not ready to marry? She can pack her things and go. A right little know-it-all she is..."

# Esin's Days
## (Indolence)

Esin felt lazy but got up in the morning and walked her husband to the door like a model wife out of a film, sending him on his way with a kiss and wishes for a successful day. She went back to bed. She was wearing a short nightie of cotton, more comfortable than slippery satin. It was Alp's favorite. "My baby doll," he'd say. She didn't like to sleep naked. No matter how much Alp insisted, she couldn't get used to it. When she went to bed at night, she had to have something on; be it panties, shorts or a T-shirt. If not, she felt too vulnerable and got cold when she woke up in the middle of the night.

Once she woke up, it was hard for her to fall asleep again. If she was sleeping deeply she could sleep till noon, and when she got up wouldn't be able to get her head straight for a long time. She needed to make some calls. And the maid was coming today. She was lying in bed, listening happily to the birds singing through the open window, undecided whether to get up or not, when her cell phone rang. It was her sister Elif.

"Esin, you won't believe it, we got Mom to eat fish."

"Whaaat? Really! How did you convince her?"

Esin sat up. She was very pleased at this news. Her mother had been battling cancer for three years. She learned to do meditation, got involved in Far Eastern philosophies, and became a vegetarian. With her constitution so weakened by medications and chemotherapy, abstaining from meat had really left her in a weakened state.

The girls were not at all pleased about this but respected their mother's decision. They didn't press her about it at first.

But she was exhausted by the slightest bit of housework and everyone was worried about her. So they began to scheme how they might get her to eat meat again. She said she absolutely would not eat red meat or chicken. The girls and their father loved fish, so they decided to try to tempt her away from vegetarianism with fish. She'd finally eaten her first fish in years, liked it very much and was happy about it.

Esin would never get back to sleep now, so she got up and headed for the galley kitchen opening onto the salon. Just then, the doorbell rang. It was the maid Döndü. Esin opened the door and went back to the kitchen. Their kitchen was modern in the extreme – embedded appliances, granite counter, and lacquered cupboards. She didn't want to fuss with bread, butter, honey, and cheese for breakfast. She poured some low-fat milk into a bowl of cornflakes.

She took up the daily papers, delivered at the door and settled into her favorite corner in the salon. This comfy armchair was her serenity corner, where she made time for herself and found equilibrium reading a little in peace. When it was cold outside, she'd throw a blanket over her knees and put her feet up on the soft, round ottoman. She munched on her cornflakes and ran her eyes over the headlines, glancing up now and then into the mirrors lining the room. Even drowsing in the morning, she found herself beautiful. A good night's sleep was better than anything.

Most of the furniture in the house was modern, though her mother-in-law's intervention had added a few antiques. They'd had an architect friend do the place. The huge mirrors were to make it look bigger; one side of the salon was mirror from floor to ceiling. There were postmodern paintings by Ismail Acar on the walls. Along the corridor, they'd hung black-and-white photographs with Istanbul themes by Ara Güler in delicate frames. It was Esin's wish that white predominate throughout. She'd been influenced by interior decorating magazines and had the house furnished in white like a hotel. According to Alp, they should use warmer tones, beige or light earthy colors and since the architect was a friend, he'd taken on all contradictions;

despite his profession. The floor of the salon was covered by a huge cream-colored rug. A wide-screen plasma TV and cinema system Alp had carefully selected, completed the furnishings. Hundreds of CDs and DVDs were filed in separate sections. At first glance, the house seemed roomy and not overly furnished.

For the first time, Esin was living in a space she herself had decorated. Was it fate? Who could tell but in the past whenever she'd decorated a lover's home, boat, summer house – from upholstery to silverware – they would immediately break up before she could enjoy it.

She looked in the mirror again and then turned back to her newspaper. It was always the same... On the top right corner of page one, there was gossip about a famous singer, and the rest was political news. There were good things going on in the country but what got into the papers was generally negative stuff. The opposition was accusing the government of something again. Page three contained all the nasty things like murders, robberies, and traffic accidents. The financial pages were full of meetings held the previous day, presentations, summits and statements made by important figures in the business world. She loved looking at the supplements printed in color. Who was seen with whom, who was invited where, who had fallen in love, who had a new album out were all in those supplements. Though most people claimed not to read gossip, everyone looked at those color supplements.

What a country! People of every class, every culture, every level of education, living together, people of every type, and every kind of happening, could be the subject of news. On the one hand, there was heavy political polemic, on the other there were beautiful girls in bikinis caressing the eye.

The profoundly religious, the conservative, radical Islamists, liberals, socialists, fascists; marginals, Ataturk-lovers, atheists, married couples, single people, live-in couples, playboys, prim and proper girls, well-mannered people, flighty types, people drowning in cash, penniless, rich, poor, fat, skinny, red-headed, olive-skinned, phony blondes – all lined up in a row. Were they really all one people or as distant from one another as could be?

Esin had been thinking about that a lot lately. There seemed to be two different kinds of people in Turkey. Two separate worlds…

On the one hand, there was a segment of people that took refuge in religion: women who covered their hair, men who went to smoke-filled coffee houses, who kept their daughters under strict supervision, liked folk songs and Arabesk music, who'd probably never read a book, never danced, never been to the theater, were not welleducated and lived sheltered lives. In recent years, she had gradually come to feel more distant from that segment which was rising with its new values from within the growing conservative middle class. On the other hand, there was a segment closer to her: women who did not cover their hair, people who were educated in private lycées and universities, had some grasp of a foreign language, who danced, who liked to have fun, who went to see films in cinemas, went to restaurants, furnished their homes tastefully, allowed their daughters to date (even if they didn't like to allow them), who enjoyed a wide range of music genres, drank alcohol, read newspapers, and lived a western lifestyle. These two segments of the population were completely separate. No one knew what they shared in common, or didn't consider that important. Even their way of believing in God, their way of viewing religion, was different. People from both these segments spoke in terms of "us" and the "*others*."

Esin finished her breakfast and left the salon. She went into the bathroom to take a shower and saw that Döndü had separated the whites from the clothes in the hamper and was forcing the washing machine door closed. There was a lot of laundry. She didn't like to use the machine half-full because it wasted water and electricity. Esin watched as Döndü put a measure of detergent into the machine. She was thinking "that's enough," when Döndü put in another measure. Esin walked up to her and scolded, "What are you doing? Don't put so much in. One measure is enough."

When Döndü was finished with the laundry, Esin took her shower. She put on a crisp, clean dress with a floral design that just came to her knees. Then she went to the computer and checked her email while making a list of people she had to call. She always did two things at once. She hated to waste time and was always in a hurry. Even so, she was a perfectionist and didn't compromise even when she did a number of things at the same time. That was partly why she had climbed the ladder to success at such a young age.

It could be said that she had a good career. She worked as a moderator and presenter at important ceremonies. If she hadn't married, she could have been more aggressive in her work but she'd understood that career wasn't everything in this life. Many of her mature friends gave themselves over exclusively to work: "No man, no relationship, especially, no husband." But not Esin.

This was an era when mothers tried to get their girls to marry as soon as possible but warned them: "You must have a profession, my girl, never be dependent on a man." Women in this dilemma struggled to be successful. To perform well at work, to be a success, to have a good life, to care for one's appearance, to be healthy, to be a good cook and find the right man… One had to be good at everything these days.

Yet people were getting married later in Turkey like everywhere else. True, among rural people in Anatolia, girls were still married off very young. Although among the "*others*," that is to say, the conservative urban segment, girls were not married very young, it was considered best to marry as soon as one finished college.

Recent changes in family law had made it possible for Esin to use her maiden name as well as her husband's. She liked that a lot. How could she change the name she'd had from birth at the drop of a hat, suddenly taking on a new identity at thirty? And for her, using two last names had a message. It meant: "I am a married woman with a career."

She did not like inequality. Inequalities between women and men, rich and poor, old and young, white and black races and even though she didn't show it, the inequality between the religious and non-religious made her uncomfortable.

Her head was filled with racing thoughts. Although people said freedom of speech had been broadened, who was really able to say what they wanted the way they wanted to say it? How could they freely and boldly express their opinions on social matters when they couldn't even tell the ones they loved exactly what they felt?

Enough! Was she going to be the one to save Turkey? Now she had to get to work and make a phone call to discuss the details of a presentation she was to give at a ceremony next week.

Driving in morning traffic, Alp had had enough of the DJ who kept blabbering on between songs on a music channel and turned off the radio. Actually, it wasn't the traffic or the radio that was bothering him.

Last night, he'd had to go to sleep unsatisfied. And with Esin looking so sexy beside him. What had gotten into her these last few days? They'd gone to sleep three times this week without making love. Or rather, Esin slept peacefully, while he lay awake.

He was young, he was a man, and he had a beautiful wife. Like every healthy male, he wanted to have sex regularly. Why else had he gotten married! Yes, he loved Esin, the first time he saw her, he thought: "What a doll!" She was a level-headed woman he could spend his life with but he did not like her reticence these days. Men were simple; they wanted their basic needs met, that was all. Dinner ready when you got home, sex ... no need to get complicated about it.

He wanted a cigarette but no, he was not going to smoke. He didn't have any cigarettes anyway. He'd given them up months ago. He had to, being with a woman as fond of healthy living as Esin.

Soon, he'd be in the middle of a chaotic stock trading session. He had to empty his mind now. He turned the radio back on but this time, listened to classical music instead of that blabbermouth DJ.

# Kübra's Days
## (Prayer)

Kübra finished the final cycle of the prayer. She folded her rug and carefully put it away. She heaved a deep, peaceful sigh and sat down on the edge of her bed.

She felt expansive, her burdens lightened. That sweet feeling of relief always embraced Kübra after prayer. After she was done, she felt liberated. All tension, all anxiety left her in those moments.

She turned off the lamp on the bedside table and got into bed. She closed her eyes and drifted off to sleep. Relaxed, light…

The dawn prayer was like no other. She had to set the alarm clock, go to bed early and wake up early, do her ablutions and perform four cycles of prayer. The ritual *namaz* was a harder form of prayer because it had to be done every day at specific times. Although it helped one to develop and renew one's self, the patience required to perform *namaz* at the required times was not for everyone.

When the alarm went off at five, she never wanted to get up. It wasn't easy to break into the deepest, sweetest part of sleep for the sake of duty. She'd say to herself: "I'd be able to get up if I had to catch a plane, so I can get up for my prayers too." She'd untangle her small body from the comforter, stagger toward the door and head for the bathroom to do her ablutions.

She'd take out the prayer rug her sister-in-law had given her, put it down in the direction of Mecca and begin the *namaz*. She took special care of her prayer rug because of the part it played in her performance of her religious duty. Like most prayer rugs it was woven with symbolic designs which brought the religious atmosphere of a mosque into the home. Hers was made of silky woolen yarns and depicted a tree of life suggesting Heaven. But she was intelligent enough to know that not everyone who wore the veil and prayed would go directly to Heaven. Everyone could sin, veiled or not.

If she missed one of her five daily prayers, she felt she'd done something wrong and was dogged by the lack of that familiar expansive feeling. She could sense that she was training herself inwardly by performing *namaz*. *Namaz* had taught her patience and will power. It was like what her American friends who did sports exercises every day had told her when she was studying in New York: they gained discipline by doing sports exercises regularly. Like sports, performing *namaz* relieved a person of internal contradictions.

She had begun praying at an early age. *Namaz* became incumbent upon girls when they began to menstruate. When a girl started menstruating, her sins began to be recorded, and *namaz* was incumbent from the moment sins began to be counted. But she had become curious about *namaz* a few years before she entered puberty and had decided to start covering her head too. Not because she came from a family where women were veiled. She hadn't been forced in any way. She read religious books, observed those around her and decided to cover her hair.

Both her mother and father prayed, and she'd been familiar with it for as long as she could remember. The religious course at school was not enough for her. She hadn't learned much of anything there. Her mother and grandmother made her memorize prayers at home. They encouraged and praised her, the way any parent would a child who'd memorized a poem.

Theirs was a large family. At large family gatherings, the children would be asked to recite prayers and applauded if they managed to recite them correctly. And they'd be asked to state the five pillars of Islam. Everyone would applaud warmly if the child could say: "To perform *namaz*, fast, give charity, make the pilgrimage to Mecca and bear witness to God's unity." That was how Kübra had memorized the prayers. First, she had memorized the shorter chapters of the Koran recited in *namaz* and with time, learned others as well.

Her grandfather would also ask the children to recite the memorized ten stanzas of the national anthem, and if they could do it, he would give them pocket money.

She was in middle school when she wanted to start performing the prayers. She read books about how *namaz* was done. She imitated the pictures and learned quickly. It wasn't hard once she had memorized the words. When her parents saw how enthusiastic she was, they sent her to a Koran course nearby.

She liked being with the girls at the Koran course. When they had got their memorizing right, they would hug and kiss each other. Sitting side by side at their desks, their arms and legs would touch and although this innocent touching made them excited, they never talked about it. What they experienced at the course was engraved in their memories. The frightening stories they heard about boys and the way the opposite sex was described as an unknowable creature, made them draw all the more closer to one another. Kübra did not like boys. She did not want to know them.

As she grew up, the habit of *namaz* became a part of her life. During her middle and high-school years in Istanbul, she wore her turban until she got to the school gate. She took it off there and went inside with her head bare. She attended all her classes with her head uncovered. The fact that she was a veiled Muslim girl who tried to perform her prayers at the proper times despite being in school, signified that she had accepted that form of religious life completely. She was not allowed to perform the noon prayer at school and so, had to make it up in the evening.

While studying at university in the States, she had asked that a place be set aside for her to pray, and her request was met with tolerance and understanding. She was given a special room where she could pray every day. The attitude of the school towards her practice of worship pleased her very much. In Turkey, one could not even think of making such a request. She would do her ablutions before leaving the school dormitory on campus and then perform her prayers when the time came. Her mother had instilled in her the habit of keeping her ablutions intact, so she did not look upon it as a hardship.[2] The university had made a place available for her to perform ablutions as well but she did not need to use it.

Now she was a young woman of twenty-five. The five daily prayers were as indispensible a part of her life as food and water.

[2] Several things invalidate an ablution – in which the hands, forearms, face, mouth, nostrils, ears and feet are washed and the top of the head wiped – among them, eating or using the toilet. To keep one's ablution intact is to avoid doing any of these things until after the prayer. – Trans.

# Esin's Days (The Summit)

As Esin arrived at one of the most beautiful of the old Istanbul palaces, she thought to herself: "What a wonderful city this is. How lucky I am to live in Istanbul!"

In the Ottoman Empire, the choicest spots on the shores of the Golden Horn and the Bosphorus were reserved for the palaces and mansions of the sultans and important men of state. Most of them had disappeared but the Çırağan Palace had been restored and expanded as a grand five-star hotel on the Bosphorus shore.

This enchanted world was enclosed by high walls on the street side, exemplifying the most superior Ottoman stone masonry. Esin surrendered her car to the doorman at the gate and let herself be overcome by the effect of its old-world palatial glory and efficient modern luxury.

She adored the place. Whether she came as a guest for Sunday brunch or a presenter at an event, she always loved being here.

Today, she was working as a presenter again. The organization in question was a very important one. Istanbul had been chosen as the "City of Culture" for that year, and the leaders of several nations and their spouses had gathered for "The World Women's Summit," hosted by the Turkish Prime Minister's wife herself.

They'd had to make the preparations in plain view, rather than in a backstage space. With delegates from several nations attending, the excessive security arrangements set limitations on what the organization could do, and no backstage space had been set aside.

Like all events involving extensive protocol, the Summit began late. Esin was used to that; things always started late under such conditions.

At last, the Prime Minister's wife entered the salon with an army of bodyguards, no less than would attend her husband. The spouses of the other heads of state walked in beside her. The first few rows of seats in the ballroom were reserved for them, their consultants, and security. From where Esin looked out from the stage, a colorful scene met the eye. Women dressed in all kinds of attire were present, even some with bare heads. There were women with modern veils showing a bit of hair, women veiled up to the whites of their eyes, women in long flowing gowns, wearing strings of pearls, silk veils and high heels.

The Summit began formally when Esin welcomed the guests, in English and Turkish. The opening speech was given by the Prime Minister's turbaned wife. She spoke calmly and softly. Clearly, she, like her husband, took speech lessons.

This was followed by a speech by the wife of the president of a Muslim country. She was young and had a modern appearance. She enchanted everyone with her understated make-up and elegant suit with jacket and skirt. So, choices could differ. Personal tastes as well as national culture were brought to the fore.

The wife of another head of state of a Muslim country began her speech "In the name of God, the merciful, the compassionate" and spoke in Arabic.

True, the topics spoken of here were more serious. The world had entered an age when women entrepreneurs were becoming known for their success on the international scene. The view of women as "the slaves of this age" had to change. The world was mobilized to remove the injustices suffered by women.

Projects to prevent violence against women were discussed and the creation of resources and means for the development of women. Women made up half the world's population, and if societies were to develop, so must women.

Some of the statistics mentioned in the speeches were genuinely chilling. One in three women in the world was a victim of violence at some point in her life; one in five was a victim of rape or attempted rape. Every year, more than half a million women died during pregnancy or while giving birth; half of the women in the Arab world were illiterate. Esin lived in a very different world. She was surrounded by women who were educated, cultured, who stood on their own two feet. Some of them had the power to make things happen. Some lived happy lives as housewives, supported by their spouses or lovers.

During the coffee break, Esin met a female journalist from Malaysia. Turkey had recently been compared with Malaysia, where sixty percent of the population was Muslim and political Islam was swiftly on the rise.

Their conversation was intense and they shared many ideas. Malaysia had women who smoked cigars on the one hand and on the other, women who wore the *hijab*, known as the symbol of "moderate female dress." Like Turkey, Malaysia was confusing. Religion was taught in schools but children went home and watched MTV. Both women agreed that Islam was portrayed as a violent, anti-social religion opposed to human rights. Unfortunately, Esin too sometimes perceived Islam as reactionary, a religion based on antiquated norms opposed to development. She realized that although she and her family were Muslim by birth, she did not know enough about her own religion. In fact, she had not made an effort in that regard.

Like many of her friends, Esin did not think much about religious issues. She would recite a prayer on special occasions, perform rituals, and leave it at that. Religion was not a focus of her life. But in recent years, disputes over religion had taken center stage, both in her country and in the world at large and had even been occasion for war. She could not remain indifferent to the subject of religion.

She was riveted, and shocked by some of the things the Malaysian journalist told her. Since Islam forbade premarital sex and the sexes were not permitted to mingle freely, homosexuality was spreading swiftly among youth, and the number of young Malaysians who defined themselves as gay or lesbian was increasing rapidly. Women and men lived separate lives. Both girls and boys generally spent their time with members of their own sex. This constant togetherness determined sexual preferences which developed in an atmosphere of intense fear.

The woman journalist also told her that the National Fatwa Council of Malaysia had forbidden girls to dress and behave like boys. This was in contravention to Islamic doctrine.

Once again, Esin felt fortunate to be living in Turkey. Turkey was not becoming like Malaysia or Iran. Turkey had its own reality. It was a synthesis of the varied ethnic roots encompassed within it. And the turban issue or efforts to outlaw alcohol, did not in themselves mean "the decline of secularism." They only raised doubts.

# Kübra's Days
## (Hikmet Bey)

Sometimes, Hikmet Bey performed *namaz* with the congregation at their neighborhood mosque.

Hazret Muhammed encouraged the performance of *namaz* in congregations and himself prayed or led the prayer in congregation at mosques or in open spaces when necessary.

The voice of the *muezzin* calling the people of the neighborhood to the sunrise prayer was heard before the day had begun. The reverberating waves of that burning voice dispelled the twilight and rose into the clouds. Hikmet Bey got out of bed to that divine summons and performed his ablutions. In the deep silence of morning, the sound of splashing water spread throughout the house. Lights came on in some of the houses in the neighborhood. Men emerged into the street on their way to the mosque.

In the street, men laid their right hands over their hearts as they gave each other old-fashioned Ottoman greetings or the more religious "Selam Aleykum," rather than a simple "Good morning." Some fingered beads. Sleepy eyes opened to gaze on the spiritual sight of worship.

Some men of the neighborhood did their ablutions at the large fountain in the mosque courtyard, preparing for the holy *namaz* to the sounds of gargling and flushing of nostrils.

Hikmet Bey took off his shoes with the others at the mosque entrance, carrying them with him as he walked across the straw matting laid in front of the door and pushed aside the heavy green leather curtain to enter. He greeted a few of the more prominent neighborhood men and stood for the prayer next to a man wearing a skullcap, who he knew from the office of the Municipality and had done work with before. They nodded to each other without speaking.

The congregation stood ready in rows. As the Imam said, "God is greatest," all moved as one, bowing, straightening up, and reciting their prayers with silently moving lips.

The day had begun with the peace of mind granted by the dawn prayer. Bodies and souls were refreshed. In a few hours, everyone would be swept up in the rush of daily life. When the prayer was over, Hikmet Bey chatted briefly in front of the mosque with the Municipality civil servant. There were no new tenders on the horizon at the moment.

He began walking home. Today he would go to work early. It wasn't worth going back to bed for a couple of hours; he would enjoy the breakfast his wife prepared and get to work.

Kübra did not go back to bed after the prayer either. She sat down at the breakfast table with her father. She dipped her toast in olive oil. Before swallowing her toast, she took a sip of tea made in the samovar. Kübra didn't like to start the day without a good breakfast. She loved the morning hours and the fine breakfast her mother made.

Auntie Kadriye helped to make breakfast but it was Nadide Hanım who made it special. She decided which cheese, which olives, and what kind of eggs would be laid out on the table. Hikmet Bey didn't eat much bread and would only nibble at tomato and cheese; mostly he just drank tea. He would have at least two or three glasses of tea and then get up from the table.

The three of them had breakfast together. Büşra was still asleep. She had stayed up late listening to music and reading her pop magazines. She didn't mind skipping breakfast but never missed dinner. When Hikmet Bey got home in the evenings, he wanted to see the whole family together. He was very particular about that. Dinner was the only meal they could eat together. The girls could retire to their rooms after dinner if they liked, and he would not complain.

The chauffeur, Cenan Efendi, was waiting at the door. He had been with the Akansan family for years. Their relationship couldn't be considered formal but Hikmet Bey seemed to have put him at a bit of a distance as the tempo of his work had increased and the company he kept changed.

Kübra sat in the back seat next to her father. Hikmet Bey gave her a look over and said in a formal tone: "You look good. Your outfit is lovely but you have on a bit too much jewelry; take some of it off." Kübra smiled at him and looked at herself, trying to decide which piece of jewelry to take off.

Kübra's father criticized her attire almost every morning. Sometimes he'd say she looked "beautiful" or "chic"; sometimes he'd say bluntly that the colors of her outfit "clashed" or that she was wearing "too much jewelry." Then he would turn away and read his newspaper. If he was not very absorbed in the paper, Kübra would retort with something like: "Your tie is not right!" Hikmet Bey did not like to wear ties but felt obliged to these days. Nadide Hanım would always check his shoes as well before he left the house, to see if they were right for his suit and properly polished and shined.

Hikmet Bey had turned away slightly from Kübra and was reading the paper. He kept a close watch on the daily news. He had not been to college but had educated himself by reading extensively and traveling a great deal as his business demanded. He knew how to take advantage of opportunities when they arose. At this hour, the trip to work did not take long, though it depended on traffic. In the fifteen to twenty minutes of the journey, Hikmet Bey glanced through most of the daily papers and read certain columnists he particularly followed.

Except for this brief time spent together in the car, Kübra and her father did not see each other at all during the work day. Hikmet Bey attended important meetings at the company and went out to see business associates. And he often went to Bahçeşehir at the other end of Istanbul. The trips to Bahçeşehir did not have to do with work; they were illicit visits of a private nature. His second wife, whom he'd married illegally in a purely religious ceremony, lived with their four-year-old son in the home he'd bought for them in Bahçeşehir. Of course, Nadide Hanım, who had sex with her husband once a week as a wifely duty and had not for a long time experienced real sexual satisfaction, knew nothing about the other woman. Nor did their daughters.

Hikmet Bey had good relations with the bureaucrats in the capitol. He went often to Ankara in his capacity as a contractor. These bureaucrats had played a large role in his rise in the construction sector in recent years. Many filled their pockets through the deals they struck with bosses and rose in their profession by virtue of their position in the loop. Thus, everyone made money.

Municipal officials, in particular, had been key to Hikmet Bey's lucrative projects, especially in the early years. Nothing could be done without the help of municipal committee members. It was they who were responsible for the granting of undeveloped land to holding companies, the building of factories on protected lands and the illegal buildings rising on the Istanbul skyline. Their names were never heard but it was they who had the authority to decide on every matter from the changing of street names to the width of sidewalks.

At the office and in company meetings, Kübra called her father "Hikmet Bey." He liked having his daughter address him that way in front of others. Most of the administrators in the company were men. Women were employed if new personnel were greatly needed. If Hikmet Bey had to speak to female personnel, he left the door to his office open, so that no one might imagine anything amiss.

Kübra went to her own office. She asked Fatma Hanım to bring tea. She sat down at her desk and turned on her computer. She liked to read newspapers online. She read all the newspapers, a habit she'd acquired from her father. She recalled that he had not always followed the news so closely; he used to read only certain publications. Now, they had news of everything, whether liberal, radical, nationalist, leftist, right wing, conservative, or militant.

Kübra made a habit of reading the regular news on the internet but she had to read the supplements in print, so as to be able to see the pictures better. The supplements were printed in color, and she found them entertaining. She was curious about who was wearing what, who was going out with whom, what kind of new image people were creating for themselves, and she'd gaze for a long time at the photographs in the supplements.

The tea lady, Fatma Hanım, came up to Kübra's desk to refill her tea glass and noticed a photograph in one of the color supplements. "Lord, these girls walk the streets naked. Have they no shame?" she exclaimed and left.

After completing her morning ritual, Kübra set to planning what she would do today.

# Esin's Days
## (On the Bosphorus)

Istanbul was, for Alp and Esin, a city that continued to amaze them every passing day. The perfect Bosphorus view from the giant windows of their salon was always enchanting. When they'd looked for a home to live in after they married, they focused on the hills by the shore in Bebek, Arnavutköy, and Emirgan but in the end, rented this Etiler flat in a modern apartment building overlooking the Bosphorus from a high ridge.

Istanbul is beautiful in every way, Alp thought. At night, with its lights reflected in the deep blue sea; its hills, its streets, its islands – all are gorgeous. If you leave for a while, you may thank your lucky stars you're free of the city's trials and tribulations but before long, you start to miss it. He and Esin couldn't do with or without it.

Alp had travelled the world and acquired rare tastes but if you suggested a fish dinner with raki on the Bosphorus, you had him.

He was happy as a child this evening because they were going out to dinner with friends at Kıyı Restaurant in Tarabya. They jumped into the car and took the long road up the shore, just so they could gaze at the Bosphorus along the way.

Tarabya is famed as a district where Istanbul aristocrats took their leisure in the eighteenth and nineteenth centuries. The old Greek name was "Therapia" and its therapeutic effects had made it a favorite pleasure spot for Istanbul's high society of the time.

Esin had often eaten at Kıyı with her parents when she was a child. The old gilded piano and paintings by Turkish artists lining the walls, which she hadn't noticed when she was small, gave the club a warm, inviting air.

The first couple to arrive after them was Ergin and his wife Seçil. He taught at a private college and lawyer Seçil was known for her calm nature. Ergin was a bookworm; he knew something about everything and took every opportunity to show off. Sometimes, he bored everyone by talking too much. Although his wife Seçil was an excellent lawyer, she was the opposite; a quiet, unremarkable looking, ordinary woman who seemed to be in her own world.

As the four of them sat down and began chatting of this and that, the last couple to join the table arrived: contractor Ahmet, almost fifty and his flamboyant wife, Mehtap. Stockbroker Alp was helping him invest his personal savings. When it came to money, Alp was Ahmet's mentor.

Mehtap was, as always, very strikingly turned out, wearing a satin dress in a baby pink shade a bit much for dinner at a fish restaurant. Louboutin stiletto heels completed her chic outfit. Although she was thirty-six years old, she'd never worked, and dressing up was her only passion. It clearly didn't bother her husband; on the contrary, he liked it. He took his beautiful wife wherever he went but as an ornament, a kind of accessory. He was not known for having deep conversations with his wife. She was not the only woman in his life, anyway; as he put it; he had a finger in every pie.

That Mehtap's life was made up of home decorating, brand names, hair-dos, and gossip was a source of enjoyment for Ahmet. It wouldn't be fair to say Mehtap was a complete airhead, though. She was an intelligent woman. She took an intense interest in her only child, the child's Moldavian nanny, school, and her lessons and homework. Thankfully, the child wasn't a girl, or she'd have signed her up for every kind of lesson available – ballet, piano, swimming, tennis, volleyball, painting – whether she showed talent or not.

There was a merry atmosphere at the table and they chose a round of first courses to accompany the drinks without even looking at the menu. The women asked for smoked fish without onions, and the men with old school. They ordered grilled eggplant salad, white cheese, red beans, seaweed salad, and shrimp to share. As always, they had the mixed green salad chopped fine and garnished with white cheese. Aside from Mehtap's white wine, everyone was drinking raki.

Ergin frowned as if something were on his mind. "So, it seems the country's stagnant economy isn't enough. We had another heated argument about the 'turban issue' today," he said, laying out the most sensitive subject of recent times.

Alp jumped in right away.

"Man, let's not bust our heads about turbans just now. Eat something first, let's sip our raki, we can talk later. But if it's the economy that's worrying you, I think the situation is bad."

He punctuated his sentence by raising his glass.

"If the stagnation is due to internal problems like 'the turban,' then I have a right to question them," Ergin said, defending himself. He swallowed a morsel of cheese and went on: "Frankly, I can't stand seeing girl students at the university covering their heads. Concessions should never be made on secularism. But part of me thinks as a total liberal and says that even if the turban is a religious symbol, a political symbol, it should not be outlawed at universities. Because there is no alternative to public education. But it should be outlawed for personnel working in government offices, absolutely. Because one has the alternative of working in the private sector."

Alp didn't want to dig up that corpse but couldn't stop himself from adding: "You're right. Nobody is forced to work for the state. Someone in the military, who becomes an officer, for example, can't decide to go around in shorts or jeans."

"If there are veiled girls who still want to study at the university under these conditions," Ergin continued, "let them study. But then they shouldn't complain later, after they graduate, that they can't get a job working for the state."

Seçil joined the conversation: "Why is the turban such a problem in this country anyway? Our religion is a religion of tolerance. Why are we so hung up on appearances? I don't get it."

"Because they're mixing religion up in politics," Esin said, and Seçil went on: "The turban issue has been debated in Turkey for years; it's nothing new. It's flared up now, because people are suspicious of the government's moderate Islamic politics. Turkey is like a laboratory for an experiment in moderate Islamic democracy these days. I want Ergin to come home in the evenings at peace with himself but these problems are not easy."

Ergin put the question to all: "All right then, do you think the turban ban at universities should be lifted?"

Alp jumped in right away: "No. Just as uniforms are worn in primary and secondary schools, there should be a dress code at universities. Why do students wear school uniforms? So that the rich should not be distinguished from the poor, so that students should study under conditions of equality as much as possible."

Esin turned to her husband: "But that's why the *others* want to wear the turban at universities, because they want an equal right to education. Damn, what an irresolvable problem it is..."

Alp agreed with Esin but went on: "A young woman finishes lycée and begins college. She's in no position to advertise what she believes at the educational institution where her future will be prepared. If you allow the turban at universities, you divide people into two camps, whether you mean to or not, and that violates the principle of equality."

Ergin seemed to want the last word on the subject he'd started: "Matters of faith are between a person and God. Secularism should not be taken as the enemy of faith. Secularism is one thing and belonging to a religion is another. The view that a secularist has no religion must change. Most of us are not against religion; we're just not interested in it. People will understand one another better when that ignorant way of thinking is done away with. And that requires more time spent reading and listening.

"Turkey is going through an interesting time. The economy is being affected not only by worldwide developments but the political uncertainty within the country as well."

Ahmet hungrily finished his plate of smoked fish and ordering another, spoke like someone who wanted it understood that he was a man of much experience.

"You're right, son, there's been a slowdown in our business too. It was great; things in the country were moving forward, and the construction sector in particular was growing amazingly fast. There were projects everywhere but something always goes wrong in this country and then we're all pulled back. You know, when I think about it, all our lives we've been hearing denunciations, accusations of corruption, theft, and backsliding. Three military coups in twenty years have left us at least fifty years behind. And the younger generation doesn't remember military coups, police beatings, and prisons. They don't even know about them!"

Alp smiled. "You can't say anything about the military, Ahmet; we have an officer's daughter at the table," he said, indicating Esin.

"Come to think of it, if we had the younger generation now that we had then, we wouldn't be dependent on other countries," Ergin said, but fell silent without developing further the theme of "youth these days."

As they went on with their dinner and their toasts, a couple sat down at the table behind them. Ahmet lifted his head to look over at the tall young woman, one of his old "friends" and her boyfriend. When his gaze lingered a bit too long, Esin watched Mehtap ask, as if out of curiosity, rather than jealousy and suspicion, "Someone you know?"

Ahmet collected himself and answered evasively, "I thought it was our friend, Metin." Mehtap had no idea who Metin was. Alp mischievously raised his glass and toasted, "To our Metin!" Esin kicked him under the table and gave him a hard look meaning, "Cut it out."

Local and global issues were discussed, glasses were clinked. Ergin looked at their glasses of raki and recalled that the drink had been brought to the Ottoman Empire from Arabia in the seventeenth century in order to get around the interdiction against alcohol because its clear liquid looked just like water.

There was a silence at the table as if everyone was lost in their own thoughts for a moment but the good mood didn't last long.

Ahmet was the sort of man who could walk in the snow without leaving tracks. His womanizing was legendary but he never let on about the girlfriends he kept on the side. As Esin was thinking about this, Mehtap squeezed a wedge of lemon with her long red-painted fingernails and ate her shrimp, holding her fork in the most refined manner. Suddenly, Esin noticed her puffy lips. She seemed to have had them artificially plumped with Botox injections. She'd used Botox before; her eyebrows were already unnaturally high, and now her lips were swollen too. Esin didn't know whether to be angry at her or sorry for her. She kept having plastic surgeries in order to hang on to her playboy husband but they did not make her more beautiful. She looked at her salad with that expression of fright shared by women who eat salad to keep down their weight.

The waiter brought the hot second-course dishes. The fried squid with tartar sauce looked superb. Seçil went ahead without waiting for the others and tossed a thick ring of squid into her mouth, yelping as soon as she did; clearly, it was still too hot.

The talk turned back to the country's problems, while they waited for the squid to cool. The men asserted their opinions heatedly, not really listening to one another most of the time and cutting in before the other had finished speaking.

It was time to order the fish. They'd already eaten so much, they had no room left for the main course. They always made the same mistake, filling up on first and second courses and then only picking at their fish. But the men had not had their fill of conversation and set about choosing fish to accompany the raki.

The conversation turned to vacation plans. Ahmet and Mehtap were taking a boat around the Göçek coast; Alp and Esin were going to Bodrum. Ergin and Seçil were planning a tour of the Italian coast.

Their table was by the window, and now and then, they paused to watch passers-by. Mehtap was delicately separating the bones from the meat of her fish when she saw a girl in a colorful headscarf pass by carrying flowers and said suddenly, "Those girls are everywhere these days."

"That's nothing, my dear, her hair is showing anyway, and her skirt is as colorful as the scarf she's wearing," Seçil said. "What really bothers me is that style they call 'wrapped-head,' which doesn't show even a strand a hair. Was Ataturk's sartorial revolution for nothing?"

Alp got interested in the conversation and added, laughing, "The turban trend spread in the 80s, after the 12 September coup. Soon you'll be wearing one too. The shariat might even be enforced. They'll tell you to cover your heads and stop going around in revealing clothes; these will be the good old days."

"Oh cut it out, Alp, it's not that bad," Esin said.

Know-it-all Ergin cracked a joke: "These people don't want the shariat, brother. Half of them would lose their shirts!"

Ahmet jumped in: "They're everywhere these days, they get all the contracts; they're taking over. However, a fault line has appeared. A fracture deep in the political skeleton. These people who had been looked down upon for years, are gaining status, momentum, and let's not kid ourselves ... power. Now, they are politically organized. Otherwise, there's money in every sector of society ... though people have different ways of earning it. It's rough for us, I can tell you. The country is in their hands."

"You're exaggerating," Esin said. "They're in power now, so they're amassing wealth. Later, it will be someone else."

"Don't say that, Esin," Alp cut in. "There used to be many more exporters. Every administration takes its turn at the trough but these guys make your hair stand on end. The old left and right hated each other but stood together when it suited their self-interest. Now there are new factions, neo-nationalists, Second Republicanists, Islamists..."

Esin was about to continue but fell silent. She felt confused lately, things seemed contradictory, and her feelings and thoughts were in a whirl.

The distinction between "us" and "them" had penetrated every cell of the social body, Esin wondered. Whatever "we" did was right, and everything the *others* did was wrong! The creation of blocks was palpable. Who was to blame for this? It wasn't clear... And maybe, it wasn't anyone's fault. It was the natural result of the process.

Seçil went on a lawyerish jag: "If we surrender democracy to tolerance, they will use their power to take things all the way. We act weak, and the more well intentioned we are, the worse they get. We've let them take power, and they rule as they like."

Everyone nodded in agreement.

Ergin agreed with his wife but couldn't help adding: "They were leading quiet, upright lives but now they are shedding their skin. They've begun to wear branded clothing, for example; they've become conspicuous consumers. They love to wear outlandish colors and draw attention. They use sexually segregated hotels. Now there are health clubs for veiled women; they've got their own gated communities with swimming pools and live in villas. They've discovered their own amusements. They've created spaces for their social life in accordance with religious values. They have their own private TV channels, press organizations, and newspapers. This, friends, is the result of the rise of green capital in the 90s."

They bought some fresh iced almonds from the itinerant seller who had walked that shore for years, and enjoyed the pleasures of raki and fish in Tarabya. Although it was not much fun to discuss the gloomy state of the country, the men always brought the talk around to politics.

They shared the bill. "If I'd got the contract, I'd pay the bill, kids," joked Ahmet, the wealthiest of them, tensing up again as he remembered how he'd lost that job.

# Kübra's Days (Thankfulness)

Hikmet Akansan did not like to waste his time and tried to make the best of every hour he had. He thought of God continually and tried to be heedful, keeping his heart awake to God.

He had no bad habits. Hikmet Akansan did not drink or gamble; he avoided such things for the sake of attaining God's peace. The type of connections he made now and then, to get things done at work, were acceptable in Turkey now. At least, no one knew about his second wife and illegitimate child. Well, if a man's heart was open, his wits soon sharpened too.

He left the office with his son-in-law, Bilal, and offered to drop him off wherever he was going. Bilal was his eldest daughter's husband. The chauffeur, Cenan Efendi, was away and Hikmet Bey was driving. They arrived in the district of Fatih, known for its conservatism. He wanted to go on alone after he dropped off Bilal; that was why he hadn't had Cenan Efendi drive him.

Bilal was in Fatih to stop by the Iskenderpasha Mosque, which was affiliated with the Nakshibendi religious order to which he belonged.

Although Hikmet Bey's father and uncle were members, he had not gotten involved with the order. His son-in-law had now become one of the congregation's well-known figures. Another important characteristic of the order was its secrecy. It was like a kind of Masonic lodge.

In Fatih and some other districts, there were perhaps some five hundred congregations. There were also small congregations which met in homes or the basements of apartment buildings. There were various kinds of new religious groupings all over the world, not just in Turkey. In Turkey, from the Islamic point of view, there is a world of orders, made up of twelve basic paths and their various offshoots. In the world at large, various Christian, Jewish, Hindu, and Buddhist orders are carrying out their activities. Religious orders are extremely varied.

Hikmet Bey loved his son-in-law; he'd never seen him do anything wrong. The young man was good company. Hikmet Bey had no doubt he had subjected his soul to rigorous examination according to the rules of the order.

Hikmet Bey drove his luxurious car to Bahçeşehir, far from the city center. On the way, he made some calls on his Vertu cell phone, a brand the jet set was never without and no one else could buy because of its exorbitant price. Hikmet Bey knew no foreign language but it pleased him considerably that the meaning of the French brand name was "virtue."

Kübra had asked to have a Vertu too; she'd seen the phone in the young bourgeois fundamentalist circles around her and longed to have it but Hikmet Bey had not bought her one yet.

He had a heady feeling of pleasure when Nermin opened the front door. Even to respond to his young wife's, "Peace be upon you, Hikmet," with "And upon you be peace, my beauty," was for him a way of flirting and a delicious way to begin the visit.

His wife stood before him invitingly. She was much more slender than Nadide Hanım, a much younger, much more pleasing woman. Her brown hair was straight and long and she'd had blonde highlights added to the ends. The expression in her hazel eyes was sad and opaque, a mixture of the slow burn time spent in waiting brings and the joy of seeing him again. She was of average height and thin-boned but had a lovely figure.

She'd put on make-up and a pretty, colorful dress in expectation of Hikmet Bey's visit. She was even wearing the heavy Trabzon hand-carved gold bracelet he had given her as her husband in this world and the next. She always received him well. He came to see her infrequently enough anyway, and must find here what he did not have at home.

They had met five years earlier. Hikmet Bey proposed a marriage by religious ceremony, merely because he knew well that for a married man to be with a woman other than his wife without it was considered adultery by religious law. She'd had no choice but to accept a religious marriage. Her pockets were empty and so was her heart. She was really taken with Hikmet Bey. She liked his quiet way and his seriousness. He was strong and successful in his business. She'd fallen in love with him.

Sex outside of marriage was considered a major sin, and Nermin had accepted the status of second wife by religious ceremony in order to make herself feel better about the liaison. From then on, she thought of her religious marriage as a formally legal marriage.

Although the Gracious Koran had been interpreted to allow men to marry up to four women, to marry more than one was not lawful. Yet those who wished to "marry" a second time, did it without the knowledge of their wives by religious ceremony and set up a second life.

Polygamy was *haram*. And to not inform the first wife was morally objectionable; it was duplicitous and disloyal. But it was no easy thing to satisfy lust! A religious marriage with a second wife was a solution which ensured that such relationships would supposedly not be counted as *haram*.

Because of the religious ceremony, Hikmet Bey saw Nermin as a wife and had come to find nothing wrong in having a child by her. Nermin became pregnant unintentionally in the first year they were together. The unexpected event caused some problems in their relationship at first but with her sweet way of talking and feminine wiles, Nermin had led Hikmet Bey out of his anger. They had a son and named him Ozan. Hikmet Bey wandered between joy and sorrow. His true wife Nadide Hanım had never given him a son; she gave birth to three girls. Now, he had a son but no one knew about it. He'd not yet given the boy his last name, and he was growing up without a legal identity. But it gave him some comfort that Nermin treated him with understanding and did not make an issue of it. Nermin never nagged him. She accepted everything as it was. She lived according to his needs as his second wife. If she had not, she would not have come this far with Hikmet Bey.

The house seemed a bit untidy. A depressingly dark brown sofa and armchair set, a worn-out but not antique carpet, a dining table for four with average looking chairs, a medium-sized TV, CD player and dozens of cartoon CDs, toys and children's books scattered about, white tulle curtains – all prevented the home from taking on a warm and welcoming air.

The little boy was asleep in his room. They went into the salon. The TV was on. She was about to turn it off when Hikmet Bey said, half smiling, "Leave it on. Make me some tea and come sit down beside me."

Nermin turned the fire down low under the tea in the kitchen to let it steep and went back to her husband. She loved Hikmet Bey enough to wait for him in this house, never going out…And their union had borne fruit. She spent all her time with her son. She bought him toys and cute outfits. She could buy things without worrying about the cost, thanks to Hikmet Bey. As the child's father, he left no need of his unfulfilled. He provided everything. He valued the woman who belonged to him. He had enough character not to wrong a woman who served him and cared for him.

As soon as she sat down on the couch, she felt something warm on her neck. Hikmet Bey had planted a wet kiss, just the kind she liked, on the most sensitive spot on her neck. As they moved closer, "Thanks be to God," slipped from Hikmet Bey's lips. He embraced Nermin and began kissing her. Things were warming up when Nermin thought of the tea on the stove. She hurried off to the kitchen to pour a glass of tea and set it down on the side table next to Hikmet Bey.

He pulled her to him with desire, as if telling her to forget about the tea. He went on kissing her. As he ran his hands over her body, he occasionally hurt her. His hands moved under her blouse and skirt as if starving, squeezing her breasts and legs. It always gave Hikmet Bey great pleasure to sense that fresh body awakening under his hands and lips. Her man's harsh movements aroused Nermin's womanhood in the same way, although they sometimes made her feel like a "bad girl." Nermin's satisfaction belied the urban legend that veiled women did not have orgasms.

The silence of their swift, savage lovemaking was broken only by deep moans. Afterwards, Hikmet Bey went to the bathroom and performed a full bath ablution.

He came back into the salon and put on his pants and shirt, along with the white undershirt he never neglected to wear. While buttoning his shirt, he went to the room where his son was sleeping. He watched the child from afar, sleeping in all his innocence, unaware of the world. The boy did not stir when he kissed him on the forehead.

Life would be unbearable without Nermin. He found a little time here and there to run off to see her; talking to her relieved him of daily cares. Nermin prepared a lovely table. Hikmet Bey had no complaints about the food served at either of his homes.

Nadide Hanım was the mother of his daughters; she had the crowning place in his life but what about Hikmet Bey's inner world? The boredom had almost killed their sex life. But he wanted to have new adventures in bed and realize his fantasies. To come here and be with Nermin was to dip into a different world.

His wife did not satisfy him. His Nadide was not enough. It excited him to find union in another woman's body. The novelty of it attracted him. There were many Muslims in Turkey who had a married life like this, merely by religious ceremony. On the *other* side, there were many couples, heterosexual and homosexual, who were not legally married but lived a married life which was portrayed in the media. Those who wished, could have sex with different people from one day to the next. No one knew whose hand was in whose pocket.

# Esin's Days
## (Jacuzzi)

Alp had spent another day in turbulent stock trading sessions and was stuck in traffic on his way home as usual. The weather was hot, the schools were closed, and people with summer homes had begun to abandon the city, so the traffic was not that bad, and he even reached his apartment building in an Etiler gated community earlier than he expected. He parked the car and took the elevator to the third floor. Out of habit, his hand went to the doorbell. There was no sign of movement inside, so he opened the door with his key.

According to old films and what he'd heard from his elders, when husbands came home, their wives met them at the door. A smiling woman at the door took away the fatigue of the day instantly. But nowadays... Once again Esin Hanım had not found time in her busy professional and social schedule to arrive home before her husband.

Alp changed into a comfortable T-shirt and poured himself a vodka on ice. Actually, he did not drink much at home. But this evening, he needed something to relax him. He took the opportunity to put up his feet and was soon lost in thought.

Why had he married? The proverb, "Age thirty-five is half the way," had been engraved in his mind like everyone else's, and he'd married before he got half-way.

He was not the sort of guy to feel inclined to marry. He'd had his fun chasing lots of women. He'd been with many girls who worked as stockbrokers and bankers. As his male friends had joined the marriage caravan one by one, he'd found himself alone. Still, he'd been in no hurry to get married and went on having short-term relationships without headaches. He even let it be known from the start that he was not the marrying kind. Girls usually didn't mind, thinking, "I'll get him to toe the line anyway," but in the end, it was they who were disappointed. Even if he really liked a girl, it never lasted more than a month. Maybe he was subconsciously afraid of love and relationships, and this was his way of avoiding them.

He'd go out at night, meet a girl, drink, have his fun, then get bored and go on to the next. He took vacations with his male friends and partied so hard that he returned tired from drink and sleepless nights.

He and his male friends had special "breakaway" destinations. Sometimes, they'd go as a group to Thailand, Russia or South America, just to have sex. Of course, no one believed their talk about how the Far East was for massages, Russia for vodka, and Brazil for beaches.

But in the end, he got tired of that life. Even if he was with another beautiful girl every day, after a while he'd get used to it and the thrill would be gone. He needed other things in his life, other things to share.

He'd been in this frame of mind when he met Esin at a party. She was not only beautiful, she was intelligent. She'd impressed him by showing she would not devote all of her time to a man. She was a self-confident woman who stood on her own two feet, she was young and full of fun.

They'd been going out for a few months, when he proposed to her on vacation after a special moment of pleasure they had in a Jacuzzi on the balcony of an Antalya hotel.

Although the flight to Antalya was only an hour, they'd arrived at the hotel utterly exhausted after the long drive from the airport to the Antalya village of Belek. When they got to the room and saw the Jacuzzi on the balcony, they filled it up right away. Esin put bubble bath in the water but couldn't get it to bubble up as she wanted and kept putting more in, though Alp warned her not to. They heaved a sigh of joy when they got into the suds stark naked, aching with the dust of the road. Esin closed her eyes and tried to relax but Alp couldn't keep still and kept running his toes over her body. She soon joined in the game, drew near him and finally sat in his lap. They kissed long and sweetly and enjoyed the pleasure of making love in the open air.

The action in the tub made the suds bubble up and spilled sudsy water all over the floor of the balcony, making it slippery. As they got out and headed for the bathroom, Alp looked carefully at Esin's face and realized how beautiful she was without make-up. He proposed to her then and there. She said yes, and when she lifted her arms to embrace him, the towel around her fell to the floor and they burst out laughing.

Having received this proposal of marriage soaking wet in a hotel room, Esin asked, "So where is the ring?" Alp explained he hadn't planned to ask her and acted on the spur of the moment.

A few days after they got back from vacation, they were at Alp's house; he went off to the bedroom as if he'd forgotten something, and when he came back, suddenly kissed Esin and left a ring with a single jewel in her mouth. When she realized what the metallic taste in her mouth was, she jumped for joy and smothered Alp with kisses. Oh well, every playboy meets his match eventually. Alp had chosen to come to his senses in his thirties and was now the man of his house. But the mistress was still not home. However much he was a modern man and tried to sand down his macho edges, he wanted to find his wife at home when he got there. Yet a helpless smile showing that he'd accepted the situation spread across his face. He took a sip of his drink.

The following evening was Alp's poker night with the guys. Like many caught up in gambling, they met almost every week in one of their homes and got lost in the game for hours.

Most of their wives could not understand why their husbands spent hours sitting at a table playing poker. There had been a play-station epidemic for a while and just when they were feeling relieved that it was over, this poker addiction began.

They'd planned the poker session for a weekday after work, and this time it was to take place on Ahmet's boat docked in Kalamış Bay.

Ahmet had two boats. He kept the larger one in Göcek and the smaller one for emergencies in Istanbul. When Ahmet wanted to play around behind his wife's back, he didn't bother with hotels; he had his casual flings on the boat. Beyond that, he used it when he wanted to relax or take care of business with Ankara bureaucrats discreetly. It was a harbour close at hand where he took refuge.

Ahmet was someone who knew how to take full pleasure in life. He had all the material means he wanted. He smoked special cigars brought from Switzerland and Beirut and drank fine wines in restaurants. He always wore a limited edition wristwatch.

Alp played poker constantly but it wasn't always possible to play with the same people. This evening, he'd brought his friend Volkan along. With Ahmet playing host and Ergin there too, it made four players for poker night.

The gentlemen sat around the table with their drinks. Ahmet could not do without his whiskey; Alp and Ergin were having vodka on the rocks, and Volkan alone was having tea. Volkan drank tea on such occasions because it wasn't healthy to play poker drunk. A man could get overconfident and lose control.

This group had not played together before, and so they first discussed the rules and limit on bets.

Volkan was the new man and asked in a low voice what the game would be but nobody heard him, so Alp repeated his question: "What's your poison, gentlemen? What will we play?"

They decided on 10–20 Come On.

The "serious players" at the table, first of all, Alp, wanted to play Duke or Texas Hold 'Em but Ahmet put an end to that: "No way, man, I play Turkish four-hand poker."

These big shot businessmen turned into little boys at the poker table.

Alp began to sort the two decks on the table for the thirty-two-card sets needed. The game began, and after two or three rounds, Volkan had taken 150 liras off Ahmet twice. Then he began joking around. He thought he had Ahmet.

Volkan had already shaken off his initial reticence at being new to the group. He picked up a napkin from the table and blindfolded himself, saying, "This is the only way to play fair with you, man; I'm going to play like this from now on." There was an explosion of laughter at the table.

At that point, Alp turned to Volkan and said, "Don't talk so big. I'll get you on the last round."

They took a bathroom break. They went down to the tiny toilet in the hull of the boat. And then the bullshit session began. They talked about beautiful women, soccer, and about money too, a little. Always cool-headed, Ahmet said things like: "You can lose money running after women but you never lose women running after money."

When the subject turned to stocks, Alp said, "Playing the market you don't always put down one and earn three, gentlemen; you can lose all." Although Volkan was an ad man, he couldn't do without the thrill of the stock market and joined in right away.

"If you go into the market like I did, without really understanding what is going on, you'll lose all your savings too," he said.

Wanting to show that he understood women well, Ahmet said: "I know women, gentlemen. You have to please her if you want her to make you happy. You have to spoil her. You don't make her ask twice. You give her presents. No woman can refuse presents, whether it's jewellry or flowers."

"You're just like Sultan Suleyman, the Lawgiver. He ruled for fortysix years and made the world tremble but he couldn't deny his wife Hürrem anything," Alp said, wanting to soothe Ahmet.

Although the game hadn't gone well for Ahmet tonight, he was satisfied to be likened to Sultan Suleyman, who'd brought the Ottoman Empire to its greatest era during his reign, and chuckled happily. He reflected on how a woman could wrap a man around her little finger. Catherine the Great, known for her beauty, cunning and mind-numbing intrigues, seduced Baltacı Mehmet Pasha and made him turn the Ottoman army back just as it was about to defeat her armies.

He refilled his guests' drinks and opened an expensive bottle of old wine. He studied the label and laughed. "A woman is like a bottle of wine, she's best lying down."

Poker is a game that crushes both the best and the worst players. Everyone was equal here. Even if you had a million dollars, or a nuclear weapon, you could be helpless and ridiculous at a poker table, as Ahmet was now.

Volkan began to take things too far, making jokes like, "Ahmet, what was the captain's name again? Why don't you introduce me to my new personnel? The boat will belong to me before long anyway."

The second and last session began. In fact, Ahmet knew it would not go well for him. The wisecracking continued to heat up. While he talked about how much he liked a new singer, the others were thinking: "He'll get his hooks into the girl for sure, and he's testing our reaction. He'll lose interest in three days."

It was the last round and like all last rounds, especially tense.

Because it was the last round, everyone placed a bet. Volkan was ahead in his winnings and wanted to take this hand too. His self-confidence was at its peak, although he'd had nothing to drink. He had a pile of money in front of him and began at 1500. Ahmet glanced at the pair of aces in his hand and hissed, "Pass."

It was Alp's turn. He remembered that he'd promised to take Volkan down in the last round and went all in, pushing the nearly 4500 liras he had to the center of the table. Volkan had felt sure of himself until that moment but now became apprehensive; he couldn't resist though, and stood pat. When they put their cards on the table, Volkan, who'd been warbling like a nightingale all evening, blushed purple. Ahmet was more pleased about it than Alp and kissed Alp on the cheeks. The game was over.

Ergin got off easy. His pedant's knowledge of poker history had helped him. Their host Ahmet was, in a word, busted but happy because Alp, not Volkan, had won the last hand.

# Kübra's Days
## (Vacation)

The plane had begun its descent. Kübra looked out at the sky through the tiny window, absorbed in watching the soaring flight of a bird in the distance. How free birds seemed to be, flying whenever and wherever their hearts desired. But in the end, they too were part of a flock. They had specific places where they came down to roost; so no creature was completely free, including human beings.

They arrived at the recently opened Hatay Airport after a flight of one and a half hours. They got into two taxis and in ten minutes, arrived at The Ottoman Palace Hotel, patronized by members of the new administration, including the Prime Minister and several others. The Akansan family had chosen to go to Antioch for a three-day vacation.

It was a luxury hotel with the splendor of an Ottoman palace as its name suggested. The magnificent entrance made an immediate impression. Walls worked in gold leaf motifs, portraits of Ottoman sultans, decorative pools in the center of the lobby...The delicate painted borders worked into the pillars had been done by a Georgian artist whose works were represented in the Kremlin and the White House.

There was something special about this five-star hotel. Chance had smiled upon the brother entrepreneurs who would be its owners while the hotel was being built and a therapeutic hot spring was found when the foundation was dug. The minerals in the water were beneficial for many illnesses.

Another family, friends of Hikmet Bey and Nadide Hanım, were coming from Kayseri to join them. The Akansans' eldest daughter, Müberra, and their other two daughters, sons-in-law and grandchild, had all come for a pleasurably healthy vacation.

They settled into their rooms, all on the same floor. Kübra and Büşra were in a suite connected with that of their parents and their older sister Müberra was in another with her husband and sons. The rooms were as splendid as the new hotel's entrance. The bedsteads and cupboards were worked with gold leaf and adorned with carvings and inlays.

The best thing to do in the hotel was to go down to the bottom floor and soak in the thermal waters. Hikmet Bey said he was going to make a few calls and sent off his wife and daughters. Nadide Hanım and Müberra got into the elevator in comfortable but veiling dresses. Büşra, like her big sister Kübra, wore the white bathrobe that came with the room and a white scarf over her hair. Slippers on their feet, they all went down together.

Nadide Hanım turned to her younger daughters and said: "Girls, what is this? Does a woman wander around a hotel in a bathrobe?"

Kübra had a ready answer: "Oh Mom, it's a thick robe, it covers everything. Our heads are already covered anyway. And when we get downstairs, we'll be on the women's side. While you're changing into bathing suits, we'll already be in the water." When they got to the spa floor, Kübra and Büşra went straight to the pool, already in their bikinis when they took off their robes, while their mother and older sister headed for the dressing rooms.

On the spa floor, there were separate pools and saunas for men and women but also areas men and women could use together. Kübra took a shower and sauna on the women's side. After she had sweated and breathed in the relaxing menthol air, she was ready to go into the thermal pool. She sat at the side and dipped her feet in the water. It was very hot, almost boiling. Büşra, very curious, came up and sat next to her. They dangled their legs down into the water until they adjusted to the heat and then lowered themselves in completely. The hot temperature of the water was unpleasant when you first went in but after a few minutes, your body got used to the heat and you felt like you were enveloped by a protective wave. They swam for ten minutes and walked in the water up to their chins. It was as salty as it was hot because it contained iodine. Kübra called out to her mother. Nadide Hanım let herself down slowly into the water in her bathing suit.

Kübra wanted to have a rubdown with a loofah at the Turkish bath. She'd made an appointment earlier. She got out of the water and lay down on a chaise lounge to relax for a while. She chatted with her mother and older sister. Nadide Hanım had worn a black, one-piece suit which concealed as much as possible. Kübra's older and younger sisters were wearing bikinis like she was.

When it was time for her rubdown, Kübra went into the Turkish bath section. A crude-looking young woman wearing a bath cloth around her waist was to do it for her. Kübra lay down on the broad, smooth bath stone at the center of the chamber. She felt like she was in the Thousand and One Nights. The attendant asked her to take off her bikini to make the rubdown easier. Kübra hesitated at first but when she saw that most of the other women around her had taken off their tops, she untied her own and took it off, keeping it by her side. Kübra bathed dail and did her ablutions, yet the rubdown with a loofah made her feel her body was even cleaner.

After a healthy session of self-care, they all went up to their rooms. Hikmet Bey and Bilal had enjoyed the thermal waters in the men's section. By the time they came upstairs, it was time for tea. Their friends from Kayseri had arrived at the hotel. They went together into the salon with an open buffet of sweet and salt pastries. The men sat at one table and the women at another. There was fresh *çökelek* cheese, bread baked with peppers and sesame and other varieties of breads on their plates. They ordered humus to share, and ate it with thin flat bread. It all tasted good with strong tea. They chatted while they ate heartily.

The following day was devoted to touring Antioch. Again, they went together. They walked the narrow streets of the city which had been incorporated into modern Turkey in 1939 and was rich in the inheritance of several cultures. The Grand Mosque and main Orthodox and Protestant churches were each within walking distance of the other on the same avenue. With the Catholic Church on a back street, Antioch was one of the finest examples of how several religions had been able to co-exist.

The homes lining the narrow streets had large inner courtyards with orange trees. Most of the street numbers were in Arabic. They also walked through the Long Bazaar spread across the city center, where the women did not neglect to buy pomegranate paste, bay leaf soap and various spices.

They had set out early and still had a lot of time. When Kübra told her father she wanted to see the Armenian village, everyone agreed.

They set out in two cars for Vakıflıköy in the Hatay province of Samandağ, the only village in Turkey to have an entirely Armenian population. Kübra had heard that Vakıflıköy once hosted the Meeting of Civilizations, and that its residents had worked hard to keep their village alive despite many difficulties.

After a short drive, they came to another village. Young men and women were dancing an ancient folk dance in the square under the shade of a great plane tree. They stopped the car to watch. A woman was selling broiled ears of corn and they bought some. While they were eating it, they learned that this was an Alevi village.

At last, they reached Vakıflıköy with a population of just 130 in thirty households. The village was famed for its magnificent natural beauty, the warmth of its people, and its organic farming.

For a short time, they walked around the sweet, orderly village with its unspoiled Armenian architecture until they came to the Armenian Church. The girls went inside, while Hikmet Bey craned his neck to have a look and then waited in the courtyard. It was small and dozens of candles were lit. Kübra came outside and was washing her hands at the fountain in the courtyard when she saw a baby lying on a kilim spread on the ground. She came closer; the baby had just woken up and gazed at her with sleepy eyes. She bent over to move the sweet baby boy's head back onto his pillow. She caressed his face and he smiled. His mother came up at that moment.

"Your baby is very sweet; what is his name?" Kübra asked.

"Kevork," the dark-skinned young mother replied.

Kübra caressed the baby again, saying his name. Most of the people in the village were old. There were almost no young people. The woman told Kübra there were only twentytwo children in the village. She was Catholic and had moved to the village as a bride.

How interesting people's lives could be! A Catholic woman comes as a bride to an Armenian village of thirty households and gives birth to her baby there...

When they got back to the hotel, everyone was tired but seemed happy. The best thing to do was to go and relax in the thermal waters.

# Esin's Days
## (Friends)

Esin was unhappy that she had not been able to get together with her girlfriends for a long while. They just couldn't find a time when everyone was free. All right, so everyone was busy but it wasn't all that hard to meet for a chat over lunch.

When people are newly married, for a while they generally see less of their unmarried friends; couples start hanging out with other couples. It was a weird social habit but that's how it was.

At last, they made a date for lunch in Nişantaşı. If they had time, they would take a look around the shops as well.

Abdi Ipekçi Caddesi was like New York's Fifth Avenue or the Champs Elysees of Paris, and as always, it was more spectacular than ever, well- kept and teeming with chic women in branded clothes, although some took their obsession with brands too far and the things they wore were just in bad taste.

Esin and her best friends Sevim and Zeynep met right on time. As always, Esin was wearing a knee-length dress which fit her perfectly and accented the lines of her body. She had on high heels which were more comfortable than they looked. Sevim was conservative and wore a full skirt with a white blouse. Her heavy necklace of large stones immediately caught the eye. She'd tied back her curly hair at the nape of her neck. Zeynep was wearing a blouse with spaghetti straps and blue jeans. Her stiletto heels looked very chic. They chose what to eat and drink from the menu quickly so as to get down to the gossip as soon as possible

They killed off some media gossip and mercilessly dissected a few of their own sex, and then the subject wandered to men. Relationships between men and women were so difficult, impossible to figure out, a bottomless pit...Women were stunned by the instability of male-female relationships and men bewildered by the almost schizophrenic female obsession with detail.

Esin was still newly married, she was happy, she had a handsome husband and things were going well.

And Sevim? She hadn't been serious about anyone since her divorce. She'd stayed away from men for a while because she lived with her daughter. She missed flirting, she missed having long talks with her lover and – no doubt about it – sex. But for a year after her divorce, she'd put her daughter first and almost forgotten about herself.

Zeynep was the only one of them who had never been married, and she was the youngest. She was a delightful, lively young woman. She had been wanting to have a good relationship for a long time. She'd had a few affairs that didn't last long, some for a few weeks and one for six months. Although many people became numb after a few bad experiences and raised the white flag, Zeynep was still looking for a grand passion. The last boy she'd seen had been very handsome and younger than her. She'd tried that too. But he wasn't enough for her. She craved the thrill of love. She dreamt of meeting someone with whom she could have a passionate affair. "You know what, girls? Love is ready there inside me, waiting to be discovered," she said and winked.

They'd finished their food but there was no end to gossip. Still, they got up from the table. Then they wished they'd had a Turkish coffee and told each other's fortunes after so much talk. Sevim wanted to go back and sit down again but Zeynep had to go to the hairdresser's to get ready for a party that night.

# Kübra's Days
## (A bad thing)

Kadriye was supposedly washing the windows but her mind was miles away. She felt really bad, her heart was aching. She almost didn't care if she fell the three stories to the ground below. That ass of a husband of hers was fooling around with another woman. With the little money they had, Huseyn was running around after women like a rich playboy.

This was occupying her mind all the while she struggled with the windows in Kübra's room. Her heart was broken. She was ashamed in front of the neighbours. While lost in thought, wondering what to do, her left foot suddenly slipped on the ledge. She seemed to see the ground rushing toward her, her head was spinning but a sudden reflex made her grab hold of the window frame. Nadide Hanım happened to come into the room at that moment and froze, her eyes wide as china plates. She thought she couldn't get there in time even if she ran toward the window and stood staring in the doorway.

"Goodness, Kadriye, be careful! Come this way. I almost died of fright thinking you'd fall. Come down and rest a bit."

"If resting would make it go away..." Kadriye mumbled. She took firm hold of the window frame and stepped back into the room.

Nadide Hanım came up to her. "What's wrong, Kadriye?"

"Don't ask, Mistress, you know I share everything with you. That Huseyn is with another woman; he's cheating on me."

"Mercy! How awful!"

"Yes, awful. I can't look anyone in the face in the neighborhood. The grocer, the fruit and vegetables man, the neighbors, I rush past them. I go home with a heavy heart."

Nadide Hanım sat down on the edge of Kübra's still unmade bed. She was going to listen to Kadriye's troubles a while.

"Forget the neighbors. What are you going to do? How did you find out?"

Kadriye heaved a long sigh and went on, her eyes full of tears: "You know my man, he paints houses. He has his bosses. When he gets a job, they all go together. The last house they went to had a lot of work. For days and days, they went back and forth to that house. There was a girl working there. He had his eye on her. The girl probably made nice ... well, whatever she did, they started meeting outside. The job was over and our man was nowhere to be seen. Turns out when he finished painting, he took the girl for ice cream. I hear they're drinking tea at sweet shops and so on."

Kadriye had been telling Nadide Hanım everything for years. If she had to go to the doctor, if her daughter had a problem, if there was something she didn't know what to do about, she always went to Nadide Hanım. Nadide tried to comfort Kadriye.

"Darling, it's just a whim, it will pass. When the work on the house is finished, he'll stop seeing the girl too. Is the man crazy? Will he take things so far as to wreck his happy home?"

"We don't have five kuruş to our name; we have debts. I hear he's sending gift minutes to her cell phone too. And we have to do without bread, while he sends minutes to fancy girls. He shouldn't give away my children's daily bread. Ah! Ah! What good can playing around do him? As if we were rich!"

Nadide Hanım was irritated by that last remark.

"What does that mean? Do such things have to do with money? Do rich men have the right to cheat? Don't talk nonsense, Kadriye. He's made an ass of himself; forgive him and let it go. He should stop seeing the girl. You're not thinking of breaking up your home at your age?"

"No, I'm not, Nadide Hanım but my head is all mixed up. I can't sleep, by God."

Nadide Hanım turned to religion to comfort poor Kadriye, even if just a little.

"Wherever you turn, Kadriye, there you find God. With God's help, you'll get past this as well."

Kadriye was not about to be comforted by that.

"I'm hurt bad, I'm so ashamed. How can I take him to bed with me now? It's not like our house is so big that I can say, 'Go to the salon and sleep on the couch.' He's never shown any interest in me anyway. He's never put two nice words together. But this is really bad. I guess I'll get used to it. I have to try. People don't take to divorce where I come from. And what will I do all alone without a man?"

Nadide Hanım sighed, and then she smiled. She rubbed Kadriye's back. "Don't be sad," she said. Then she went downstairs.

Street shoes were not worn in the house. They usually wore slippers but sometimes the girls went around barefoot. Nadide Hanım had the stairs carpeted so they wouldn't catch cold. Footsteps were not heard on the stairs.

The two-storey house had plasma televisions in both the salon and the family room. Calligraphic tableaux hung on the walls. There was one in a fancy frame in the entrance hall with "Allah" written in Swarovski rhinestones in Arabic letters against a velvet background. The floors were covered with Hereke carpets. The dinner table in the salon seated twelve, and could be opened out to seat twenty-four. There were only four members of the family living in the house but they had many guests. They needed the big table, especially during Ramazan for breaking of the fast dinner parties. Large, showy chandeliers seemed to reflect the wealth of the homeowners and also, somewhat, their parvenu tastes.

Nadide Hanım went into the kitchen and checked the refrigerator; she was wondering if there was enough food for dinner. The weekend was almost here. If only she'd cooked fine dishes and the desserts the children most liked... Strangely enough, a wicked thought suddenly occurred to her while absorbed in these cooking plans.

"And if my Hikmet did the same bad thing... If he went with another woman..."

# Esin's Days (Reaction)

Esin's cell phone was ringing. It was an agency calling to ask her to do a presentation in English. She asked about the nature of the event and stated her price. A Kuwaiti investment firm was going to organize a large event in Istanbul for their foreign partners. There would be meetings during the day and a fashion show in the evening.

A half hour later, they called to confirm the deal. They didn't try to get her to lower her price. Esin was delighted to have a good piece of work.

The day before the event, she met with representatives of the foreign firm and the Turkish company organizing it. They went over the program and cleared up questions she had about various things. She talked with two Kuwaiti representatives, one a young woman in a black headscarf and the other, a middle-aged man. The woman had not overdone her make-up, despite her black eyeliner and red lipstick. She had her headscarf arranged so that her hair was invisible. She was wearing a loose blouse and pants. She worked in the public relations section of the company and her English was perfect.

When the meeting was over and everyone was about to leave, the woman asked Esin what she was going to wear for the presentation the following day.

"Don't worry, I'll wear something appropriate."

"Please don't wear anything low-cut, and we would like it if your skirt were below the knee."

"I've done many presentations like this before and know what to wear. I can judge what is and is not appropriate. As I said, you have nothing to worry about."

Esin was poised and reassured the woman in an even tone, making it clear that she understood their sensitivities.

The next morning, the hotel's grand meeting was filled with the wealthiest businessmen in the Middle East when Esin arrived. There were two hundred attending. She saw a few women here and there as well. Bosses of the Kuwait firm's partner companies who made decisions involving millions of dollars had been invited. Most of them had flown to Istanbul in private planes. Esin was wearing a navy blue suit with a knee-length skirt. It fit her perfectly and showed the lines of her body. Closed-toe navy blue shoes completed the chic outfit. She kept her daytime make-up light.

The evening event was more colorful. The round tables in the large dining hall were decorated like brides. The runway for the fashion show had been cleared after rehearsals and was ready.

Esin looked over her cue cards backstage; she straightened her hair in the mirror and checked her make-up.

The models all had their hair done the same way in a French twist, and their make-up was almost finished when a scream rang out. The dresses for the show, created by a famous, mustachioed transvestite fashion designer, had been judged too revealing, and when he saw the shawls which had been brought in as a solution to the problem, he hit the roof. Apparently, his assistant had agreed to the firm's demand without asking him. The firm had objected to bare shoulders and backs and had shawls sewn to match the dresses. The famous designer was shouting menacingly at the Kuwaiti representative.

"This is the secular Turkish Republic of Ataturk. Do you think you can come here and do whatever you want? What right do you have to change my designs?" The representative was trying to calm him down but to no avail.

Esin was afraid the argument would get out of hand. She had to go on stage in a moment to announce the show. She was riveted to the spot, watching the debacle by the door leading onto the podium.

The designer had calmed down to some extent and collapsed into a chair, panting. But he began shouting again as soon as he caught his breath: "Let them go to Paris and try this on Jean-Paul Gaultier's runway if it bothers them so much! They won't get away with it. But they think they can do whatever they want in Turkey."

For a moment he seemed to simmer down but then said, "No, girls, we're not going on!" He would not give up.

"My maternal grandfather, my grandmother, and my father all came from different regions. I am a citizen of the Turkish Republic. I am a child of the Ottomans. We will never be an Arab country. You Arabs can't come here and pass judgment on us!"

Now the representative from the Turkish organizing firm tried to reason with him, saying the evening would be ruined and begging him to start the fashion show.

Esin was still waiting by the door, not knowing whether to go out on stage or not. It was long past time.

Things turned out all right in the end. Esin went out on the podium and smiling modestly, announced that the gorgeous outfits had been inspired by Ottoman designs and adapted for contemporary Turkey. The audience gaped stupidly and twittered. Esin could not believe her eyes. With all the presentations she'd done, she'd never come across such a bunch of stiffs. These men probably spent so much time thinking about their millions, that they could not enjoy life.

One by one, the models came out in those colorful shawls. On the return, almost all of them said things like, "I let my shawl slip and showed some shoulder, serves them right." They kept kissing the designer on the cheeks and trying to calm him down. As he sent them out again, he looked each dress over one last time dejectedly and straightened the shawls.

At last, the show was over and everyone rushed out. On the way home, Esin, tired but happy, kept thinking about the designer's reaction. Statements he'd made in recent interviews did not square up with what he said when he was yelling that evening. He was from a prominent family. He was a city boy, raised by nursemaids. He always talked about how he grew up listening to classical and French music.

Today, almost sixty, this famous fashion designer had begun his career making contemporary versions of traditional shalvar baggy pants. Although he'd been brought up in western culture, he tried to revive interest in things Ottoman and this was reflected in his designs. In recent years, something had come over this homosexual designer, who openly declared his sexual preference and named his boyfriends in public. Although he lived a life of extremes, he felt an affinity for the conservative religious party and made statements emphasizing that he was a sympathizer. Perhaps his sexual preference and life style pushed the boundaries but he repeatedly claimed to be a conservative. True, he expressed his conservatism not in terms of religious principles but his fidelity to classic Ottoman culture. He was closely involved in politics. He defined himself as a liberal democrat with an affinity for the conservative party, saying that he looked up to the prime minister as a father and found the president a very warm and kind man.

He shocked everyone when he aired his views on the turban issue as well. He began to support veiled women, saying, "If I were a woman, I would wear the turban too." In his opinion, no one should interfere with what a person believed or how they dressed.

Why had he changed? What had happened to him? Did he express such views in order to find work in the present political climate, to get contracts and design uniforms worn in state institutions? Is that why he sent such signals to those in power?

He had, for example, designed the airhostess uniforms for the national airline. He was successful with his first contract but despite his partisan statements, the next contract was given to an upscale, fashion-forward Jewish firm and then to a successful, modern female designer. Truly, Turkey was an interesting country.

# Kübra's Days
## (Design)

Kubra performed the morning prayer and drifted back to sleep. A few hours later, she awoke to the bitter sound of the clock alarm.

She picked out something appropriate to wear from the closet. She put on a light-colored, ruffled blouse, buttoned up to the neck, a long matching vest and loose, dark trousers. She went to the mirror and applied light make-up. She used a light-coloured, sheer foundation cream. She spotted on some cover under her eyes and spread it with her finger. Then she put on a thin coat of eyeliner around her green eyes. She didn't use any eye shadow. She was about to put on some lip-gloss but decided to leave it until after breakfast. She had to go to the hairdresser's soon. She needed to have her layered cut trimmed. Her mother needed her highlights done too. They would go together at the first opportunity.

She gathered her long brown hair up on top of her head with an elastic band, drawing out hair from the sides to hang free under her scarf. She arranged a thin black under-bonnet over the gathered up hair. She had bonnets in every color but usually wore black. Sometimes she wore a brown one if her outfit was completely brown. A bonnet served more to keep the scarf from slipping than to conceal her hair. It was impossible without one; a silk scarf would not stay on.

On top of the bonnet, she draped a famous branded scarf she'd bought on a trip to America with her parents. As it was an antique scarf, she did not tie it with a traditional knot. And leaving the scarf to hang free in the back gave a girl a "grown-up" look, because older and married women wore it that way. But young women like Kübra tied the scarf in back, creating a more compact, flawless look. This type of knot was nothing new. When Kübra was a little girl, she used to practice tying a scarf that way in front of the mirror because she thought it looked chic. True, styles of tying scarves had changed somewhat. There were fashions for tying them at the side, in the front, in the back or fastening them with pins.

While she was studying in the States, and years later as well, she'd gone to New York and bought Italian and French scarves at a better price than could be got in Europe. She liked to shop in New York not only for the prices but because the greater variety available made it easier to find what she wanted.

Her father was in Ankara, so there was no need for the family to have breakfast together. Her mother had set the table just for Kübra. She ate only a little bread and cheese and a few olives. She left her tea glass half-full. She said goodbye to her mother and went out through the garden where her father's company car was waiting for her.

The morning papers had been left on the back seat but Kübra did not feel like reading in a moving car. She gazed out the window and looked at passers-by. People were hurrying off to work. Most of them were frowning, or you could say their faces had no expression; they were still half-asleep.

She'd begun to work for her father shortly after returning from her university studies in the States. People in the circles they traveled in had at first been quite shocked that the daughter of such a conservative father would have gone to study in America. But Kübra's desire for an education was so strong that she had been able to overcome her father's objections; although she'd wanted to attend college in Turkey, she was determined not to discard the turban. So, while at college in the States, she had lived in a well-guarded girls dormitory.

Although the construction business had, at first, seemed to her a crude kind of work suitable for men, her interest in the selection of materials and interior decoration made her grow to like it in time. She loved design.

When she arrived at work, she said good morning to the few people she met and went into her office. As always, Fatma Hanım brought her tea. Kübra plunged straight into her work without even glancing at the newspapers.

She was to choose the kitchens for a new housing project. They were going to offer buyers kitchens with built-in appliances in accord with the latest design trends. A three-dimensional model for the kitchens had to be produced as soon as possible. There was a meeting with the interior decorators that afternoon. They would decide upon the materials, colors and design of the kitchen cupboards as well as matching handles and counters. Hikmet Bey had stressed that the project would be addressed to middle-class customers and so the materials must not be too expensive and high in quality. But they should still be attractive and competitive with similar projects.

Kübra worked backwards, choosing the materials which should have come last first. Now she would select cabinets to match the counters. The education she'd received in the States encouraged her to act freely. While thinking about her old school, she remembered Esin, who had studied communications at the same college. Esin turned heads when she walked across campus. She was a very attractive girl. Kübra liked it that a Turkish girl got so much attention. She'd even felt proud of Esin from afar. Sometimes, Esin wore short skirts; Kübra liked it when she didn't take her revealing dress too far.

She wanted to show off the creativity she had discovered at college. Conservatives were very fond of ostentation. Because their homes were the only thing they could show off, they spared no expense.

There were varied materials available for kitchen cabinets. The cupboards themselves could be melamine-coated chipboard or medium-density fiberboard and the doors, paneled, laminate or lacquered. She was a bit unsure about that. She took a break ... in any case, she would be making the decision with the other members of the company working on the project at the meeting that afternoon. She didn't want to put her father in a difficult position as she had last time, when he hadn't liked the project and they had to start over. Kübra had a tranquil nature but she could sometimes lose herself while focusing on a project. The more she learned, the deeper she got into it, the more pleasure she got out of it. She wasn't an engineer or an architect; her family trusted the education she had received and her instinctive eye for things. She was getting better at design all the time.

The firm that would build the kitchens was going to offer models according to each unit's measurements. Their computer program would show the finished kitchens in three dimensions, and they would decide how to arrange the plumbing, the box frames and outlets. Kübra would, of course, be free to make the changes she liked before the production stage.

It all turned out as she'd expected, although the meeting with the interior designers lasted longer than she'd thought it would. Their plans were overly classic. She couldn't change the computer simulations with her pen but when they were printed out, she made copious corrections and asked for a great many changes in the project.

Kübra had been able to act more freely at the meeting because her father was not present. When he was there, she could not do as she liked; she felt inhibited. And there were men in her father's business circles who would not even shake a woman's hand; their fanatical style of piety was such that they did not recognize a woman's right to express herself. Kübra did not like such extremism.

Although she covered her head, Kübra was a modern veiled woman who felt comfortable wearing trousers. Now, in her authoritarian father's absence she laid out her demands. The architects were shocked that an apparently frail, veiled young woman could be so decisive and self-confident.

In business circles abroad, no one concerned themselves with a person's beliefs and convictions; they paid attention to the work at hand and focused on finishing the project. A Jew, an atheist and a homosexual could work together on the same project. In Turkey, however, people said things like: "He's a communist, I won't work with him," or "He's religious, he can't get along," or as in Kübra's case, "She veils her head. How can she get the job done?"

It was as if the turban could only be worn by a helpless, vulnerable little girl. People thought she interfered with the work because her father was the boss. And Kübra really was delicate-looking. But at the meeting today, she'd shown off her knowledge, her ability to think ahead, and her vision. If she had sensed even the slightest negativity toward herself, she would have said: "O esteemed, well-educated, well-traveled architects, I veil my head, not what is inside it."

She was determined that the changes she wanted be made. Those supposedly madcap architects would just have to be a little more creative.

# Esin's Days
## (Shock)

After talking with Sevim on the phone, Esin waited for her to come over. Sevim was going to leave work early and come straight to Esin's house because she had a lot to tell her.

Sevim was older than Esin. She was like a big sister as well as a friend. She was protective of Esin, maybe partly because she had a child of her own. She lived with her fifteen-year-old daughter. Her motherly soul was expressed in her friendships too. She had a slightly plump figure and a beautiful face. Her hair was very curly; her curls were legendary.

The doorbell rang. Esin pressed the buzzer to let her into the apartment building. She listened while the elevator came up. Sevim rushed out, all upset.

Before her friend was even through the door, Esin asked: "What's happened, girl? Tell me right now, I'm about to burst."

"Give me a moment to catch my breath," Sevim said, taking off her sunglasses. "Oh, before I forget, I should call my daughter and let her know I'm at your house," she added. She had a warm talk with her daughter on the phone and then threw herself onto the couch in the salon. She got straight to the point, not wasting time with chit chat about her day.

"I got to know this guy. We really liked each other, though we didn't let on at first. I thought this was it; I was finally going to let someone into my life but it turned out to be hopeless."

"Why hopeless all of a sudden, darling, tell me about it, there must be a solution."

"No, there is none, Esin. Still, I've come to tell you about it; let's see if you're as shocked as I was."

"I'm listening, sweetheart."

Sevim said she wanted a coffee with milk first and brushed past Esin to the kitchen to make it herself. Esin didn't want to drink anything just now.

She sat down in the big armchair facing Esin and began to talk: "You know, I met someone named Hakan three weeks ago. You haven't seen him; he's very handsome. He makes you look twice. He has a very good body, does sports. It's the first time for years, especially since the divorce, that I've been attracted to a man."

"Don't I know it! Didn't we try so hard to find someone for you? You kept talking about your daughter, saying you didn't want anyone."

"It's true. And Hakan didn't impress me at first. There was a cold breeze blowing when we first met. I didn't even like his voice; it didn't seem manly at all. Anyway, a little while later, we began calling each other and sending each other phone messages. We even got together a few times, just for dinner or to sit in a cafe."

"Right, I know all that. But you didn't tell me much about what you felt for him."

"After a couple of dates, he started giving me these looks and smiles and acting more masculine. I liked those looks and I kept him in a corner of my mind. When he sat across from me, it was as if he was waiting for me to say something. He's very proud. He didn't make a pass. He liked me but we weren't letting on."

"So he was building up the image of a proud, smooth guy. There are a lot of them like that, don't you think? So?"

"Wait and you shall hear. Every time we met, we got a little closer. We looked into each other's eyes, we laughed, we talked, you know. We'd broken the ice. I kept thinking, "My God, what's happening to me?" We'd see each other and then he wouldn't call for a few days. I went on with my normal life, as if I was very busy. But it was hard. He'd gotten under my skin. And when he didn't call, it made me more interested. I hadn't wanted anybody but there was an electricity between us."

"But he confused you, of course. That's how these things go. The less the guy calls, the more the woman wants him to. So he was a cool type."

"Yeah, cool and cute. He has such a body, I was burning for him, I swear. I just wanted to be near him, that's all. Just walk down the street with him. It wasn't just me; he liked being with me too. I was very excited. When we were together, it was high voltage, very obvious. Then just when I thought he wanted me, he disappeared. When he didn't call, I thought about him more than ever and began to feel bad. I was about to give up on him when he sent me a message.

"And that's the worst kind," Esin said. "The ones who pretend to want you. They're both there, and not there. The ones who turn up just when you're about to forget them. They make it seem like you can't do without them. You should tell these types about Shakespeare. He said that most people are afraid of love because they're afraid to lose."

"If only that were the case. Anyway, then we got together again. He began to show his feelings more openly. I thought the best thing was not to push it, give it time. We drank some good wine and talked. But he held out hope and then ran away. There was something evasive about him, as if you couldn't trust him."

"And of course, you were hooked, isn't that so, my lovely friend?"

"Oh don't ask, Esin. It was like sparks were flying from our eyes. I hadn't felt like that in so long. I thought I'd be in the clouds if we slept together. But unfortunately, a voice inside kept telling me we'd never be together. Just when I was thinking my daughter was old enough and I could start to live my own life, the guy makes no move. I was so upset. He started to act mysterious, like he was very busy. He broke a few dates, saying he had too much work to do, and it was taking longer than he thought. I was about to decide not to see him anymore when he turned up again. Then he even went away on vacation. We didn't talk for days. I began to imagine things, of course... I thought he must have a girlfriend he couldn't shake off."

"What happened when he got back from vacation?"

"He came back but it was the same thing; he'd call, then not call. He wouldn't call me if I didn't call him first. I was about to go crazy. I'm lonely, Esin. I feel shut out, like no one wants me. I kept forgiving him for some reason I don't understand."

"It's your motherly side. You're very compassionate, my dear Sevim. If it were me, I'd have long since sent him off with his nonsense."

"It's not so easy, Esin. I couldn't stop thinking about him. Then I was cold to him for a while; I didn't call. Yesterday evening, there was a message on my cell from him: 'What are you up to?' I wrote back: 'I'm taking it easy. I'm tired.' Then he wrote: 'So you won't accept my invitation to dinner, my smiling one?'"

Esin straightened up in her seat. "And you went out with him?"

Sevim was a little annoyed. "Yes, and all dressed up. I couldn't decide what to wear. I was so excited on the way, that my heart was in my mouth. There he was before me with that muscular body and gorgeous face. I melted."

"So, very nice, two good-looking people having dinner."

"I relaxed a bit after a couple of glasses of wine. While we were talking, he let it slip that he really liked me. And somehow, I got the courage to ask: 'So why do you keep calling me and then disappearing? Is there someone in your life?'"

"Bravo."

"Now, listen well. He's had a lot of relationships, some brief, some long. He said he loves spending time with me, that he trembles when he looks at me, and he even said that he's dying to make love to me. He adores my curls."

"Wow, that's great! He even tells you right out that he wants to make love to you."

"Yes, everything seemed wonderful. But there was a catch. He's been with someone else for a year and a half, and they've even been living together for five months."

Esin was so upset, she jumped up and then sat down again: "Oh no! What bad luck! So how is he going to break up with the woman?"

"What woman! His lover is a man!"

Esin's face turned completely white.

"The things that happen to me ..." Sevim said sadly. "I went into shock."

"He just said it like that? He admitted it?"

Sevim went on miserably, barely able to get the words out: "Two years ago, he met someone abroad, a man. The guy pursued him for months and finally had his way. 'He took me out of myself,' he says. The guy laid siege to him. They have a strange relationship. His family found out and didn't like it. Then I turned up. He thought of going to a psychologist. He was trapped. He didn't understand how he could feel that way about a man. He even told me: 'I find life where others fear to tread.'"

Esin listened to her friend wide-eyed. She went to the kitchen and got a huge glass of water and drank it all in one shot. She signaled with her head for Sevim to go on.

"He was very honest with me. Before this guy, he'd only been with women; he's had several relationships. Then this guy came into his life and he found out he liked being with a man too. 'We have a different kind of bond,' he says. It's more an emotional than a sexual thing. On the other hand, I'm the first since – I mean the first woman he's liked since. He's even started to be obsessed with me, he can't stop thinking about me. He wants to run his fingers through my curls and make love to me for hours. He's caught in between."

"That's all very well but what are you going to do? If you're not really stuck on the guy, show him the door, girl. Your rival isn't even female. How will you know what to do? I don't know how to advise you; I swear I'm struck dumb."

"I'm a bit worn down, I think. His not calling got me ready for something bad. I was shocked but I didn't let it show. I went on quietly eating my dinner, you know? I even told him that it was something to fill the emptiness of life. 'It must fill an emptiness in you,' I said."

"Aww, Sevim, now you're going to make me mad. This tolerance of yours, the way you try to help everyone, it kills me. The man's a homosexual. All right, but that is not an illness. Anything can happen to a person in life. But this is really too much. You're not going to go on with this weird relationship, are you?"

"The truth is I didn't end it. I think I'm going to try to make it work. I'm going to make him leave that guy and be mine. I have no idea how. I don't know what homosexuals or bisexuals do, what they feel. Look Esin, I think love has two sides. There's taking and there's giving. The first way, if what you are taking gets cut off, you suffer. The other way is surer."

Sevim was amazed that she didn't feel angry despite the fact that he was with a man. She wanted to help him, make him confront his true feelings. It seemed a strange relationship was about to catch fire.

Esin could think of nothing else to say but: "Well, darling Sevim, what can I say? If you will get more pleasure than pain out of it, go on and have it but if the lion's share will be suffering, stay out of it."

They talked about it a bit more ay but couldn't get anywhere. It wasn't something they knew much about. Clearly, Sevim liked the guy enough to let his troubles into her life. She had another coffee and left, sad but excited at the prospect of embarking on a new relationship.

When Esin was alone, she couldn't stop herself from wondering what would it be like to have a relationship with someone of the same sex. What did men feel when they were with men and women when they were with women? Could a woman come between two men? Or a man between two women? Sevim hadn't been gone two minutes when the doorbell rang again. Esin got up and opened the door. It was Alp.

"Don't you have your key?" she asked.

"I wanted my one and only wife to open the door, so I could feel a little like a man," Alp said, giving her round hips a naughty, resounding slap.

Having her hips touched roused Esin and she wanted to have sex. What she and Sevim had talked about had already got her going. A woman and a muscular, handsome man ... To make love with someone of the same sex ... To lose yourself ...

She gazed into her husband's eyes and began unbuttoning his shirt. Alp stood still, surprised and pleased. He was not going to miss this chance. His wife looked more beautiful than ever, she was undressing him and he liked it. "My, my, my husband's great big arms look so good, you can see the muscles even with his shirt on."

She felt him take a deep breath and began kissing his almost hairless chest. She planted kisses and little kitten tongue bites. Her lip and tongue movements got harder until she was passionately and hungrily kissing her man.

At first, Alp let Esin enjoy making love to him but now he could not hold back any longer. He began running his hands over her curves. They kissed wildly, breaking the dance of tongues for an instant to start again. She undid his belt and unzipped his fly and he got his legs free from his pants, pulling off his boxer shorts in one quick motion. Esin was wearing a thin house-dress; she hadn't put on a bra. He seized the skirt, pulled it up over her arms and head and tossed it aside.

At that moment, neither of them wanted the other completely naked yet. Esin had on only her white panties and Alp his shirt. When Alp ran his fingers over the edge of the white material and squeezed that hot softness, he realized there was no need for more foreplay. He pushed her panties aside, grasped his wife's hips in his hands and slowly lifted that maddeningly alive body onto him.

All this happened as they stood in the hallway. They had time only to close the front door and began making love without even getting as far as the salon. It was a bit harsher than usual, but they neared a climax with love and feeling.

They kept at it a bit longer, standing up, and then Alp dragged Esin toward the big armchair in the salon. Now they were more comfortable and moaned in pleasure. Alp wasn't going to be able to hold out much longer and growled, "Come on, baby."

Esin hated when he said that. She did not like to have the timing of her orgasm set by someone else; it ruined the whole thing. If she was going to come, she was the one to know when. She needed to concentrate ... to focus on herself before she could allow herself to completely release. That stupid expression he used, made her lose all desire.

Alp had already come and was mumbling, "But baby, if only we'd come together ... I couldn't hold myself back ..."

# Kübra's Days
## (Samet)

They were formally promised to one another a few weeks after Samet's family came to ask for Kübra's hand. Although the parents on both sides had decided the engagement should take place as soon as possible, Kübra found a thousand and one excuses to delay the event and succeeded in putting it off. But in the end, Kübra and Samet got engaged in a simple ceremony at home.

Kübra glanced at the ring on her finger while getting ready to see her fiancé, Samet.

Samet had been much influenced by the quoted in the Imam and Preacher's manuals, "The best of you is he who learns and teaches the Gracious Koran." That is why he had memorized the Koran and attained the rank of *hafiz*.

As a *hafiz*, Samet had been the pride of his school, the honor of his class, and the favorite of his teachers. He was a quiet, unobtrusive young man, stayed out of trouble, and never offended anyone. He was a bit placid but he spoke with his heart.

Sometimes, he'd found it a burden to be a *hafiz*. Thanks to the administration at his school, he'd been much sought-after for neighborhood funerals. But he'd liked that it got him out of attending school once in a while.

After graduating from the Imam and Preacher's lycée in Konya, he moved to Istanbul with his parents and got his university degree there. He was going to graduate, fulfill his obligatory military service, and marry Kübra when he got back.

His choice of university for an advanced degree was controversial. He went to Kazakhstan to attend one of the universities which the Nurcu community, gaining strength in Turkey with every passing day, had founded abroad within a supposed "moderate Islam" framework.

The Nurcu community's leader, now, long a resident of the United States, had been accused by some of being a reactionary who wished to destroy the Turkish Republic and set up an Islamic state based on the *sheriat* in its place. Others averred that the community was content with the established order and aimed only for economic expansion and influence through education in the religious way of life. Turkish schools were being opened everywhere around the world. Teaching was done in the local language or English but classes in the Turkish language and Islam were encouraged. Some people would even find it cute for a Chinese or an African kid to speak Turkish. Whatever anyone might say, the university Samet attended was part of an efficiently functioning global organization which had attained an incredible degree of financial power.

Kübra was dragging her feet, downhearted. She did not feel at all like seeing Samet, didn't want to talk to him. Yet shouldn't a young woman about to marry run joyfully to meet her fiancé, full of shy excitement? And wasn't love a desire to be with the one who would be the man of her life?

Kübra had not even spent much time getting ready in front of the mirror. Yet shouldn't she have given hours of thought to the clothes and jewelry she would wear for such an emotional occasion? But she'd chosen something in a hurry and carelessly put it on.

First she'd thought she'd wear a green outfit. But the colour green did not suit the way she felt. Instead, she chose a lilac blouse and matching skirt.

She had read a great deal about colors. She spent a lot of time pondering the language of color, both because of her work and because she took a special interest in it. She knew which colors firms used for which purposes, how color influenced the buying habits of customers, which colors added energy to an environment and which gave a feeling of calm.

Green was the color of trust. So, today she had no need of that! She did not want to feel safe, to feel she was under the protection of anyone. Especially not Samet; she did not want him to approach her that way. She'd put aside green in favor of a dark lilac tending to purple. In other words, she was in an unsettled psychological state. Purple was like that; even the specialists had not quite determined what it meant. Some said it represented creativity and the power of thought; others that it symbolized balance. Another specialist said that it calmed the heart and reduced fear and anxiety. But for Kübra, purple meant infinity.

Today, she didn't want to worry about the unpleasant realities of life; she wanted to be in the realm of abstraction... But she couldn't have put off Samet any longer. According to those around her, and the ring on her finger, she was Samet's fiancée. "And according to me as well!" she couldn't keep herself from thinking.

She struggled with a profound inner dilemma. She felt tormented seeing Samet. She was caught between tradition: her family and friends on the one hand, and her own true self on the other.

Samet picked her up from her house. He'd come in his car. As she was about to sit down in the front seat, she saw a single white rose left for her there. She thanked Samet shyly.

Even just sitting next to him made Kübra uncomfortable. How would they live together under the same roof? They chatted about the weather, friends in common, falling silent now and then and arrived in Beyolu instead of going to Baghdad Boulevard as they'd planned.

Beyoğlu's Istiklal Avenue was full of life. They walked for a while, and then went into a cafe. Kübra sat in the chair Samet politely held out for her, and she kept her eyes down as he sat across from her. He rubbed his hands together as if the weather were chilly and his hands were cold. Nerves made him make that slightly strange gesture; he did not know how to behave at that moment.

Kübra asked for orange juice and Samet, for tea.

Kübra kept averting her eyes from him, glancing down at the table or gazing off in the distance. Samet met Kübra's coldness by trying to make as sincere an impression as possible; he talked a little about the Master's degree he'd just completed. He'd studied international relations for his B.A., and his M.A. was in business administration. He told her about his life in Kazakhstan, the atmosphere and the food at the merely ten-year-old school. He said that the old capitol, Alma Alta, was quite different from Istanbul but had a population of two million and was rapidly becoming the most developed city in Central Asia; it had many shopping malls, restaurants and hotels offering a rich style of life.

He tried to get Kübra interested in the subject.

"Kübra, look, you'd be surprised, the center of the city is a perfect grid, just like Manhattan. All the streets are either vertical or horizontal. The buildings on one side of the street have odd numbers and those on the other have even numbers. The easiest way to specify an address is to give the names of the intersecting vertical and horizontal streets, just like in New York."

Kübra remained indifferent. Inside her she kept repeating, "Happiness should not be built on a lie." The man sitting across from her could have sensed her true feelings from the expression on her face but clearly, it either did not suit Samet to do so or he had no empathy. While she should, as a grown woman, have expected from men, the understanding and approval she had not gotten from her father as a child, she realized she would find her spiritual goal not in another person, especially not in Samet but in herself.

Kübra pulled herself together, thinking of the honor of her family, and gave Samet a slightly forced smile.

Samet asked for his second strong tea.

"Kübra, is something bothering you? You seem distracted."

"No, I'm fine, there's nothing wrong."

But inwardly, she was uncomfortable and frustrated. It was as if she were wearing a mask on her face. A smiling mask face stuck on top of her own.

"Are you worried about my military service? A pre-determined time passes quickly, you know. I'll be back before you know it. And when I return, if it please God, if it's our destiny, we will make a home together."

This last sentence embarrassed Samet and he lowered his head.

Kübra felt shamed by his sincerity.

"I should be comforting you about your military service but you are comforting me. Forgive me, Samet."

They sat in silence for a while. Samet asked for the check.

They drove down to the sea. They parked the car and began to walk along the shore. They walked side by side. They were just two people walking side by side. At one point, Samet stole a glance at Kübra's right hand, and seeing the ring on her finger, he felt better. Kübra would be his in the end anyway. She would rise to the rank of woman of his house and mother of his children. And what a beautiful girl she was. Both outwardly and inwardly, she was well mannered, cultured, an ideal little lady to marry. Pious, chaste, veiled, pure; an educated girl from a good family.

Samet was dying to hold her hand. But although they were in their mid-twenties, they had not even really kissed. Their wedding night would be the first contact with the opposite sex for both of them.

In conservative circles, where young couples did not have sex before marriage and most of the girls were virgins until they were married, it was frowned upon for a veiled girl to even walk hand in hand with her boyfriend. Although physical intimacy was becoming more common, most girls did not go all the way.

For turbaned women, even to smoke cigarettes could lead other people to form strange opinions about them. At the very least, people would say, "Look, they smoke cigarettes too." The environment of hostility toward veiling meant that turbaned girls had to tread carefully.

Kübra and Samet had once almost touched hands before he went abroad to study but she immediately pulled her hand away. When they were saying goodbye before he left and were left alone for a moment, he had managed to embrace her and kiss her forehead. Samet was in awe of Kübra's shyness. But Kübra had read enough novels to know that unhappiness began when the touch one was used to was lost.

In this country, the bourgeois youth of Etiler and brand-loving generation of Baghdad Boulevard were on one side, and the youth of Ümraniye and politicized groups of Armutlu on the *other*. The way they talked, the things that bothered them, their expectations of the future and life styles were completely different. While Samet couldn't even hold his fiancée's hand, other underage girls were beginning to have sexual relationships with men. True, young girls in very conservative circles who wanted to keep up with the millennium age, had sex with their boyfriends but shortly before their wedding day, secretly had their hymens sewn up. The practice was widespread in both Turkey and Iran. Two days before her wedding, a veiled girl would go to a private clinic to have her hymen sewn, and when the groom saw blood on the wedding night, he thought he had pierced his bride's hymen. But the blood was from the tearing of the stitches.

They walked along…just walking side by side. Samet spoke of how much he had missed Istanbul. He meant to hint that it hadn't been only Istanbul he missed but his beautiful Kübra as well. They walked along, gazing at the city's magnificent view a while longer. Then a light breeze came up. As it got stronger, a sudden reflex made Kübra's hand go to her scarf to straighten it. At that moment, a light rain began to drizzle as well. Kübra was happy the weather had turned bad because now she had an acceptable excuse to go home early.

# Esin's Days (Aphrodisiac)

Esin was going to have trouble choosing the right outfit for the evening. They were going to two different parties, one a cocktail and after that, a wedding. She had many beautiful dresses lined up according to color and occasion in her perfectly organized closet, and usually she could dress very quickly. Her habit of getting dressed quickly was something her husband Alp particularly liked.

He'd had such bad experiences with women before they got married. How could it take so long for a woman to get herself ready! What could she be doing anyway? Shower, creams, hair, make-up, clothes, perfume ... They weren't having plastic surgery to change themselves from head to toe! It had always driven him mad that women spent so much time getting dressed. At least Esin was not like that.

But Esin was having trouble making a decision this evening because she was going to wear a very revealing dress that made it impossible to wear a bra; the dress all but exposed her breasts to view. Her husband had particularly asked her to wear it!

Where had Alp acquired this new way of thinking? No sir, women with small or medium-sized breasts should not wear bras; those padded, wired bras didn't look natural at all; Esin had beautiful breasts, what was there to hide? She should be proud she had such firm breasts ... she should take a look at those foreign actresses and models, they did not wear bras like casting molds.

Oh well, the truth was, it didn't take long to convince Esin. It even flattered her feminine pride but it was going to take some time to find the right kind of dress with thin straps for this new kind of décolleté. She knew that if she took too long, Alp would go crazy waiting in the salon. However much he might rummage through his financial magazines, he hated to wait.

She decided on a colorful, short, one-piece dress in a geometric pattern with thin straps. She tried it on and thought it looked very good. She put on her chic copper-colored stiletto heels which buckled around the ankle. She took her gold portfolio-style clutch purse without a handle, the kind men usually said looked like a large wallet. The most it could hold was her ID card, lipstick, the security card she'd pulled off the invitation that came in a huge envelope, and if she really pushed it, her cell phone. She left her hair loose; she'd had it styled at lunchtime. She put gold rings in her ears to match her purse. She exchanged her everyday white wristwatch for a gold one and her white diamond necklace with the first letter of her name to which she'd had a jeweller add the first letter of her husband's name after they married, for another elegant necklace with a gold chain.

They left the house, a very chic and attractive couple. Their tanned skin, their youth, their magnificent attire, all gave them the appearance of a well-off husband and wife. When they walked by hand in hand, everyone turned to look. And it was not just for show; they really were a happy, lovely couple.

The party was on Water Island at Kuruçeşme. It was a site possessed of all the latest accoutrements of enjoyment, located between two continents right in the middle of the blue waters of the Bosphorus separating Asia and Europe. It made you feel like you had arrived at a luxury vacation land. Alp drew up to the park on the shore and left the car with a valet. They joined the other guests, most of whom had also arrived in private cars, to board the small ferry going back and forth to the island. Esin gazed at the Bosphorus as they crossed over in a gently blowing breeze. Who could tell how many people had crossed these waters over the centuries? What all they had experienced... Love and war... If these waters could speak...

The boat drew up to the island and the guests began getting off one by one. Alp behaved like any gentleman would and took Esin's hand to help her on shore.

They felt good. They glanced over the assembled guests. The eye was dazzled by the latest fashions, open-toed shoes with pencil-sharp heels, expensive handbags, jewels, colors, and top brands. It was a virtual contest in chic, though the eye was caught here and there by frumpish women who looked like gift-wrapped packages in their dresses festooned with huge bows. There were rich women flush with jewels from head to toe.

The guests had drifted into the space in small groups. Bored couples, arrogant-looking types, workaholics ... Everyone was checking each other out, from people who kept smiles firmly stuck on their faces as they pretended to listen to each other, to couples holding a "we are happy" pose. What a strange affliction it was; to be unhappy at home but try to appear happy in public ... How was living merely for others any different from being locked up in a jail cell? There were the maniacs who appeared ultra modern and civilized from outside, but beat their wives at home ... Yet both wife and husband tried hard to present a picture of domestic bliss when they were with others.

And there were the types busy rushing up the ladder to fame. Because most of them had no real foundation, no cultural accumulation or proper education, when they made it big, they would suddenly become madly impressed with themselves, spoiled and unprincipled. They wanted to break away from their old friends, from the circles in which they once mingled and forget them. At a certain point, they would become insatiable and lose the ability to control themselves. After that, everything was permitted in order to get more. Life in a world of falsehood turned people into little monsters who ate away at a person's insides and took over their souls.

What should be said about the men who arrived at the party after their wives because they had too much work to do? Workaholics who went about their jobs obsessively but could not find time for their families. They would lose it when they didn't have problems to solve at work. There had to be some insecurity and fear underneath such love of work; "working" was simply a means of escape.

In this group, you could also run into idealists who chose the less well-travelled path. They were not wealthy but they were respectable.

Before long, Alp and Esin ran into some people they knew and began chatting. Some time passed with small talk like, "It's so humid today," "The traffic was dreadful," "Have you lost weight?" and "What's to become of this country?"

At brilliant cocktails like this where fame joined with power, people generally stood sipping their drinks and munching on snacks while they threw smiles about. . Women got all dressed up and usually arrived on someone's arm. Some people ran from party to party, making you wonder if they had anything in their lives but cocktails and parties.

The following day, photographs of the guests would appear in society magazines. Silly things were written about the famous women, most of whom had had plastic surgery and posed with a self-confidence derived from money and power. While the women showed off in gossip rags, their husbands made the covers of business magazines.

Esin and Alp were going on to another party this evening. They wouldn't have missed their friend's wedding at the seaside mansion of Esma Sultan.

This historical mansion located next to Ortaköy Mosque bore the name of the daughter of the Ottoman Padishah Sultan Abdülaziz. Esma Sultan married Çerkez Mehmet Pasha when she turned sixteen, and the mansion was given to her as a wedding present.

Esin and Alp made their entrance, striking yet not showy. They saw a dazzlingly chic party of guests in the garden, where the ruins of an ancient cistern, Turkish bath and stable were still in evidence. Some of the women were in long gowns and the men in tuxedos.

Esin had chosen an outfit appropriate for both of the parties they'd attend that evening. Alp touched his wife's bare shoulders and back, smiling with eyes full of love. Esin too was pleased with her cavalier and responded graciously. The chic group of guests at the mansion seemed to give both of them an extra air of refinement.

The gay breeze of a summer's night and the magnificent view of the Bosphorus boosted everyone's mood. The splendor of the mansion's interior, renovated with glass and steel, was enhanced by the luminous play of light. Alp and Esin strolled through the open space, stopping to chat when they came across people they knew. Everyone was chic, everyone was smiling. Then the bride appeared in her pure white gown like a swan beside the tall groom. They walked toward the marriage table to applause. The bride was clearly nervous, yet threw kisses everywhere. It was a civil ceremony carried out by the Mayor of the province. The bride stepped on the groom's foot to another burst of applause. There were smiles and laughter all around when the marriage document was signed and delivered to the bride and she raised her hand in a victory sign.

After the bride and groom danced to a romantic song, other couples joined them on the dance floor edged with decorative white flowers.

This time Esin and Alp passed on the dance and headed straight for the bar.

Esin normally did not drink much but this evening she was going to keep pace with her husband and enjoy the evening. She asked the waiter for a mojito but Alp intervened.

"Have a straight drink, my beauty. At crowded events like this, the cocktails are thrown together in a rush and the mojito won't be any good."

So Esin asked for a whiskey on the rocks. Alp looked at his wife wide-eyed. The little lady was not good at holding her drink, and she was starting off the night with hard liquor.

Esin had one whiskey, then another and her head began to spin. She was not used to alcohol and got drunk right away. Alp then stopped drinking himself, since he would be driving them home. When they went out together, Esin drove on the way home because Alp drank, and having to watch what he drank spoiled his pleasure. This silly crowd was unbearable without alcohol. He told himself it didn't matter and asked the waiter for a vodka on ice. Esin sidled up to him and gave him a mischievous wink: "Don't drink too much ... a drunk man isn't much good for anything!"

Both of them were feeling no pain, laughing and flirting. Seen from afar, they made a perfect picture of gaiety. In that sense, they were no different from anyone else. The difference was that when you looked more closely, theirs was a much warmer version of the same tableau. Alp was planting kisses on his wife's face, forehead and lips while she caressed her beloved husband's arms. Enraptured, she turned to him and began talking baby talk.

"I want to spoil you ... Come on and treat me nice ... You wanted me to go around without a bra like this and my breasts are tiny under my dress, like a little girl's ..."

Esin was high and had begun to talk nonsense. But Alp liked her baby talk; it made him laugh. They left the party soon after. They hadn't danced because they wanted to get home to their bed as soon as possible.

In their condition, neither of them could take the wheel, so they left the car there, intending to pick it up the next morning. They jumped into a taxi and were home in no time.

They tore off their clothes and stretched out on the bed. They'd thrown their clothes all over the bedroom. At this hour, in this condition, they weren't about to put them away! They did not speak as they began to caress each other. A bit of alcohol affected Esin like an aphrodisiac, she took much more pleasure in making love and gave her partner the same. Now every touch on her skin, every wet kiss, had an incredible effect; wherever Alp touched her body, waves of pleasure swelled up and broke to melt on an endless sandy shore, followed immediately by new swells.

Sometimes, while Esin was making love, she felt like a bird was flapping its wings inside her. The bird would gradually grow in size and ferocity, then turn into a hawk and take flight, spreading its wings as wide as could be. At that moment, the marvelous moment the French call "the little death," Esin seemed to experience immortality.

Now they were lost in pleasure. A thirsting filled the room and Esin burned as if with fever. She locked her fingers around her husband's neck and pulled him to her.

After wonderful foreplay Alp did not hesitate to enter wonderland. The moans rising from their intertwined bodies mingled with the silence of the night.

Esin began to lose consciousness, making sounds between a moan and a scream. Alp bit her ear slightly, saying half proudly, half anxiously, "Don't be so loud, the neighbors will hear. Esin paid no attention. On the contrary, roused by the alcohol, she yelled loudly in English, "I don't care!" Alp was shocked; his wife was so hot tonight!

After a while, he slowed his tempo.

When they had both calmed down, before she drifted off into the sleep of angels, Esin took the trouble to get up, go to the bathroom and have a shower. The water pouring over her was not about to wash away the traces of the magnificent sex she'd had. Since she couldn't go to sleep without taking off her make-up, she did that last thing too, tired as she was, and put on her face and eye cream.

She was happy. She got into bed with a smile that said she wanted always to feel the way she did right now.

# Kübra's Days
## (Farewell)

His friends picked up Samet at the door of his home in Fatih. They set off in a convoy a few cars long, honking their horns. A blaring tape made the Military March echo down every street they passed through. The windows of all the cars were open and the boys hung out, waving Turkish flags and shouting, "God, God," "O God," "In the name of God," "God is greatest," and, "Our soldiers are the greatest soldiers of all!" There was no one left in the neighborhood who did not know that Samet was going off to do his military service.

At last, they reached the bus station. Samet's mother, her white prayer veil on her head and tears in her eyes, said farewell to her son. Only yesterday, he'd had his hair shaved in military cut by the neighborhood barber. He was wearing a T-shirt, jeans, and sneakers chosen at random. His mother had carefully prepared white undershirts, underpants and socks and packed them in a cheap suitcase, thinking it would get lost while he was in the army.

Kübra was there too. Her fiancé Samet was going to Balıkesir to fulfill his duty to his country. He would have basic training as a candidate reserve officer for three months at the Nineteenth Infantry Brigade Command in Balıkesir province and then be appointed by Ankara to the as yet undetermined location of his new post.

Since there were no flights to Balıkesir, Samet was to go by bus. Kübra wondered why his family did not drive him to Balıkesir themselves. In that family, everything absolutely had to be done according to custom; even Samet's departure for his military service would be done with the same send-off ceremony every other boy had.

The night before, Samet had gone with his male friends to a folk music bar to celebrate. He was still tired from the night out, and his mother wept incessantly. She kept wiping her face and eyes with the white handkerchief in her hand, making the red tracks of her tears more obvious and sniffling loudly as well. This was her way of saying farewell to her one and only son, the apple of her eye.

Like all young men leaving for military service, Samet was sent off to the accompaniment of zurna horns and drums.

The customary scenes of military service send-offs were all repeated over and over again – tears, applause, shouted slogans and a thousand and one mixed feelings. Young men were leaving on assignment to different locations. A storm of emotions difficult to describe reigned; it was painful to see a father weeping as he did a line dance to the tune of zurnas and drums. While his friends tossed Samet, son of the nation, into the air from a blanket, his dear mother's heart skipped a beat. Each shout of "Our soldiers are the greatest soldiers of all!" was like an arrow planted in her heart. Samet's delirious friends encouraged him with their shouting but his mother's heart shed silent tears.

There was one more person standing there in silence: Kübra. This was the first time someone close to her was being sent off to the army. And the one going on this journey was her fiancé. Yet, Kübra shared none of the emotions of that exuberant crowd. She felt only the sorrow of sending someone off to fight. But it was not like she was saying farewell to a lover she would burn for, waiting impatiently to see him again. She couldn't pretend. Her feelings for Samet were far from those for a lover her heart longed to be with; he was more like a friend or a cousin. She looked toward Samet's mother and watched her for a while from afar. Kübra didn't feel like this woman was her mother-in-law either.

Samet embraced his mother and father and kissed their hands. When it came to Kübra's turn, his feelings too were unclear, and he gazed at her for a long time, not quite knowing what to do. Since they were not yet married, he did not kiss her. Kübra smiled a tight-lipped, awkward smile. "Have a good journey, Samet. I will come to visit you. Go with God," she managed to say.

Samet's closest friend, Refik, performed the rituals of military farewell with excitement as if this were his first. He'd sent off two close friends the year before.

In the moments before the bus was to leave, the joyful scene at the terminal turned sorrowful. Mothers rushing for the buses to hug their sons one last time, friends and family stampeding to say goodbye, all brought the general chaos to fever pitch.

Samet stood at attention, saluted, and got on the bus. He slumped into one of the back seats and furtively wiped his tears away. Refik stood in front of the bus and led the crowd in the national anthem.

The bus took off and everyone went on waving goodbye until it disappeared from view. They shouted the slogan, "He's off to the army, and he will return!" The families of the other soldiers were waving too, and not one wave was unreturned.

Samet's friends went up to his mother one by one to say "May god reunite you, Auntie," and hugged his father, Memduh Bey.

Samet gazed out of the window throughout the long journey, lost in thought; he just could not fall asleep. About six hours later, they arrived at the province of Balıkesir. Young men going off to do their military service were advised: "Don't wander about on the first day, report for service at once, and your discharge will come all the sooner." Samet was told this too but he didn't listen. After he got off at the Balıkesir terminal, he wandered around, wasting time. He dragged his feet, not wanting to report to the barracks right away. He caught a minibus and headed for the town of Edremit, where the brigade command of his service was located.

While strolling aimlessly through Edremit center he was thinking of nearby seaside towns like Akçay and Altınoluk but soon remembered that his destination was a military base, not a beach.

At six o'clock in the evening, he caught a taxi and went to report to his unit. Thousands of young men were waiting in line to register. His turn did not come until three in the morning but there was still no place to sleep and no bed. He spent his first night in the army on a palette on the floor.

They were woken up at 5a.m. He started on a difficult day with two hours' sleep.

The privates who had not yet had their heads shaved, went off to the barber. Then they went on to the uniform depot. Despite the confusion at the depot, Samet managed to find trousers, shirt, hat, parka, and boots to fit him. Now he was a real soldier.

Once he was told which barracks to go to, he chose his bunk.

The squad commander gave a "welcome speech" to the new soldiers. He explained how they would spend their days in the military, the rules of dress, and hours of rest. He asked if there were any questions and after a few soldiers asked things like where one could make phone calls, Samet raised his hand.

"May I perform the Friday prayer?"

The commander was used to that question.

"You cannot perform the Friday prayer here. This is like a workplace; we have a job to do, we have duties. You will have no time for Friday prayer but we do have a small mosque. You can make up your missed prayers in the evening there."

They had fifteen minutes of free time in the evenings. Some soldiers lined up at the phones to make calls with jetons or phone cards. So, on some evenings, Samet would call his family and Kübra and on others, he would catch up with his five daily prayer routine.

One of the hardest things about military service for Samet was having to shave every morning. In Istanbul, Samet kept a short beard but here he was forced to shave every morning for a whole year. And Samet, who observed every detail of his religion, including the precept of embarking on every action with the right foot, had some difficulty marching starting with the left foot but was obliged to get used to it in a short time.

Before meals in the mess hall, all stood while the staff sergeant on duty came and led grace. The prayer for grace was written on a panel hung on the wall; the sergeant would read out each line and then the soldiers would repeat it all together.

"Thanks be to our god."[3]

"Thanks be to our god."

"May our nation abide."

"May our nation abide."

"Good appetite."

The final phrase was not repeated. Instead, the hall shook as the soldiers shouted in one voice, "Good health!" The first time Samet heard the prayer for grace, it made his hair stand on end. The soldiers discussed it amongst themselves. "I am a Muslim," Samet said to the soldier sitting across from him, "Why should I say 'god' [*tanrı*] and not 'God' [Allah]?"

"Probably because 'Allah' is Arabic and *tanrı* is Turkish," his young friend answered. Another soldier next to them who had studied Turkish Language and Literature at university, joined in: "*Tanrı* is a pure Turkish word, and it is not incorrect to use it here. But it may be wrong to specifically avoid using the word 'Allah'. In Turkey, words have had symbolic meanings for years. Your reaction to '*tanrı*' has a sociological basis, not a scientific one. It's like using the Turkish *devrim* for 'revolution' instead of the Arabic *inkılap*; we can use the word *tanrı* without falling into such complexes. There's nothing wrong with it."

Samet was angry. He didn't have any complexes. But his even-tempered nature won out, and he swallowed his anger because he was in the army now.

---

[3] The term for "god" here is not Arabic "Allah," specific to monotheismbut the Turkish *tanrı*, which can refer to any god. The state policy of using Turkish in preference to Arabic terms developed with the secularizing reforms of the 1930s. – Trans.

For a few days, he struggled to get accustomed to this new world. But with time, he began to like the army. He was learning so many things in his basic training.

It was not like men who'd done their military service had told him; the army did not "make his mother's milk rush back up through his nose"! Or maybe the conditions at this base were better than at others. He'd been anxious about doing his service at first but when he'd heard he would be sent to Balıkesir, he felt better.

At most training bases, they had traditional Turkish hamams rather than showers. When he started bathing in the *hamam*, two guys in the unit from Istanbul shocked everyone by slipping out of their boxer shorts and coming into the bath stark naked. Everyone was staring at them. They didn't understand why, and looked at each other nonplussed. A corporal screamed, "Hey, are you perverts? You can't come in here naked. Put on your shorts immediately!" But the two young men had showered that way at sports clubs for years.

Some commanders and sergeants were easy to get along with when you talked to them one on one but they were merciless in the way they treated the unit. They tolerated no mistakes. The head sergeant sometimes seemed to be a reasonable man but woe to anyone who abused his good intentions. One of the first lieutenants ground them into the dirt. Samet's arms and legs were covered with cuts and bruises from thorns but he didn't mind. The more problems the privates created, the harsher their superiors became.

Samet found himself in the army and felt like a real man. It brought action into the monotony of his life and he was gaining experience not to be underestimated.

Three weeks had passed. The oath of the enlistment ceremony was to be sworn the following day. The soldiers were told what to expect and were warned: "This is the Turkish Armed Forces. We have certain standards. Your mothers, wives, sisters, and friends will come to the ceremony tomorrow. They must take care with their dress. Those dressed inappropriately will not be allowed to attend."

The warning underlined a tacit understanding that while the traditional headscarf would be allowed, the politically symbolic turban-style head covering would not be tolerated.

Samet's mother was not the sort of woman to wear a tightly bound headscarf. When she went out, she covered her head with the same loose prayer veil she wore at home. Though Kübra wore a turban that could invite comment, she was not coming to the ceremony. She said she had a great deal of work and had to finish certain designs on a deadline. Only Samet's mother and father would attend the ceremony.

All the parents, proud and highly emotional, took their places at the parade ground to watch their sons. The new soldiers arrived, marching in line. They were put through their paces – "At ease!" "Attention!" "Present arms!" "Attention!" "Shoulder arms!" "Attention!" – and stood at the ready in a ceremonial stance.

The garrison commander, the Gendarmerie captain, the governor and the mayor now arrived. The ceremony began with a moment of silence and the national anthem, followed by speeches and the oath of enlistment.

Quite some time later, Samet was granted his first shopping leave and went off to Balıkesir with his army buddies.

On the previous day, the prime minister had been in Balıkesir and given a speech at the opening ceremony of a new housing development. A man in the crowd shouted at him: "We want no funerals for martyrs!" The prime minister's response had shocked everyone.

"The army is not a place to slack off!"

The phrase was made much of and debated for days.

Samet and his friends were on shopping leave, drinking tea when they heard the prime minister commenting on the event on the TV in the cafe: "All Turkish boys do military service. Terror is a trial. To be sure, no one wants to see the funerals of martyrs. But in the struggle against terror, there are sometimes martyrs, and there will continue to be. As a man with the burden of responsibility, I must share this reality with you. Throughout history, we have talked of many things, shared many things too countless to number. But we have always said this: 'Go, my son, go and become a veteran or a martyr.' We have dyed our sons' hands with henna and sent them to the army."

Samet and his friends looked at one another and went on drinking their tea in silence.

They left the cafe and began to wander the streets. They walked very stiffly as they passed through the marketplace in their uniforms, glancing at the girls around. There was a water fountain in the city center. Samet wanted to wash his face. Two young women wearing country-style head kerchiefs were standing at the fountain, one of them singing a folk song in a burning voice about a longed-for lover in the army.

The song was sad enough to break your heart. Clearly, the young woman was waiting for her lover to return from the army.

As Samet splashed water on his face, he thought of Kübra. Was Kübra longing for him like that in Istanbul? Was she missing him? Deep down, he knew that was not true but could not accept it and forced himself to drive away the feeling.

Soon Kübra would visit him at the base. Then he would know what she felt.

Samet's father, Memduh Bey, was driving his wife, Behiye, his older brother, and Kübra to Balıkesir to visit the base. Behiye Hanım could not contain her excitement at the prospect of visiting her son with her future daughter-in-law. She was probably the person who most missed Samet and wept for him while he was gone. Memduh Bey was excited as well, though he didn't let it show. Like every father, he wanted to be proud of the son he'd brought up. So, before he left, he had his hair trimmed, had a shave, and had his wife iron his trousers. Kübra's feelings, however, had not changed a bit.

Kübra sat in the roomy back seat of the car with her future mother-in-law. She joined in the conversation now and then but there wasn't much conversation anyway. It was hard for her to spend so much time with a woman she had nothing in common with. In short, she was finding the journey difficult. She had no opinion of Behiye Hanım, positive or negative. It was just that since she could not look upon Samet as her future husband, she could not show any sincere interest in his mother either.

Behiye Hanım asked after Kübra's parents and her older sister and niece, of course. Kübra kept giving short answers like, "They are well, praise God."

Finally, the real topic was breached. Taking care that those sitting in front should not hear, Behiye Hanım got down to business.

"My darling girl, Samet's military service will be over in less than a year. After he has returned, when will we marry you two, with God's permission?" she asked.

Kübra averted her eyes and looked out the window for a few seconds but she knew she couldn't keep the woman waiting for long.

"Samet is a man of gentlemanly and intrepid character. Now he is doing his military service. God willing, if it is our fate, we will discuss these things when he returns."

Behiye Hanım was disconcerted by this evasive answer but mature woman that she was, did not let it show. She sighed inwardly, thinking, "Young people these days..."

They arrived at Edremit and drew up at the brigade command where Samet was stationed. Soldiers with rifles held ready at their hips directed them to the reception building at the front of the visitors' sector.

Samet was waiting nervously inside for his mother, his father, his uncle, and fiancée. A pair of smiling eyes, a letter or a telephone call had so much meaning for a soldier. Though the military might make a man tougher, it could also make him sentimental and more likely to reveal his inner feelings.

In accordance with the general procedure for visitors, the soldiers on duty at the reception asked the gentlemen and two veiled ladies with him for their identification. One of the soldiers was eyeing Kübra or rather, her head covering. Since visitors were not taken onto the base proper but remained in the reception building, the style of head covering and dress was not important. So the soldier on guard duty did not want to give the wrong impression but he did not take his cold gaze off the politically symbolic, tightly bound turban.

The party of four was taken inside. Soldiers visited with their families in a large room like an abandoned nightclub with only a few stools made of plastic to sit on. The guard called for Samet to come in. As Samet entered the room, his mother stood up and hugged him tightly, her eyes immediately filling with tears. Samet inhaled his mother's warm scent and kissed the hands of his father and uncle. It was Kübra's turn. Hiding his nervousness, Samet held her by the shoulders and greeted her with his eyes. He was not about to embrace and kiss a girl he was not married to, a girl who was still only his fiancé, in front of his family.

They sat together for about an hour, drinking tea. Samet's mother asked him constantly about his health, what he was eating, how he was sleeping. The woman was all a fluster, and Samet kept kissing her soft hands, trying to calm her down.

At no time were Samet and Kübra alone, and he spoke mainly to his family. Kübra sat there silently like a bashful bride. The visiting hour was almost over when Memduh Bey realized this and got up, saying, "Come, wife, brother, let's leave the young people alone for a bit."

Kübra's heart began pounding. If she had not been left alone with Samet, she could have got through this visit without letting her feelings show. But now?

For a few short moments, Samet asked his fiancé how she was and what she'd been doing. Kübra averted her eyes and answered in monosyllables. Finally, Samet asked the question which was always on his mind: "Have you missed me?" Kübra swallowed. The answer was no but one could not say that to someone in the army, far from his family and home. She didn't answer yes or no. Silently, her eyes went to the ceiling of the slightly damp room with paint peeling off the walls and stayed there. The man sitting across from her did not hear the voice in her heart. For Samet, everything in life had to be in balance and according to rule, everything kept within bounds. In Kübra's eyes he was someone ordinary, who would follow the rules and could, respectfully, faithfully, be happy with his plans for a definite future. She lowered her head and with an expression on her face that did not show her feelings, her eyes cold but her words warm, said, "I've missed you."

That was all. She'd told an innocent lie. She could not have said more. She could not have gone on romantically about how she longed for him as desert sands long for water.

# Esin's Days
## (Wildly, madly)

When her plane landed in Istanbul, Zeynep's heart was singing with the joy of the past few weeks. She already missed her lover, or rather the man she had recently decided to marry. They'd only said goodbye a few hours before.

The evening of the day Zeynep last saw Esin, she met an Italian singer at a party and fell in love at first sight. They slept together and stole each other's hearts. Raffaello was fascinating. After he returned to Italy, he invited Zeynep to come to Milan and they spent a week of love together happily like something out of a film. A typical Italian man, Raffaello had exhibited all the nuances of the art of love.

She caught a taxi at the airport and headed home. She was dying to drop off her suitcase, run to Esin's and tell her everything, down to the last detail. She was going to share the dream she'd lived with her closest friend.

Of course, she'd not been able to resist calling her mother from Italy. Her mother had been very happy to hear the news at first but after hanging up the phone, became distraught with worry that her daughter would settle down in a foreign country. Italians are Christian, and her daughter was a Muslim. So what would their children be? Oh, the trouble they would have!

"Come on over, right away; we're waiting for you. Sevim is here too," Esin said on the phone, "You'll both tell me all today."

Sevim was sitting in Esin's salon in a plain T-shirt and pants with her curls gathered up carelessly on top of her head and no make-up on, drinking cup after cup of coffee and relating again the tale of her relationship for which she could find no happy ending.

The first man she'd let into her life since her divorce had turned out to be bisexual. He couldn't give up the man he was living with, not now. Sevim had grown tired of this dilemma and put an end to it. She had a daughter to take care of, whom she loved more than anything; she had no energy for such madness. She was sad about it but that would pass. Life had taught her that.

They were sadly listening to music and had turned up the set so loud, they did not hear the doorbell when it rang. Esin noticed the light blinking on her cell phone. It was Zeynep.

"Open the door, girls. Don't you hear the bell?"

Zeynep rushed in with all her joy and undiminished energy, despite the fatigue of her trip. She hugged and kissed her girlfriends. They turned down the music.

"You won't believe what I have to tell you. Italy was like a dream."

Zeynep sat down in an armchair, oblivious to the pain on Sevim's face. She told the whole story, grinning from ear to ear, ending with the surprise news that she was going to get married very soon.

They all jumped up, shouting and yelling, hugging each other and hopping around in the middle of the salon. The amazing, unexpected news made both Esin and Sevim very happy.

Esin ran off to the kitchen and grabbed a bottle to celebrate; she poured out drinks for her friends. One drink was not enough for Sevim; she asked for another. While Zeynep was flying with happiness, Sevim was drowning in sorrow.

They began making plans right away. Where would the wedding be? The Italian wasn't insisting on a church ceremony which was only a formality but it would be good if they had one; they would celebrate in both cities anyway. Zeynep was not going to change her religion. Raffaello's position on circumcision was not yet clear. They wouldn't force their children into either religion. When they grew up, they would be free to make the decision themselves.

"Ooo Zeynep Hanım, so you've even talked about that, God be pleased," Esin said. You'll join the European Union before Turkey does. Our girl is going to Italy as a bride. You'll have to get a house with lots of rooms; we'll come and stay with you."

Sevim had slumped back into her despair after the first thrill of hearing the news. Her love had ended before it began, and the pain died down only to flare up again. It thudded inside her like a fist to her chest. It seemed the constriction she felt might let up a bit if she could take a few deep breaths. She sipped her sweet drink and sat there in her armchair.

Esin gave Zeynep a short version of what had happened to Sevim. They tried to get past it by saying, "Every cloud has a silver lining." But Sevim was listless, her eyes filled with tears. If you touched her, she'd cry. That's what the pain of love is like.

In female solidarity, they tried to comfort their dear friend. They listened to the sad songs of famous Turkish pop singers. Zeynep even got up at one point, holding an imaginary microphone in her hand and sang, "Do not weep; life is not worth those tears of yours!" But they saw that Sevim could not pull herself together. Esin had a suggestion: "Come on, girls, we're going to Bebek. Look, Sevim, my sweet, in these situations, the best medicine is a walk by the sea. That's what I always do. A walk will relax you. Come on now, let's go ..."

They walked down the hill to Bebek. Even that short walk made Sevim feel a bit better. The pain inside her lightened with every step. Like a cold shower, it hurt at first but she got used to it. They could see she would begin to liven up before long.

When they got to the shore, they weren't sure which way to go. They decided to walk to the right, which was the quieter side. Sevim looked up at the sky and said, "If you don't have a man to watch the sunset with, you're alone."

Esin hadn't quite understood what she meant and asked her to say it again.

Sevim turned her red-rimmed eyes back to the sky.

"You know that color of the setting sun? If there's no one beside you when you see that color, it means you are alone. You're tired after a long day and it's time to be with someone. If you can't share that moment, woe is you."

Esin understood but she wanted to boost her friend's morale, so she laughed and said, "It's not always that way, Sevim, my sweet. Look, the sun is setting now; is my husband with me?"

They walked further down the shore and stopped at a dumpling shop. Sevim sprinkled lots of sweet red pepper on hers. When she noticed Esin and Zeynep looking on in shock, she said, "Sweet red pepper has happiness hormones in it, just like chocolate." And at last, she laughed.

# Kübra's Days
## (Moving House)

Most of the furniture had been left at the old house and some of it given to neighbors and friends in need.

The Akansans were a charitable family. Whenever Hikmet Bey completed a successful project, he would sacrifice a ram and give the meat to the poor, and as a wealthy Muslim, he made charitable contributions on religious holidays. He did not fail to donate money as well as wheat, barley, raisins, and dates. In addition, he fulfilled a basic religious duty by paying the ten percent tithe on his earnings every year, giving it to poor Muslims. Hikmet Bey believed that when he helped his relatives and those in his social circle and neighborhood, his own wealth was sanctified and multiplied.

As Hikmet Bey's business grew, the family became dissatisfied with their old neighborhood, Ümraniye. In this world, a man who began to earn more, first got himself a new house and then a new car. To have more money meant to raise one's standard of living a step. Nadide Hanım led the way and the Akansans left the Ümraniye home where they'd lived for years and moved not far away to Çavuşbaşı in the district of Beykoz, where conditions were better. Once having got used to the Anatolian side of the Bosphorus, it would have been all but impossible for them to break away from there completely. The children had been born and raised here.

Nadide Hanım and their faithful housekeeper, Auntie Kadriye, were exhausted by the move. Packing up the house and unpacking in the new villa had been emotionally and physically exhausting. But Nadide Hanım was all smiles when the move was over.

Now, they lived surrounded by greenery in a large villa with a big garden, three storeys high counting the terrace. Their new home with its beige facade and roofed terrace enclosed with lattice-like iron bars on the windows, making another room for gatherings, was a structure signaling the wealth of the family living there.

The home was quite ostentatious, and every piece of furniture was arranged as symmetrically as possible in accord with principles of Islamic décor. The floor was laminate but the rich Hereke and Iranian carpets were still there. The sofa and armchair set was one they had seen in the Dubai home of people they knew, and they had liked it so much, they ordered one of the same. The new conservative bourgeoisie greatly admired the luxurious residences and villas of Dubai. Most of the interior decorators in that country were Italians who'd had no trouble working out the principles of Arab décor and were now applying them. It was the Arabs who had encouraged famous brand names like Fendi and Versace to go into the furnishings market.

The framed Arabic prayer carved on leather hung over the entryway to the salon. New crystal gewgaws had been purchased and planted where they would be most visible. Although the two vases, one very large and decorated with Swarovski rhinestones, the other more delicate, had no flowers in them yet, they stood in all their glory on top of the dresser with drawers. Not only the vases but the sides of the armchairs, the cushions, and even the designs on the curtains were studded with rhinestones. Even the skirting was worked with silver thread. Swaying lamps decorated with rhinestones hung from the walls. There were several decorative silver objects as well. But unlike Esin's house full of mirrors, there were few mirrors here; it was not considered a good thing to gaze at images and mirrors were used only in the guest bedrooms. It was an extremely showy home. It reminded one of a luxury furniture showroom.

The conservative sector had invented its own high society and did not lag behind other wealthy groups in spending and seeking to obtain every luxury, money could buy. They bought branded clothing, drove expensive cars and now, aimed to furnish their homes with the splendor of palaces as well.

Of course, the Akansan's home did not lack a sauna bath. . They had the terrace enclosed with special materials to turn it into a space for prayer and religious discussions. Carpets, low divans, small oriental-style side tables here and there … It truly was a comfortable, refreshing space.

Today, Nadide Hanım was to receive the first visitors to her new home. She had never lacked for visitors in her former home either. The ladies would sit and talk for hours, eating *börek* salt pastry and drinking tea. They got together once a week, pooling funds for a gift to the hostess. Having a "day" was a practice of social solidarity among the ladies.

Nadide Hanım was known for her calm nature but when she was having guests, something would come over her and she would become a jack-in-the-box. She had made many preparations this time as well. Fresh flowers had been placed in the Ottomanesque vases. The hand-painted porcelain dining set was in evidence. The towels in the toilets and bathrooms had been changed and new toilet paper put out. On the edges of the sinks, beige, clamshell-shaped dishes of fine-grained limestone that seemed sprayed with ocean sand, held freshly unwrapped soaps. The house was so new it still smelled of fresh paint.

The delicious smell of freshly baked *börek* pastry filled the house. Platters filled with tomato bulgur pilav, plump rolls and sweets stood ready on the kitchen table. The stuffed grapevine leaves had been rolled. There were a variety of dishes Turkish folk accustomed to snacking in the afternoon especially liked.

When the doorbell rang, Nadide Hanım turned to Kadriye: "Mercy, Kadriye, serve them well, let's not be shamed before the ladies."

They greeted the guests at the front door together. Kadriye gave a pair of slippers to each woman as she came in. Street shoes were taken off and slippers put on. Each guest carried a box. These were the housewarming presents. Some brought decorative objects and others, sweets such as Turkish Delight, baklava, and chocolate.

They went all together into the salon and settled into armchairs. The room filled with polite phrases: "Please come in, sit there, come over here." Kadriye's head spun as all the women inspected the house, while she took the boxes inside and opened them one by one and put the sweets on platters and carried them into the salon.

All at once, the house came alive with chatter as the women praised Nadide and wished her well. "Mercy, my dear Nadide Hanım, all happiness in your new home. How beautifully you've furnished it." The splendor of the new house impressed all the guests. "Who did the interiors? We should use him too," Münevver Hanım said. And she did not fail to go to the same interior decorator the very next week and say: "We are re-doing our house too. Whatever they paid you, we will pay more. Money is no object, just design something better than what you did for them."

As the ladies looked around, the conversation centred on children and then began to turn to furniture, clothes and jewelry. At last, they tore their eyes from the chandeliers, rhinestones and gold leaf and moved on to the usual pleasantries.

To Gülten Hanım's "How are you? Are you well? You must be tired out," Nadide Hanım responded, "May God bless us with goodness." Then she got up and passed the platter of salt pastries round to the lady guests.

Nadide Hanım turned to Şeyma Hanım, who had five grandchildren: "What have you been doing? How are the girls and the grandkids?"

Slightly plump, with several broken teeth, Şeyma Hanım related how happy her grandchildren made her. "How is your grandchild?"

"Well, we only have one, after all. We dote on him. Kübra and Büşra love to play with him. Now we'll have another, God willing. My elder daughter, Müberra, was going to come today but she'd promised to bring her son to see his paternal grandmother. And she's pregnant, of course. We are excited to be having a new grandchild."

Kadriye brought another platter from the kitchen: stuffed grape vine leaves rolled very thin…"Don't be shy, eat them with your fingers; don't waste forks now," she said, making the ladies feel more at home.

Gülten Hanım, who wore no make-up, laughed and said: "The more we eat these, the fatter we get. Our husbands won't look at us, by God."

With this, the subject turned to husbands. "How is your husband? How is his business going?" They went on to talk of how they had met their husbands and gotten married. This in turn brought them to reminisce about their younger years.

Gülten Hanım's parents had wanted to marry her off as soon as she graduated from lycée but she had resisted. She went to college and became a teacher. She had not practiced her profession for six months before her marriage to a well off man was arranged. Then she'd taken up the turban and become a housewife. All her years in school had been in vain.

Şeyma Hanım had loved Turkish music and played oud when she was young. She'd realized one could not practice music as a profession but hadn't wanted to study anything else. At twenty, she lost her heart to a boy in the neighborhood and got married. She had three children and five grandchildren. She spent her time bringing up her grandchildren.

Münevver Hanım came from a prominent rural family. There was no end to the lands they owned, and she'd been married off to a cousin so that the property would stay in the family. Later, she had settled in Istanbul with her husband. Her husband sold the agricultural products of the lands they owned. He did not let her work but had both of their children educated well.

The five veiled women could show themselves off to their husbands only within the home and never neglected to go to the beauty parlor to have their hair dyed. Not all of them but those who'd been around a bit more, bought fancy lingerie.

Their husbands were out all day with unveiled women. The way to tie them to the home lay in keeping them happy behind closed doors. But unfortunately, it was not always easy. As their first sexual experience had been with their husbands, and they knew no other men, their sexual lives were monotonous and irksome. There were no surprises in bed for them, and they did nothing to surprise their husbands; their sex never went beyond the classic movements and customary positions. If their husbands asked for the slightest variation, they would frown and mope, and under no circumstances would they do what their husbands wanted. That would not go with the classic style of playing hard to get. They lived in a world of limits, and their sexuality was limited too.

Nadide Hanım constantly urged her guests to eat more. "Now, now, don't act like a guest, come on and eat something."

When Kadriye brought the delicious tray of cheese *börek* into the salon, steaming with the fragrance of milk, they all cried, "Ahhh, God bless your hands!" and ate with relish, sipping their strongly-steeped tea.

Then came the rumor that the notary in the old neighborhood had cheated on his wife. "I'm amazed at you, by God; the man has several children. It's just gossip," Nadide Hanım said.

"No, no, they say he's seeing another woman," Münevver Hanım declared.

"But it's probably a whim; it will pass. The man has children; is he going to break up his home at his age?" Şeyma Hanım changed the subject: "When will our daughter Kübra be married, if destiny allow? Praise God, she's become so beautiful too."

Nadide Hanım sighed. "Samet is a good boy, a gentleman. But our girl doesn't seem inclined. I am worried. It won't be long, if destiny allow. Especially, considering Samet will soon be back from the army. His father wants to go ahead immediately." She reflected for a moment. The girl really was getting older, why was she still not married?

Auntie Kadriye cleared the dirty plates and brought in the fruit. The ladies did not feel much like eating anymore. They expressed their gratitude and got up to leave. But first, Nadide Hanım took them on a tour of the house, stopping in each room to talk about the furnishings. Well, they'd spent so much money, of course it was her right to show it off!

But the Akansans were relatively modest on that score. The things people did! There were men who told their decorators, "Make me such a salon that people will think I have fifty million dollars," and women who said, "Line the bathroom ceramics with Swarovski rhinestones, Mr. Architect; I will pay for it myself," and the next day, plopped down ten gold bracelets and a purse full of gold coins on his desk. Clearly, they too wanted to live in European-style houses now. The number of people seeking a "*residence*" style of life was increasing rapidly.

# Esin's Days
## (In Bodrum)

Esin put a few slices of apple on her small plate and sat down next to Alp while he read his paper. They chatted in the VIP lounge with a few people they knew before taking their seats on the plane. Everyone must be going on vacation, they were all smiling.

They descended to Milas Airport after a fifty-minute flight. The heat hit them in the face the minute they got off the plane. They were both feeling good because they'd caught the scent of vacation. An advertising billboard caught Esin's attention while they were waiting for their luggage. The latest season of a famous Italian clothing line had women wearing colorful scarves bound around their heads, showing only their bangs. When an Italian designer did it, it was called "style," but when Muslims covered their heads, it was called a "political symbol."

They got their bags and left the airport. Yes, vacation had begun. In fact, they would only know on the way back if they'd had a vacation or an exhausting bit of fun.

They jumped into a taxi and headed for Bodrum, the land of vacation where nights became days and days became nights.

The hotel where they were staying was in Torba. The number of boutique hotels in that district had increased in recent years. People who came to Bodrum to enjoy the action, only stopped off at their hotel rooms to sleep and spent their time in the sea and the sun, eating and having fun.

Esin put on her bikini and slipped their things into her beach bag. She didn't forget to bring a book to read. She couldn't stand to sit in the sun for hours without a book. During her years in lycée, instead of reading, she'd put in her ear buds and listened to the Gypsy Kings all the time. She thought it was the best music for summer vacations.

Vacationing often both in Turkey and abroad had made them change their habits a bit. Alp, especially, wanted to try all water sports. He'd go water-skiing and jet-skiing, though Esin didn't like him to, and he and his friends rode the Banana like children. While he ran on the treadmill at a health club in the evenings Esin would take yoga classes.

But in Bodrum, all that seemed like too much trouble. Here one ate, drank, swam, and had fun. That's what most people did. Even conversation didn't go beyond where one had been last night, whether one had been at the beach party, how much one drank, and how much fun one had.

Esin ignored Alp objections and brought her bikini top with the underwire foam cups. Alp wanted his wife to wear the simplest, skimpiest kind of bikini and bra. He made fun of her when she came out of the sea, took a shower and wrung the water out of the foam cups in her bikini top. Eh, it wasn't easy to give up old habits.

After spending the day taking in the sun and swimming, Alp and Esin put on their comfortable beach clothes and hopped into a taxi to Türkbükü. They met up with friends there. Everyone was tanned and in good spirits. The alcohol consumption went through the roof. They ate dozens of stuffed mussels sprinkled with fresh lemon juice bought from itinerant sellers. The area was riotously loud, with blaring music adding to the general noise pollution.

Esin and Alp went along with the crowd and gave themselves over to pleasure, spending hours amusing themselves. That evening, they were invited to a cocktail party at the swimming pool of a villa belonging to people they knew. They had already had quite a bit to drink. They drank and danced a bit more and then went back to the hotel. They took a shower, got into their crisp and clean summer outfits and went off to the cocktail in Yalıkavak.

The party's summertime venue was past the Yalıkavak marina in one of the large, freestanding villas on the hill. It was a stone duplex with a huge swimming pool. The grassy lawn landscaped by a talented architect was decked with flowers and went on as far as the eye could see.

The guests had begun to fill up the villa in the cool summer breeze. Waiters wearing white shirts, white gloves, and pressed trousers, circulated with trays of drinks and hors d'oeuvres. They all had permanent smiles stuck on their faces and bent forward politely, offering guests the drinks and hors d'oeuvres on the trays. Finally, Alp's favorite came around, sushi with wasabi and ginger. Alp took up chopsticks, dipped his sashimis into soy sauce and tossed them into his mouth.

Just then he saw a hand wielding chopsticks with particular expertise reach for the sushi platter. The owner of the hand that caught Alp's attention was a famous painter. He seemed to be saying, "I wield a brush like a master, and I can create miracles with chopsticks too." They greeted one another. Alp and Esin had been to a few of the painter's openings.

The painter was also known as a Social Democrat and wherever he went, the conversation would be sure to find its way to politics. People who occupied their minds all day with money matters, the difficulty of making a living, TV series and soccer matches, had to lift their heads now and then and step back to take a look at the big picture of the nation and the world as a whole. The painter was a person like that, sensitive and forward-looking. He took every opportunity to exhort intellectuals in particular to wake up.

"While we stand here watching the sunset, drinks in hand, my friend, elsewhere in the country, the sun really is setting. We are heading straight into darkness. No one gives a damn. Not the media, not the civil society organizations that should be applying pressure through lobbying, not youth, not the opposition, not the army ..."

Army brat Esin joined the discussion at this point: "What? The army's goal and regime is the protection of secular democracy and the essential values of the Republic. The army is pressuring the government, and severely too."

The painter turned to Esin: "They avoid such forays. Their warnings smell more like conciliatory slaps on the wrist, Madam. That dark mentality has been waiting to take its revenge on the enlightenment spirit since the founding of the Republic and won't change its course because of such things. They're doing the *shariat* tango, two steps back, one step forward."

Esin sipped her fruit vodka cocktail and returned to her mute young lady mode.

The painter went on, looking at Alp and glancing, however briefly, at Esin: "As if the reactionary laws coming out now and the formation of cadres in government offices were not enough, they are supposedly flirting with the European Union. They calculate how to get into the EU by turning our beautiful Turkey into a middle- eastern country. The EU both uses us as a market and tries to partition our country. And for the government, running the EU race is an excuse to neutralize the army."

Alp thought over what he was hearing and ended up agreeing: "Why don't you say it: the holy skullcap is off and they are bald. In this age, such populist, demagogic and illegal activity is intentional. But this is Turkey. There can never be an Islamic state here. No philosophical or religious movement can take Turkey back. We are a country trying to integrate with the EU and the USA, to march forward with the world. It is impossible for Turkey to go one way while the world goes another. Whatever line the internal political movements and formations take, Turkey will go where the world is going."

Just then, Esin pointed with her finger to say she was going to join a group of women laughing loudly in their spaghetti-strap Missoni and Cavalli dresses. These ladies had worn plain sandals on their pedicured feet to go out and stand on the lawn. She wasn't about to go on pretending to listen to these two men, engrossed in talking politics. She'd decided it would turn out to be a "difficult days lie ahead" Turkish classic. She went off to enjoy the evening.

The painter indicated that he didn't completely agree with Alp and listed examples of USA and European provocations.

Alp continued to defend his view: "Great states like the US will have plans for us, of course. Just as Turkey wants to have its say on its own demographic; I mean, its neighbors... We want to be a prominent actor in the Middle East, the Caucasus, and the Balkans. Turkey is a large, strategic bridge, and the US has to use us to protect its interests in the region. It can't realize any of its projects without crossing that bridge."

While the gentlemen were thus plunged in heated conversation, their host Fahri Bey came up. The thick cigar he had lodged between his porcelain teeth with a broad smile and everything else about him, said he was enjoying a pleasurable summer's evening with friends. Only yesterday, he'd taken his boat out of the marina to drift from bay to bay with friends. They'd enjoyed a day of fresh breezes, brilliantly shining sea and lots of sun.

They left off talking politics and spoke of the more refined pleasures of life.

Esin tried to join in the women's conversation. Who the girl in the skimpy bikini sunning herself on the beach all day was sleeping with; how the cheap model, who did not hesitate to run around with married men in her time, had used her profession to find a rich husband, finally got her hooks into a man and was promoted to the status of wife; how to lose kilos of belly and hip fat most quickly; whether it was better to buy the new season clothes in Milan or London... Subjects that didn't much interest Esin. She asked the way to the bathroom. A maid gave her directions.

Esin slipped inside the villa, wobbling a bit, and took a look around. The house was very large and had little furniture. There were big abstract oil paintings on two of the walls. One was by the famous painter she'd talked to in the garden. The tiled floors were paved with a ceramic that had the look of natural stone. She used the guest bathroom, washed her hands and dried them on the tiny guest towels. She went back outside and returned to the maidens' group. They had moved on from gossip and were now talking about the success Turkish artists like Orhan Pamuk and Fazıl Say were enjoying abroad.

At least, no one at this party by the pool fell into it, despite the alcohol flowing like water, and the evening passed without incident. Esin and Alp thanked their hosts and left the villa happy. When they got back to their hotel, they were both dizzy with exhaustion. They washed their faces, brushed their teeth and went straight to bed. They couldn't find room on a flight Sunday evening and instead, returned on Monday from the vacation they'd started on Thursday. They were both tired. They were supposed to come back rested but the real vacation was during the quiet hours they spent at home after they returned.

# Kübra's Days
## (The Contract)

"Whatever the burden may be, we will take it on," Hikmet Bey said, looking into the eyes of his bureaucrat friend with the thin mustache sitting across from him.

Another big project was being put out to tender. Last year, Hikmet Bey had gotten the contract for construction of an overpass and completed it successfully; under discussion now was the construction of a new unit for a ministry, not a municipality.

He had put his signature to fine projects for several municipalities. His specialty was more construction than product and service procurement or consulting type work. He bid particularly on tenders for underpasses, bridges, roads or infrastructure, and he got most of them. He submitted his work in full on the date promised. Some firms broke the contracts they received by hiring subcontractors who hired others in turn, parceling out percentages of the tender. One firm received the contract while others did the work. Hikmet Bey did not sell off the contracts he received for a commission. He was conscientious; he did the work himself, and he did it as it should be done. He was good at his work, and he had friends in high places where decisions were made. He did not always have to conform to the terms of the contract. Other firm owners like him also enjoyed such privileges.

Contractor Hikmet Bey did not begrudge his support either. He rewarded those who facilitated his work. He supported the bureaucrats, their families and friends in various ways according to the size of the project and the amount of the work. He paid for their vacations abroad and private school tuition for some of their children. He sold them units in his housing projects at symbolic prices. He had sold a two hundred thousand lira home for thirty thousand. But these were small gestures compared with the money he earned. He always remembered what a close friend had told him: "Eat but do not eat alone or they will not feed you."

As he expanded his business, he sensed a giant-sized passion for new horizons growing within him. It was clear that construction work would soon not be enough for him and he would begin forays into the energy sector. That was where the real money was. He was preparing for a collaborative initiative with an Arab firm. The Arabs were, after all, the only ones not to be affected by the global financial crisis.

The rise of the Islamist sector was a phenomenon not limited to Turkey alone but a reality for most of the oil-rich Muslim countries as well. In Asia, even the Japanese were badly affected by the crisis, while the Arabs were still standing tall.

Although they had not been very close as classmates at the Imam and Preacher middle school in Kayseri, Hikmet Bey's friend had now risen quite high in government circles.

They had both been teenagers from conservative families and had not neglected their religious education while preparing themselves for life.

Hikmet Bey and his bureaucrat classmate had been students at their Imam and Preacher school before it became a normal lycée issuing legally recognized diplomas. In any case, when Hikmet Bey was eighteen, he moved from Kayseri, the city where he was born and raised, to Istanbul.

Running across old classmates from these schools which had proliferated with the claim to provide a religious education based on respect for humanity, thought, freedom, morality and cultural heritage, could bring opportunities in later years.

Hikmet Bey's Imam and Preacher school classmate now worked in a government ministry which needed to create a new supplemental unit. Hikmet Bey always kept his ears open, and he'd already heard about it. He was going to bid for the tender after making the necessary preparations.

Several firms were making sealed bids, among them the firm of Esin and Alp's close friend, contractor Ahmet. One received an approval of the bid with prequalification documents, and the papers were submitted according to regulations. One was informed when the decision was made. If Hikmet Bey took the necessary precautions, he was never surprised by the decision on the tender.

As in every age, certain individuals abused their authority in their own self-interest and made benefits available to their supporters, awarding tenders to their friends.

Every step of the way – the writing of the specifications, preparation of the offer, setting of prices, and approval of the project – went according to deals set in advance. Certain persons would be aware of the relationship between the officials and firms concerned.

True, the website of the Public Tender Commission was very detailed, stating the number of tenders on offer, bids made, contracts announced, and complaints about them transparently. But that did not mean that certain deals slipped through unnoticed.

That was why Hikmet Bey was now meeting with his old classmate after so many years. But even if they were friends, everything had its price. His friend at the Ministry, aware of the significance of the supplemental unit project, hinted that the amount of the bribe should be raised by saying, "There is great interest in this tender, and your chances of winning it may not be high."

Hikmet Bey got the message and said only, "Look, the tender is very important to us. Whatever the burden may be, we will take it on." And he did not forget to add (using his Kayseri accent for emphasis), "Don't underestimate what I am willing to pay."

This conversation ensured a tacit agreement. "May God be pleased," Hikmet Bey said, giving thanks for what they had done and for the bureaucrat of the day who acted within the bounds set by his master. He was used to regarding such money matters with resignation.

There had always been corruption, and there was corruption now. The religious sector had risen to prominence by way of political developments. An unmistakably religious entrepreneur movement was growing stronger economically. A nouveau riche was being formed. Money had changed hands according to the conditions of the day. The religious were in conflict over the practice of divine law; they lived in compromise. Most could not practice what they believed. Worldliness was a part of the life of today's Muslims. It was now considered acceptable for even the religious to stray and allow themselves to be compromised for the sake of the money they could earn from government tenders. They neglected their prayers as they worked more in order to conform socially, in order to own more, and they cheated. Appearances were more important in business today. The faith of most believers was being shaped by worldly desires.

Hikmet Bey did not conceal his rise in the business world. He'd long since forgotten his great-grandfather's maxim, "If the way is short and the reward great, fear it." He did not mind that the phenomenon he was party to was called "Islamic capital" or "green capital." He just kept on taking care of business. He chatted for a while with his old schoolmate, now new business partner, about other things.

"As you can see, the distance between center and periphery is now almost zero. The dynamism makes those who suppose they own the established order and guard the values of the Republic uncomfortable. Those who today rage against us, the nouveau riche, weren't they themselves the nouveau riche of the 1950s and 60s? Maybe in twenty years we, the stars shining bright today, will hate the nouveau riche of the future!"

Those who ran the country said it was their duty to struggle against corruption but the rumors of their own corruption were legion. It was as if their corruption was particularly overlooked. They got vacant lots cheap from villagers, fixed their zoning status with the municipality and sold them at astronomical prices to big companies, sharing the profits with each other. They steered things their way and turned a five-fold profit on an empty building lot! Well, it wasn't easy to say no to such opportunities. Who wouldn't want a seaside mansion on the Bosphorus or a million dollars in their bank account? They pulled strings and put a million dollars in their pockets. Of whom should the people complain? To whom?

So the horrific reality created by the maxim, "The wealth of the state is an ocean. Only suckers don't drink," went on and on, while now, we had to cope with: "Prayer in the mosque and capitalism in the shop!"

Bids were being hurriedly prepared both by Hikmet Bey's firm and Ahmet's. If Ahmet could find the way to do it, he'd be just as eager as Hikmet Bey to take on the burden, whatever it may be but unfortunately he had no friends in the municipality. Hadn't he entertained more than a few bureaucrats in his time when those from his own circles were wielding power? Everything in turn.

# Kübra and Esin
## (Wedding Dress)

"Come on, we're going to be late. Hurry up!" Kubra cried, the tone of her voice projecting panic, happiness, and wonder all at once. Her friend, Ayşe, was getting married in two months and Kübra was almost more excited than she was.

It wasn't the idea of getting married that excited her, but the details of dress, flowers, jewelry, and the henna night. She loved arranging for every detail of an event. Kübra had good taste. Her close friends always sought her opinion about clothes, colors and designs. She knew best what fabric and color went best with any given season.

She and Ayşe jumped into a taxi and drove to Teşvikiye. They were both more chic and colorfully dressed than usual. Some people said a veiled woman should not attract attention. She should not overdress. But the way young women dressed today was freer, more original, and noticeable.

There was very little variety available in ready-made veiled outfits, so young women who wanted originality in style, combined them with clothes produced for unveiled women.

Kübra had on a silk scarf in a violet check print and a long, loose, beige blouse and trousers. She wore low-heeled, partially open-toed shoes. Ayşe had on a brown dress and a square-shaped striped scarf wrapped around her head.

A famous woman fashion designer was making Ayşe's wedding dress. They had come for a fitting. She too had the right to look striking on the most special day of her life, rather than make do with just any wedding outfitter in their neighborhood.

Ayşe's first thought when she decided to marry had been about a beautiful wedding dress that would make her feel like a swan. She wanted to be like a swan, all white from head to toe. The woman designer had at first not warmed to the veiled bride designs ordered from her in recent years but in time, saw that she could develop her talents in this way too and earn money. In any case, veiling was not just a head-covering and loose coat. There were also evening gowns, engagement outfits, and wedding dresses. Furthermore, the conservative rich no longer had their wedding dresses made by stores in Fatih; they were now going to famous designers as well. A new potential for customers and earnings had emerged.

The woman designer had worked hard on the headpiece of the delicate lace dress with the rhinestones Ayşe had asked for. She herself preferred to design gowns with simple lines in high-quality, chic material. For, if a dress was too elaborate, it drew more attention than the bride.

She'd designed the long-sleeved gown so that the bust was closely wrapped. The taffeta skirt was full and puffy. She didn't want the turban to sit on the bride's head like an ordinary scarf; it should have an air of its own. Ayşe's hair was going to be teased and raised up high with a round cloth ball on top or the hair would be combed back and completely concealed in a white bonnet to give it a sleek look and a pure silk veil with lace and rhinestones would be tied in a manner appropriate for evening dress.

Ayşe and Kübra left the fitting as pleased as they could be. They began to walk up to Nişantaşı from Teşvikiye. They wanted to look at the shops while they were in the neighborhood.

While they were still strolling on the sidewalk, two unveiled women passed by and looked at them disapprovingly. They whispered to each other: "Those types make me sick," one said. It made Kübra and Ayşe uncomfortable. They never had any problem in their own neighborhoods, their own districts or their circles. There, unveiled women weren't much liked. But what was dear Ayşe to do? She wanted that woman fashion designer to make the dress she would wear once in her life and since wallets opened for a wedding...

Her mother-in-law was a wealthy woman with good taste. She too wanted everyone to be enchanted by the wedding dress. The signature of a good designer should be felt at a wedding. She and Ayşe got along very well. So far, Ayşe hadn't liked any of the more conservative dresses. She thought most wedding gowns for veiled women gave the impression that the bride was wrapped up like a package. And it seemed to her banal to play down an unveiled design by putting a bolero over it.

They turned into the street by the police station, intending to go up Abdi İpekçi Caddesi. They had just reached the corner when Kübra saw Esin.

Esin was crossing the street toward them. She had just stepped onto the sidewalk and seeing two veiled young women before her, wondered what they were doing in Nişantaşı when Kübra spoke up: "Hello Esin, how are you?" Esin was surprised; Kübra was sincerely pleased to have run into her so unexpectedly. Esin collected herself and answered, "Oh, I'm fine. How are you? What's up?" The two of them looked each other over.

"Ayşe is getting married soon; we've come for her fitting. We were just strolling around."

As Esin studied the two young women in their fine, elegant clothes without prejudice, she really was confused for a moment. She thought she should say something to break the silence. She was already feeling a bit embarrassed at how prejudiced and tactless she'd been when she ran into Kübra at the award ceremony.

"I have a business meeting but I'm early," Esin said. "Would you like to sit somewhere and have a drink?" She wanted to hear about the fitting of the wedding dress and find out how the *others* did such things.

They walked a little and sat down at a relatively empty cafe. Esin ordered a cappuccino, while Kübra and Ayşe asked for orange juice. Esin began to examine these two girls who led a kind of life she knew nothing about. How they had done their make-up, what kind of watches and jewelry they had on, how they had done their nails. But they were just two young people made of flesh and blood like she was. And unlike their elders, unlike their mothers who stayed at home and couldn't get along with their husbands, these young women were educated and kept up with the latest technological advances; they tested their religiosity with worldly values. Still, Esin couldn't keep from studying them.

True, Kübra was also studying Esin wide-eyed, though she tried not to let it show. Ayşe wasn't paying attention. Her mind was on her wedding dress. Should it be a one-piece outfit, rather than the two-piece they had now?

Esin asked a few questions, wanting to relax these rather shy young women but she could not keep a slightly ironic tone out of her voice. She felt she'd made them more uncomfortable instead but in fact, they were used to this kind of insinuating talk.

Ayşe was even more timid because she didn't know Esin at all. So Kübra started to talk about the wedding dress: it had such-and-such kind of material here and rhinestones there, such-and-such part of it was gathered…At that moment, Esin realized that to be a bride was every young girl's dream. Everyone had a right to be excited and pleased.

Esin looked around as if she were afraid that someone she knew might see her sitting with veiled women and get shocked.

Then she talked a bit about her work, telling them about ceremonies where she'd acted as presenter. She was going to present at the buyer's meeting of a conservative group again and was about to say, "I'll be working for your people," when she stopped herself. It was weird that everywhere, no matter what, there were always *us* and the *others*.

The half-hour drinking coffee went faster than any of them guessed. Both sides learned something about a different world. Esin paid the check; it was only three drinks. And she could be considered the host. The veiled girls had come to *her* Nişantaşı.

# Esin's Days
## (Spark)

Ahmet had met beautiful red-headed Irem one day when he had just again transferred funds into the bank account of his daughter, Melike, who no longer lived at home, and he was thinking dispiritedly about how their relationship was now just a matter of money.

Lovely Melike, daughter of his first marriage, was now twenty-years-old and Ahmet spoiled her with a mixture of guilty feelings and tenderness; he could not disappoint her, he never could say no to her. She got along well with his new wife Mehtap and with their young son.

Ahmet was immediately smitten when he saw the wavy red hair scented with exotic perfume. He met Irem by accident in a cafe and with the skill of a practiced rake, got her cell number right away. Soon, they began seeing each other and became lovers.

She drove him out of his mind. She was beautiful, attractive, and intelligent. They could talk about anything and never get bored. Before long, just talking was not enough; they began to touch; touch led them to bed, to unforgettable lovemaking, and they could not get enough of one another. Now Irem was having an affair with a married man, and Ahmet had a lover young enough to be his daughter.

He was the kind of man who thought love was a matter of taking the bodies of others on loan. It did not matter to him if he pleased the women he showered gifts on in bed; he made love selfishly. He had many one-night stands but this one was different. Irem had really become his mistress. He missed her, he longed for her; most importantly, he could talk to her. And this time, he gave pleasure as well as taking it.

Ahmet had begun to experience at forty what he could not have in his youth, and he was quite pleased with the situation. He loved, he was loved, and they had fun. He slipped away on vacations with his beautiful lover, more and more often using business trips out of the country as an excuse. Because his wife Mehtap knew nothing of his work and was not part of the business world, these trips of his seemed normal to her.

Ahmet had now got rid of everything that annoyed him in life and could stroll hand- in- hand with his sweetheart on the streets of foreign cities. He kissed her in public at tourist sites. He took great pleasure in ardent kisses. They spent passionate hours at hotels where they would not run into other Turks. They made love over and over and over again, drifting off to sleep in close embrace. It was in these moments of close embrace that Ahmet felt bad. Despite everything, he had not gotten used to the idea of deceiving his wife Mehtap so freely as to embrace another woman with such intensity of feeling. Not yet…

Irem knew she could never have a life with Ahmet. But she went on with the affair anyway. She didn't nag him about it; she accepted the situation in silence. Even if her feelings were stormy, she didn't trouble her man. She didn't put her hand in the fire. She stayed with her married lover, never knowing what kind of place he'd made in his mind for the two of them.

Ahmet was content to have it that way. He had no intention of marrying again even if he should divorce Mehtap. When he looked at Irem, he saw a fiery young woman confused between reason and emotion, questioning herself though she appeared untroubled.

# Kübra's Days
## (The Henna Night)

There were no men in the salon, only women washing and blow-drying hair, having their nails filed and manicured, their bodily hair waxed and eyebrows plucked. A sign reading "all our employees are female" was displayed in the shop window. Most of the customers were veiled women, and it put them at ease to know that there were no men working in the salon. They took off their headscarves as soon as they came in.

Ayşe's wedding dress was already legendary and all her friends had descended upon the beauty salon to get ready for her henna night.

Twenty years earlier, the majority of customers at beauty salons in conservative neighborhoods had been unveiled; very few wore headscarves. Since the mid-1990s, the percentage had doubled. By the 2000s, seventy percent of the customers were wearing the turban. The reason for this transformation was not, as many people supposed, an increase in the numbers of veiled women but in their patronage of beauty salons. In the past, people reasoned that since veiled women were veiled, they didn't need beauty salons. But the thinking in conservative circles had changed: veiled women wanted to show that they were as well groomed as unveiled women.

They went to beauty salons not only to have their hair but their turbans done. There were several different models of turban, varying in color, print, shape and the way they framed the face. The model most often used for evening dress was the "sultan." This kind of turban was gathered and tied in front, and various types of accessories could be pinned to the knot. But the girls going to the all-women henna night were having their hair done to show off unveiled.

Kübra had her long brown hair pulled back at the nape of her neck and held by a clip with the same type of rhinestones as on the neck of her gown. Her dress was closed at the neck, fell to the ground and had an open back. Most of the other girls had their hair curled or blow-dried to be wavy. Most of them also had their make-up put on too heavily. Kübra did her own make-up; she used a salmon-colored lipstick that went with the orange-flower print of her dress.

Girls put an incredible amount of effort into their dress for the henna night. One never went to such an event without spending time at a beauty salon. A veiled woman had to make extra preparations to go out for the evening. An unveiled woman just put on a dress. And she did not have to change anything when she got where she was going. But veiled women had to have outfits for both indoors and outdoors. Since a veiled woman could not be seen with her hair uncovered outdoors, she covered her head and – if it was revealing – her dress. When she was indoors, she took off her headscarf and her coat or sweater.

But care had to be taken when choosing both. Tasteless dress was not acceptable; as the saying goes, "A plain gun barrel underneath and grooved on top." The combo shouldn't seem like two separate outfits that did not match; they had to go well together. There should be a harmonious air to the whole; a woman shouldn't look like a walking heap of cloth.

The traditional henna night was held in the bride's home a day or two before the wedding, and was usually attended by only close relatives and friends. But in this new age, both modern and conservative people rented a space outside the home for the henna night. Of course, only those with deep pockets could manage it.

Only girls and women came to the henna. The sex of those doing the serving varied according to the guests. A young woman at a henna night could not take off her scarf if the waiters were male. The same went for the deejay. So, since most of the guests at a henna night were veiled women, those serving would be female too. Later, if desired, the groom's side would join them.

When Kübra was invited to Ayşe's henna night, she asked right away if she would be able to uncover her head. The issue was obvious. She would dress accordingly.

The henna night was being held in one of the ballrooms of a large hotel near Şişli. The whole floor had been set aside for the host. Everyone on the floor was female, so the women could go about freely unveiled.

Kübra wore a gossamer-thin jacket in a tone matching her long dress with narrow straps. She tied her scarf loosely so as not to muss her hair-do. When she got to the floor where the henna night was being held, she went to the lavatory and took off her scarf and jacket. Each of the women did the same as they arrived, taking off their loosely tied scarves in front of the mirror. They went into the lavatory with one identity and came out with another, going in veiled and coming out with beautifully styled hair.

The entire floor was done up for the festivities. The salon where the henna was to be done was enchanting. Although the companies serving the conservative sector were few, their parties and ceremonies were more sumptuous. Weddings were designed to seem as if they were being held in palaces and henna nights left nothing to be desired either.

Guests were traditionally served dried nuts and drinks. The beautifully dressed women were laughing and showing off their jewelry to one another. They danced singly and in lines, letting off steam until the henna was applied. Kübra danced gaily with her friends and let herself go. At one point, she began sweating from dancing so much, she had to sit down to rest a bit. At least, her hair was tied firmly and leaping around didn't ruin it. Everyone in the room was enjoying themselves and she joined in again.

At first, the bride appeared in a chic gown. But just before the henna was to be applied, she went into a special room set aside for her and changed her clothes. She put on a long kaftan made of the type of velvet known as *bindallı*. A red veil was put on her head.

Now the men were going to join the henna ceremony. The bride's close companions were informed and they announced to the others that the men were about to arrive. The women went off and covered their heads. They put on their jackets and shawls and returned to the room.

Two chairs were placed in the center of the room for the bride and groom. The henna was then prepared and set out on a tray decorated with candles.

Each of the young women in the room was given a candle. Kübra entered first, carrying the henna tray, followed by Ayşe. The other women began to walk in a circle around the empty chairs, holding their candles and singing folk songs.

Then the bride and groom took their seats. The women continued to sing tender folk songs, the intention being to get the bride to cry.

While the henna was being applied to Ayşe's hands, one of the older women said, "The bride is not opening her hand." At that point, someone from the groom's side put a small gold coin in the bride's palm. When the application of the henna was finished, the bride's hands were bound with gauze and slipped into gloves. The same was done to the groom.

The groom and the other men left when this part of the ceremony was over. The red veil was taken off Ayşe's head and henna was distributed to the guests. The women returned to singing folk songs and dancing, now left alone to enjoy themselves. They'd taken off their veils as soon as the men left.

The hour was quite late but no one felt like leaving. They were enjoying the rare chance to dance and laugh together. They kept on dancing and leaping around, singing and taking pictures until one o'clock in the morning, when they finally began to leave one by one. Kübra was the last to leave her best friend, Ayşe.

# Esin's Days
## (The Kuwaitis)

Esin was sitting in the big salon of her apartment, checking her email on her laptop. There was a familiar name among the messages in the inbox: an Arab name ... She realized who it was after she thought for a bit. "Ah, it's that guy from Kuwait," she said to herself. Ebraheem was the public relations officer of the company that organized the eventful fashion show where she'd presented a few months before. In the message he said he had left that job and was going to set up his own company. He was planning to establish a chain of döner kebab shops here. He was coming to Turkey the following week and wanted to see Esin if she was available.

She wrote back that she was.

One week later, Ebraheem and his two male friends from one of the richest countries in the world, were in Istanbul. Ebraheem called Esin on her cell phone and asked where they should meet. Esin never liked going to tourist sites and wanted to show them something new, so she suggested they meet in Bebek. They found a table overlooking the sea at Divan, one of Bebek's classiest spots.

Esin ordered a selection of chocolates from the restaurant's pastry shop. Ebraheem was reaching for one when his friend said something in Arabic and he suddenly withdrew his hand.

"What's wrong?" Esin asked, smiling when he answered: "What if it has alcohol in it?"

"These are not the kind with liqueur inside; there's no alcohol, relax ... But are you really so vigilant about it? I mean, enough to worry what's in the chocolate you eat abroad?"

Ebraheem and his friends had lived a fast life when they were young. They'd drunk alcohol and even smoked pot. But when they reached their thirties, they gave up such worldly pleasures and got married. Their wives were veiled. Now they fulfilled the commands of Islam and they had no complaints. That was what they believed at the moment.

The Kuwaitis kept talking on and on. When Esin asked them to tell her more about the way of life in their country, one of the friends with whom Ebraheem planned to open the döner kebab chain, spoke up: "Kuwait isn't strict like Saudi Arabia or Iran. People don't pressurize each other."

"They don't in Turkey either," Esin said. "In Turkey which is a non-Arab country in the region like Iran and Israel, there are veiled and unveiled women in the same family. We're used to different preferences."

Ebraheem went on: "Anyone can veil if they like. My wife is veiled but my sister is not. People don't meddle with each other in my country."

Esin thought that unlikely and pressed him: "So there's no pressure; you don't feel any social pressure at all?"

"We have a kind of *hijab*, that is, women cover their heads. It can be colored or not, worn with a bonnet or puffed out... Some women don't wear one at all. People don't meddle with *others*. Just now those puffed-out models are considered too sexy. They're not really appropriate for Islam. The Gracious Koran prescribes a style of veiling that doesn't attract attention."

"Really? That kind of veil has just begun to be seen around here recently. So, it's sexy! Oh-ho, better not tell the people here."

The young Kuwaiti man continued where he'd left off: "But of course we have social norms for morality. And you can't really drink in public; people drink at home. You can find everything on the black market. But we have a lot of freedom of speech!"

Esin knew that the real problem was how one saw the *other*, and this surprised her. "You can talk about everything? Isn't there anything sensitive you can't talk about?"

"We can't speak ill of our Emir. Other than that, we can talk about anything."

"Well," Esin said, "you can't really badmouth the prime minister here either, and you can't draw caricatures of him. It's obvious that most of the mainstream media either take his side outright, or at the very least, dilute their criticism. But within the awareness of many individuals, chaos in the society has been steadily increasing."

Ebraheem turned to Esin. "You should take a look at your own country rather than wear yourself out asking about ours, about how our women veil. And I think Turkey should be talking about its own economic and education problems rather than the turban. Our literacy rate is ninety-three percent. What is yours? How many days have we been here, and we haven't run into anyone who can speak English properly. We try to talk business, tell people what we're looking for, and they act as if they already know everything without even listening. Turks think they can pull anything off."

Esin laughed. She said he was exaggerating about the English; it wasn't that bad. "You were looking in the wrong places. There are plenty of well-educated people in this country who can speak English."

He saw that Esin was defending her country now. Then she reminded them about the controversial advertising campaign urging people to pray, put out by the Kuwait Ministry of Islam.

The "Pause Campaign" emphasized how important it was for everything to come to a halt with the call to prayer. People should pause to perform their prayers. In other words, the basic theme was that whatever you might be doing, be it work or play, when the call to prayer starts, you should pause and answer the call.

In the first ad, two boys are playing a computer game, and the call to prayer is heard at the most exciting moment in the game. Everything around the two boys stops at that moment. One of the boys is holding a bag of popcorn, and a kernel falls out and freezes in the air. Then the voiceover says: "When you hear the call to prayer, stop and pause. You will continue what you were doing after the prayer."The boys get up and walk by various objects frozen in time as they go to do their ablutions and then stand for prayer. Afterward, the frozen objects begin moving again, and they continue with their game.

There was also an ad aimed at girls in which two ladies are shopping at a huge mall when the call to prayer begins. Everything stops and the same voiceover is heard.

The two women perform their prayers and then continue their shopping where they left off.

Islam was defending its traditions with creative measures aimed to influence youth. Whatever the country, popular culture required that youth, above all, must be influenced if a system of thought were to be imposed. A Muslim boy may play computer games, a veiled young woman may stroll through the shopping malls of American culture.

They could have discussed the advertising campaign for hours but Esin brought the subject to a close with an example of a similar phenomenon in Turkey.

"There are eighty thousand mosques in Turkey. They are usually empty except during Friday prayers and the special *teravih* night prayers of Ramazan. Three out of four people don't perform the five daily prayers. It's mostly the old people in a neighborhood who do the morning and evening prayers. Many, many mosques are being built today but they're empty. Now, groups who want to fill the mosques and make them centers of social life again mount 'Muslims to the mosque' campaigns, like the 'Girls to school' campaigns we used to have."

Ebraheem asked, "And so, how many schools?"

"Sixty seven thousand."

In fact, Esin wanted to continue the discussion. Were there people who saw those ads and went to mosques to pray? Was spirituality something to be forced in that way?

# Kübra's Days
## (The Birthday)

"Blues here, yellows over there, and reds there," Kubra said to herself, arranging the decorations in the salon. Then she stood back and looked it all over.

It was something else to celebrate a birthday at home. The birthday girl should get all dressed up, and make sure everything in the house was ready too. It was tiring and took some deft managing of time.

Since Kübra and her friends did not drink alcohol, they couldn't go to just any nightclub. Nor could they go to a restaurant and enjoy themselves the way they really liked to. They were too old now to have a party on the top floor of a fast-food restaurant. On such special occasions, they wanted to go to an all-women place, where they could show off their hair-dos to one another. So, for women who veiled, getting together in comfort at home was a great way to have fun.

Kübra was happy but at the same time, a bit nervous. She'd spent hours with her mother at the patisserie choosing the birthday cake. Nowadays, one could have cakes made in any shape, like works of art. Kübra loved color, and she'd had a cake made of tiny squares in different colors like a patchwork quilt.

She wanted to add some balloons to the decorations. Her sister Büşra had blown up as many as she could and left them in the room. Kübra was entering her twenty-sixth year but at heart she was a child. After all, it was her birthday, and she had fine days to come.

She went into the kitchen and looked over what Auntie Kadriye had prepared. Sweet cookies, salty pastries, chips – everything was ready to offer the guests. While Auntie Kadriye was slowly carrying the platters to the table in the salon, Kübra ran to her room and changed her clothes. She put on the yellow dress her mother had bought her for her birthday. It had thin straps, sequins on the sides, and came to just above the knee. She'd just got back from the beauty salon. She'd had her long brown hair waved with curling tongs. She had her make-up done at the salon, specially for today. She checked her hair in the mirror and went downstairs. The doorbell rang for the first time while she was coming down the staircase.

Her mother had wanted to stay home that day, and Kübra saw she wouldn't be alone with her friends. Her cousins and several adult female relatives had also been invited.

The first to arrive was her older sister, Müberra. Their cousins Esra and Selma were with her. Then, one by one, her friends arrived. Newly married Ayşe had not been able to help her closest friend Kübra with the preparations this time as she had last year.

All the women arrived very dressed up. As soon as they set foot in the house, they looked for a mirror to take off their scarves and sweaters or raincoats. Every one of them looked like a renowned young soloist about to go out on stage. They'd all come from the beauty salon. Their hair was styled, swept up, curled. The bracelets on their arms and the earrings hanging from their ears added color to their flashy and revealing, outfits.

Close friends talked incessantly, lined up on sofas for three like beads on a rosary. They kept their knees drawn together, accustomed as they were to sitting respectfully before their elders. Each of these young women had different reasons for veiling. One, because she was pressured by her family, another, because that's all she'd ever seen around her, another because she'd wished to wear the veil when she got older, another because the man she would marry wanted it that way... A few women stayed standing up, talking with newly married Ayşe.

They spoke about her legendary dress, made by the famous woman fashion designer, about her henna night, and the wedding. One of them had practiced kissing with her closest girlfriend, so she would know how for later. She was talking about that, half shyly, half boldly, while the others listened fascinated.

The girls usually talked about happy things when they were together. Most of the time, they got together in their homes, in cafes, or at summer homes. They were frank and sincere with one another, but they did not dream up new things to do; for example, they'd never suggest taking a vacation together.

The cake arrived while they sang "Happy Birthday to You." There were twenty-six candles. Kübra had a candle placed in each of the different colored squares. She had creativity in her genes. That was why she was happier in her work as time went on.

She blew the candles out to applause. Each of them kissed Kübra in turn and wished her well. "You were born years ago on this very day," "Now you are more experienced," "May everything be as your heart desires." Kübra was a happy girl today. They fussed over her, and she felt loved.

There were clean glasses by the cake and large bottles of cola and orange juice. As the hostess, Nadide Hanım asked each girl in turn whether she wanted cola or orange juice. Those who could find a place, sat down and began eating their cake.

Kübra's friend with the big nose, Merve, had passed her driver's test. She was very excited about getting her license, and was waiting for her father to buy her a car. She kept telling her friends about it.

The salon was humming with conversation and the sounds of forks striking plates. Suddenly, they noticed they had no music on. Merve turned on the music set and put on current pop songs. Those who had finished their cake got up and danced.

The music was lively and the girls couldn't sit still. Those who were sitting down clapped their hands in time.

They took pictures and put them up on the digital screen right away. If they didn't like them, they took more. Everyone wanted a picture with Kübra. They posed with their arms around each other's waists and their heads tipped slightly to the side.

Kübra enjoyed herself with her friends and family. Every birthday girl was happy when people made a fuss over her. It was even more fun when she opened her presents. She showed each gift to her friends, very excited.

At one point, Ayşe sidled up to her. "How is Samet doing in the army? What will he get for you?"

"He phoned and congratulated me," Kübra said, without lifting her head from her packages. Then she realized her disinterested tone might give the wrong impression and said, "Who knows when we'll see each other. Who cares about presents?"

Samet had considerately sent a lovely gift.

# Esin's Days
## (Energy)

Esin was soaked in sweat. Long, deep breaths had given way to shorter, shallower ones. Maybe it wasn't right to push herself so much. Sometimes it was painful to stretch one's will power to the maximum. But she had to do it. Even if it felt like a duty, she felt really good when it was over. She was virtually pumping adrenaline. And that shower afterwards was the greatest pleasure of all.

Esin always felt guilty if she didn't exercise for a few days and had thrown herself into the gym early in the morning to make up for the days she hadn't been.

She took very good care of herself. She made an effort to stay young. She'd played outdoor games and ate healthy since her university years. She avoided fatty foods, particularly fried foods. In Turkey, where tea and coffee were drunk all the time, she'd become a green tea addict because she believed it strengthened her immune system and burned fat. Her friends nicknamed her "Ms Will Power." Well, if they didn't want cellulite they should exercise and eat properly too.

She warmed up, walking briskly on the treadmill. She chatted with a Jewish girl she knew who used the treadmill beside hers. She had a lot of non-Muslim friends at her gym. Those girls had gotten interested in the Kabala recently.

Then she went into the weights section to do the "super set" program her trainer had prepared for her, made up of exercises to be done consecutively in pairs without resting.

She began with the leg and hip exercises. She always put those off. Take up the weights, squat over and over again ... Gather the grapes, mow the grass... In fact, the best exercises for the hips were the ones where you squat without weights, using the natural weight of the body. After she'd done double sets, huffing and puffing, she went on to the part she liked: exercising the arms. She used three-kilo weights, not too heavy, working her arms, triceps, chest, and shoulders. The loud music playing in the salon helped to motivate people working out and really put Esin in the mood.

She went into the back to do another one of the harder parts of the program: abdominals. She did dozens of sit-ups on the ab rocker. She was already tired by the time she got to the abdominals but she wasn't going to give up. She would do every little bit of her program today too, and in the end, she would feel really good about herself. Wasn't it always like that? She did her duty rhythmically for an hour and when it was over, she left the gym reborn.

It wasn't right to force her body too much all at once. Exercise should be done in the right dosage, resting the muscles on alternate days. She tried to go to the gym three days a week without fail but it wasn't easy to keep the same discipline up every single week.

She ended with some cardio in the salon furnished with machines of the latest technology. She did the treadmill in a twenty-minute program of increasing difficulty. While the muscles of her body came back to normal after working with weights, her metabolism sped up and Esin continued to burn calories after finishing her weight workout. While on the treadmill, she glanced over some weekly and monthly magazines. The treadmill was the ideal place to read such magazines. Her attention was caught by a story titled "A Healthy and Peaceful New Life." People today had begun to be interested in Far Eastern philosophies and purification methods to relax not only their bodies but their souls and minds and this had even become a noticeable trend. Some people did yoga, or meditation, breath therapy, Reiki, or worked on opening up their chakras.

One shouldn't get too involved in meditation. There was a fine line, and if you crossed it, people around you would soon call you "crazy." Of course, once you reached higher consciousness through meditation, it was up to you how much you cared about what other people said.

People were trying various ways to empty their minds and reach higher consciousness in order to connect with the higher power on a higher dimension. "Changing dimension" like that had a Sufi side to it, for sure but some said it took you away from religion. They claimed these new doctrines, all rooted in ancient Chinese philosophy, took the place of religion.

So why did people feel the need for a religion? To purify the spirit, have a relationship with God, to feel a sense of belonging, devote oneself to something, to conform to social morality, to take refuge with a sublime protector in difficult times, give thanks in good times, pray for what one wanted, in short, to feel good... Everyone had his own reason. Belief should not be challenged. Esin thought everyone should believe as they chose, or relax with meditation techniques if they wanted. We all had a feeling of faith within us; if we didn't fill the emptiness with religion, we filled it with other things.

Another article in the magazine asked an impressive question: "If you could sum up, what would be the turning points in your life?"

What had been the turning points in Esin's life? Probably, things that happened while she was still in school: graduations, prizes she'd won... Then meeting her husband Alp and marrying him. She was only thirty. She couldn't know what awaited her. She'd have to ask herself that question again when she was older. Maybe she would have a child, maybe she would find someone else who would turn out to be the love of her life and leave her husband; maybe she would get a super job offer. Maybe, as Nazım Hikmet said, "Our most beautiful days are the days to come."

She left the exercise area and went to the locker room. She got undressed and put her sweaty clothes in the laundry bag. She looked in the mirror as she wrapped herself in a towel. She liked the way she looked right after exercising because the blood rushing to her muscles made her body look more shapely but Esin thought she was a good-looking woman anyway; she found herself beautiful and sexy. She was aware of herself… She knew her own value.

She went into the sauna. She sweated once more after working out and took her shower, humming songs. While she was creaming up her skin and getting dressed, the heavy perfume two girls who'd just come in were wearing almost made her head spin. She was very sensitive to scents, though not as much as Grenouille! Her sensitive nose immediately sensed the smell of a cigarette smoked hours before, the smell of sweat, of damp on a towel, or the freshness of food. What use was this skill to her? None at all! It even made her uptight for no reason sometimes. Hadn't she made her mother suffer because of it? When she was still living with her family, she used to drive her mother crazy with complaints like: "Mom, this sheet isn't completely dry," or "This blouse smells of damp." The poor woman would wash and dry the towel or sheet again. And she'd iron them too but Esin's nose would still catch wind of something. When she realized she was choosing her boyfriends according to their smell, it even frightened her a bit. Sometimes, she just couldn't get interested in a guy, though everything about him was good: he was cultured, educated, had money, was compassionate, and polite. When she didn't feel that warmth and closeness, she would cut it off right away. Years later, she realized that what had driven her away from one guy and attracted her to another was the smell of his skin. What they called "chemistry" was, in her opinion, just smell. She could only be with a man whose scent she could breathe in.

Esin claimed that one could tell from the nape of a person's neck whether or not one would get along with him in bed. If you could take pleasure in kissing someone's neck, take in their scent and feel aroused sexually, the rest would be smooth sailing in Esin's opinion.

And so the nose, and especially the place where the nose joined with the cheek, was in Esin's experience the true secret garden where she could sense the true scent of a lover's skin.

Once, when Esin was kissing a boy she'd just begun to go out with, the smell of his beard made her dreadfully uncomfortable. She seemed to smell the oils his beard had soaked up, and later, hadn't wanted to see him again. In Esin's personal world, hygiene affected romance and the erotic, just as it did every other area of life.

These were things she had learned by experience, and they'd almost become principles for her. Oh, and there was the matter of kissing. If she didn't feel excited by a first kiss, nothing good could come of the relationship. According to her, it was impossible to love someone with time, to fall in love or feel passion that way. There was love at first sight, with the first touch, or not at all. You couldn't make it happen after that.

The girls who had just come into the locker room undressed and put on their workout clothes. But they still had their make-up on. One of them put on more eyeliner, and the other, more perfume. She even kept on her drop earrings.

Esin couldn't help being annoyed and muttered to herself, "Offf! You're here to work out, why all this vulgarity? As if men didn't know which women were natural and which overly dressed up!" In the workout room, there were a few parvenus like that but also girls whose natural beauty caught your attention. Flat stomachs, slightly muscled arms, firm thighs. Esin liked to examine people. She memorized every detail about a person in an instant.

Naturalness was a characteristic to be sought. Whatever anybody said, a man pictured how a woman would look in bed. They didn't like lots of make-up, they didn't like nail polish like people thought... Anyway, what did Esin care? That evening, she was going to the opening of an exhibit with her husband. She was determined not to spoil her calm after her workout with unnecessary things and people she didn't know. According to what she'd learned at breathing seminars, she should love everyone, forgive everyone, and leave everyone free.

# Kübra's Days
## (Fasting)

It was dark outside. The sun was not up yet. A few houses with their lights on were visible in the distance outside the window. The Akansans' home was now in a wooded area, in a quiet neighborhood. They loved Çavuşbaşı. The noise and confusion of Ümraniye was in the past.

No one spoke much, everything went on in silence. Nadide Hanım was still preparing the food. She spooned the stewed fruit she'd made from dried fruits into cups. It was a rather rich table for a before-dawn Ramazan breakfast meal: Salami, sausage, eggs, honey, clotted cream – that was just some of what was on the table. Care should be taken that the before-dawn and after-sunset meals of Ramazan – the month of fasting which Muslims considered an extremely important part of worship, should not be overly showy; one should not forget Islam's prohibition against waste. The food taken before dawn should be light but filling, so that a person could do the fast all day in good health. The energy needed for the day should be provided. The amount and kind of fluids taken was also important.

"Let's not eat so heavily at this hour, Hanım," Hikmet Bey said, "We are going back to sleep again. One should not wear out the heart. Come and sit with us. There's little time anyway."

Nadide Hanım did not object and came to sit with her husband and daughters.

Although Kübra and Büşra had come to the table in their pajamas, they were as alert as jinn. True, it had been very hard to get out of bed but they didn't dare skip the meal before the fast. Sleep was so deep in the hour before dawn that they had not wanted to get out of bed. Kübra, especially, had trouble, thinking how she'd have to wake up again a couple of hours later to go to work. Fasting did not require that you get up for the early meal but it was the practice of the Prophet and a blessing as Nadide Hanım reminded her daughters every Ramazan.

First they had soup. Then a meal of tomatoes, cucumbers, unsalted cheese, honey, and clotted cream like a normal breakfast. No one ate much of the salami or sausage. The girls had eggs too. They finished with the stewed fruit. A few moments before the morning call to prayer, they drank large glasses of water. Then they brushed their teeth, made their intention to fast, and went back to sleep.

Kübra got into bed but couldn't fall asleep right away. She propped up her pillow and sat up in bed for a while. She planned what she would do that day. She was going to go over the details of the new housing project and call some friends to wish them a beneficial Ramazan. They were going to decide on a day to meet at The Fez Factory for the Ramazan festivities. And she was going to call Esin and invite her to the after-sunset Iftar meal. After all, Esin was an old schoolmate.

Kübra realized she'd been thinking about Esin a lot lately. She turned off the light at the head of her bed and flattened out the pillow. She had Esin in her mind's eye again just before she fell asleep.

She had some difficulty getting up again in daylight. It was not easy to sleep for a few hours and get up again. Well, it was the month of Ramazan. The body had trouble for the first few days but then got used to it. And because it got darker earlier every day, the Iftar meal kept getting earlier and it was easier to keep the fast.

Since they didn't have to worry about breakfast, she and her father went straight to work.

It was a long day. There was a lot of work piled up. Kübra did not often have meetings and visits like her father did. She did most of her work in her office at her computer, at a table, or sometimes at construction sites. Kübra was a bright girl who did her work well but her father didn't much like her going to construction sites. The workers, the craftsmen, everyone was male. And it was not appropriate for a young woman, the boss's daughter, especially a conservative young woman, to be in such an environment.

When she'd made some headway, she called Esin on her cell. She made small talk for a while and then told her why she was calling.

"I wanted to get together, Esin. Our meeting in Nişantaşı was so short. I'd like to invite you out too."

"It was nothing, Kübra, just coffee. But of course we can meet. It isn't like I don't find your conversation interesting."

Kübra continued unfazed.

"All right but this week it's not coffee. I'm inviting you for the Iftar meal. We'll go somewhere that has fine Turkish food."

"But I'm not fasting. But all right, we can meet as you say. I will leave my husband alone for a night. But I'm telling you from the start, I can't fast."

Kübra smiled at the other end of the phone.

"That's all right, it's no problem. So, shall we say Thursday? I'll let you know where."

When she'd finished her conversation with Esin, there was a smile on Kübra's face.

As the hour for Iftar approached, Kübra felt slightly listless. They left work earlier than usual.

They were all gathered around the table again at home for the after-sunset Iftar meal. Nadide Hanım had cooked lots of dishes while fasting. She and her daughters set the table together. The eagerly awaited smell of hot *pide* bread wafted through the room. That was one of the nicest things about Ramazan. They turned on the television. A ribbon at the bottom of the screen read, "Iftar time in Istanbul." The call to prayer was heard then. They all prayed silently: "My God, I have fasted for you and I am breaking my fast with Your nourishment." Then they drank water first and ate a few olives.

The Iftar table was cheerful. Afterwards, they drank tea. Throughout the rest of the evening, they snacked on sweets, dates, and fruit.

Hikmet Bey turned toward his wife but did not look at her as he said, "Nadide, I won't be home for Iftar tomorrow. I'll break my fast out." He was going to have the Iftar meal at Nermin's home.

Nadide Hanım said only, "All right, fine." She did not even ask where her husband would be.

After Iftar, Kübra went upstairs to her room on the top floor. She put on a comfortable housedress and stretched out on her bed. She felt heavy after the meal. She closed her eyes and rested for a bit, then took a novel from her bedside table and began to read. Her eyes were tired after a few pages. She thought about what restaurant to take Esin to. She was about to call Ayşe to ask what she thought but decided not to at the last minute. As a new bride, Ayşe must have much keeping her busy. Instead, she called her friend Merve and got a few suggestions.

# Esin and Kübra
## (Iftar)

Both women were in front of their mirrors trying to choose something right to wear for the restaurant tonight. Esin, in her Ulus apartment, was thinking of wearing a knee-length dress as she always did; something clingy with short sleeves and a V-neck. On the other side of the Bosphorus, Kübra, at her house in Çavuşbaşı, was trying to decide whether to wear a long skirt or pants.

At the last minute, Esin gave up on the idea of wearing a close-fitting dress that showed the lines of her body. Since she was going to an Iftar meal, she decided on pants and a chic blouse instead.

Kübra was thinking a long skirt would make her look like a mature, even old, woman and chose pants with a black and white-striped blouse she kept for special occasions. She didn't tuck the blouse in but rather left it loose over the pants. She completed the outfit with a thick black belt and black shoes.

Today, she put on light make-up, although she sometimes didn't wear any at all. She had no nail polish on; she never wore nail polish because she did the ablutions for prayer several times a day. She could, at least, add some color to her face. She put black eyeliner around her green eyes. She got right up close to the mirror, careful not to let her hand tremble as she gave definition to her eyes and put a light blush on her cheeks.

Esin had told Alp the day before that they would not be together that evening. Alp was going to take the opportunity to go out with his own friends. He wasn't about to cut off his mates just because he was married. He missed being with the guys. But Esin was understanding about that. She didn't smother her husband; she didn't interfere with every detail of his life. Alp had no eyes for any other woman anyway.

Esin was an interesting person. One day, she'd go to fancy parties to see and be seen and the next, have an Iftar meal with a veiled girl. When you thought about it, she was really full of life. She loved all the colors in the rainbow and the harmony they made too. She knew how to keep variety and contradiction in balance; sameness bored her. She wanted to learn new things. She liked to have different kinds of people tell her their lifestories. She thought that learning and observing matured her.

That was why she'd accepted Kübra's Iftar invitation. None of her friends wore the turban. She knew nothing about the world of such people. Most in Esin's circle didn't know much about veiled women. They made fun of the *others*, based on what they'd heard; it was all rumor, gossip, and suspicion. And Esin knew that the *others* also knew very little about the lives of people like her.

Alp dropped Esin off in Beyoğlu and went to join his friends. Kübra called a taxi from the stand near her house.

When they got to the showy restaurant where traditional Turkish cuisine was served, it was ten minutes to the Iftar hour. Kübra had made a reservation. They sat at a table for two. At first, she'd planned to bring Esin to Şehzade Mehmet Sofrası in the conservative district of Fatih but then, decided on Beyoğlu, thinking Esin would be more comfortable, that she wouldn't feel a stranger here.

The table was laid for a traditional lftar. Tomatoes, cheeses, olives, honey in the comb, clotted cream, *pide* bread, *pastırma* salami, dates, two bowls of sour lentil soup, and glasses for tea and water.

Esin politely waited for the call to prayer to finish before touching anything on the table. She didn't even drink water. She was showing respect for her fasting friend.

The wind blowing outside was the first topic of conversation. Summer had suddenly come to an end. One more season was behind them. Was time passing faster or what? The warm days of summer had passed in the blink of an eye.

The call to prayer sounded. Kübra recited "Bismillah" inwardly and broke her fast with a glass of water. For some reason, Esin could not take her eyes off her. But Kübra was just a normal person and she was breaking her fast as everyone else did.

Esin had fasted only twice in her life. Once was years before, her first experiment with fasting. She spent most of the day sleeping because she was so afraid she'd be hungry and thirsty. The other was a year ago, on the day before the Night of Power toward the end of Ramadan. A few of her friends had fasted that day too. They'd done it as a social sort of thing. During the day, they'd phoned one another to ask how it was going. When they broke the fast together that evening, they were all in a good mood.

Esin was thinking of all that as she began to talk: "You know what? I have fasted twice in my life. One time I slept through it, so I don't count that. The other was the day of the Night of Power. You know how all sins are forgiven on that night, so we fasted thinking we'd take a short cut to good deeds. Is that right, I wonder?"

Kübra smiled and finished what she was eating.

"Look, dear Esin, the Night of Power is more virtuous than the master of all days, Friday, and the nights before sacred days. It is the most holy night in Islam. It is said: 'Whoever spends the Night of Power in sincere worship, all his past sins are forgiven.' But of course, this does not mean that one is purified of all sins by one night of worship."

Now, Esin smiled. "And we thought we'd got off with one day's fasting and prayer. I'm joking of course ..."

That made Kübra uncomfortable, even if it was a joke. Esin realized this and tried to smooth things over.

"Oh Kübra, excuse me, I say everything bluntly like that. And I make jokes. Even about religion ..."

And she added, smiling: "I won't be struck down dead, will I?"

This time, Kübra's teeth showed in a broad smile. Esin really shot straight from the shoulder. She said whatever came into her head. She was very at ease about expressing herself.

"You can relax with me," Kübra said. "Say whatever you like, it won't bother me much. But please take care not to talk about sensitive things in front of all and sundry. Very devout people might be offended."

Esin raised her hands and hooted like a ghost, continuing to smile.

"I swear, if we go on meeting like this I will tell you straight out what I think about religion. And there's so much I don't know; maybe you'll even teach me."

"You can ask what you like. Of course I'll help as much as I'm able."

Esin took the opportunity to raise a subject she often argued over with her friends but never could sort out.

"People who live the way you do, performing all the commands of religion – are you all going to Heaven? I mean, even learned theologians and people who've been to Mecca make mistakes; they do wrong, perverse things. Are their hearts pure? People in my circle don't pray, they don't veil but some of them are good as angels, their hearts are very pure. So which is right?"

Kübra's manner became serious.

"Such people, unfortunately, do not understand the true Islam, dear Esin. But among the religious, there are people who lose their way, even if not many. You, for example, let us say you are a pure young woman, honorable, faithful to your husband, you give alms to the poor, you do not envy others, do not gossip. In short, pure of heart, let us say ..."

Esin didn't know whether to frown or smile. "What do you mean, 'let us say'? That's how I am," she said and then laughed.

Kübra continued ...

"All right, it's good that you're pure in heart but if you are Muslim, which you are, shouldn't you obey the commands of your religion?"

Esin had her answer ready: "Yes, I am Muslim. I was born in Turkey. It says 'Islam' under 'religion' on my birth certificate.

But that doesn't mean that I, under the conditions we live in today, should do like people did long ago, does it?"

"Excuse me but God did not make religion only for the old days...There is no specific time limit in the Gracious Koran, saying it expires on such and such a date. What nonsense! God forbid!"

"All right, in your opinion how many kinds of Muslims are there in Turkey? Everyone is different. It's with you as it is with us... excuse me for saying 'you' and 'us'; there are different styles of life at different levels."

"Yes, that is very true. In the segment of people you call modern, there are extremes too and people who live more normal lives. Among devout people, there are some who pray five times a day, some who just cover their heads, some who never leave the mosque, some who pretend to be religious to pull off some business deal, and some who try to bend religion to their own ends. In the end, we are all human. Nobody knows what is in another's heart."

"There are people who've turned cold on religion in this country too. Some even ridicule it. And most are like me, caught in between."

"And how is that?"

"I believe in God. I respect all religions and faiths, not just my own. But I can't perform all the requirements of Islam. If you look at the basics, I don't do much anything in life connected with religion except be well-intentioned and pure in heart."

"That's what I thought. I knew you thought that way. Yes, there are different levels of religious faith in Turkey and styles of life accordingly. Those who almost hate religion and ridicule people who live their lives according to Islamic principles, reject religious commands and look down on the devout; they see them as small-minded. They think religious people are all ignorant. These people who virtually curse religion are the opposite of people like me who govern their lives, their actions and their dress according to religious commands. Polarization is the result."

"I think the polarization comes not only from us but is produced through the influence of external forces as well. The other day, my husband was talking about how the great powers manipulate certain countries. What-all is there going on in the world that we know nothing about? There is so much hidden behind the reasons shown to the public, even for wars."

Kübra agreed with Esin. They were getting to know each other better; somehow, finding common ground.

Kübra took a sip of water from the glass in front of her. Esin ran her fork over her plate and popped a few morsels into her mouth. When she finished chewing, she began to speak again: "All right then, let's put that topic aside for now. Here's another question for you: Do you all know the Koran by heart? You're supposed to have very good powers of memory. All those prayers, verses from the Koran ... When there's a question of religion, you have a quotation ready right away with a citation to prove what you say."

"First, can I make a correction? When you say 'you,' who do you mean?"

"Well, I'm not the only one who says that ... 'You,' you know, you Muslims ..."

"Aren't you Muslim?"

"Yeah, of course, I'm Muslim too. I'm a moral person by my own right. I pray for things I need, though not all the time. But you know, you cover your heads and the men act more religious too. I mean 'you' in that sense."

Kübra took a spoonful of yoghurt. Esin paused at that point and said, "I'm sorry. You're eating; we can continue talking later." She looked over the dishes on the table. The sour pomegranate-walnut paste looked delicious.

"No, I'm fine," Kübra said. "Fasting doesn't make you attack your food. It's best to eat slowly. I'm going to ask something. All right, so when do you remember that you're Muslim?"

"When I get on a plane! If it starts to shake even a little, I start off with 'Ashadu ...' and recite the formula of witness to the faith right away."

"So, when you're scared. So when you feel afraid, you seek out a power to take refuge in and that is God, of course."

"Well, yes. But that doesn't mean I live my life according to religion. I pray when I think of it. I take refuge in God when I feel bad."

"But isn't that selfish? I mean, to seek out God only when things are bad?"

"It's not selfish. There are times when I'm grateful too. To each, his own. Everyone believes and practices their faith in their own way. I don't cover my hair, I don't veil, I don't do the five ritual *namaz* prayers. I don't think those things go along with our times."

"Have you ever done *namaz*?"

"Yes, when I was small, my mother had me and my sister perform *namaz* on religious days. We wrote the instructions for ablution on a piece of paper and hung it over the bathroom tub. We'd do our ablutions following the instructions. That piece of paper would get soaking wet. Then we'd put on a thin head covering made of something like gauze. My sister and I would pray, imitating our mother's movements. We'd giggle and laugh. The prayers we didn't know by heart we'd read out of a book, or just move our mouths in whispers as if we were reciting. If you count that as *namaz*, yes, I've done *namaz*."

Kübra just said, "Hmmm," with a teacher-like air. She went on eating. She wanted to talk about these things but she was also hesitant to do so. She did not feel like teaching religion to an unveiled modern woman who didn't value it. And today she'd wanted to enjoy herself with Esin, not debate religion.

Esin thought one of the things that made her and many others like her cold to religion was the way religious doctrine was presented. The family, one's circle of close friends, the communication media and even many religious people didn't really explain what religious values were. That was why every Muslim did not embrace religion to the same degree. And the differences in degree became a subject of dinner table debate.

The waiter brought fresh plates to the table. Small sample portions of various Turkish dishes were placed in the center. Vegetables in olive oil, stuffed grape leaves, fresh green beans, dried red beans, "slashed-belly" eggplants, eggplants stuffed with ground meat – it all looked appetizing.

Kübra took the waiter's interruption as an opportunity to change the subject.

"Did you go on vacation this summer?"

Esin's mind was still on what they'd been talking about and she was confused by this suddenly ordinary question.

"We didn't take a very long vacation. Both me and my husband had work to do. We got away on weekends to Bodrum, Antalya, and so on."

Kübra found the word "husband" strange, coming in the natural flow of Esin's conversation. The woman sitting across from her was married. The Esin who everyone at school turned to look at as she walked down corridors, swinging her hair and yes, her hips, was now the woman of her house.

And Kübra was not yet married. She was engaged to Samet but somehow she just could not say "I'm engaged." She even sometimes forgot that Samet was in her life. If they didn't meet, if they didn't talk on the phone, he was not someone she thought about every moment, someone she longed for. Was she going to be able to say "my husband" so naturally, the way Esin did? She couldn't even imagine living together with Samet in the same house. She had no plans for the future and what had happened was a blur.

"And you? Where did you go for vacation? Hey, I've got a real question – where do you all go to swim? Do you sunbathe?"

Kübra smiled through Esin's childish questions. While she answered, she popped pieces of succulent braised lamb into her mouth from a dish of clay-baked shepherd's pilaf studded with raisins.

"We have places we go, of course. I went with my family to Sapanca. Then we stayed in a wonderful hot springs hotel in Antakya. My parents went back to Kayseri, though I didn't go with them this time. As for sunbathing and swimming, no, we can't do that at regular hotels. As you know, you can't do that all wrapped up like a package. We can sunbathe in swimsuits at the homes of friends who have pools where no one else will see us."

"Well, it's not a stupid question, is it? I mean, you don't let your hair show, so going around in a bikini, God forbid," Esin said, giggling wickedly. "You're not mad at me, are you?" For an instant she threw Kübra a loving look.

Kübra smiled and said, "I'm not mad, Esin. As I said, you can relax around me. I'm used to being regarded as strange in this country. In America, as you know, people like us didn't have such troubles. There everyone is free. Nobody interferes with you."

Esin picked up the thread right away. "True but is the American system like what we have here? You can't compare Turkey and America in freedom of belief. The experience is very different. America is a geography made up of people who fled religious oppression; there are many different religions there. It's free. There's almost nothing preventing people from living according to their religion. There, human rights apply to everything. People of different races, religions and ethnic groups live together freely as equals. True, there are still racial problems in the US and it's not like there's no discrimination in politics or behavior but it's really different."

"Esin, please, let's not get into racism. For many years, Americans have been fanatical about race and ethnic roots; they're branded a 'racist nation.' Blacks were made into slaves and oppressed. Do you remember, there was a boy at our school from Los Angeles. When you asked him where he was from, he'd say, "I was born in LA, I'm American. But people didn't think that was enough, they'd insist, 'But where are you really from, where's your family from?' And when he said his family was Mexican, some people looked at him differently; they laid down an invisible line of difference."

"Oh, yes, I remember him. He was handsome, a dark type."

"There's no need for me to give more examples. Now they have a black president. That's a first. Anyway, you know very well, racism is something else. But here in Turkey, we are all Muslims, we're one people. I don't understand why they see us as different. Are we bogeymen?"

"Look, you say 'us' too. So, you too agree that there are two different segments of people. Unfortunately, that's the way it is. And I don't see any integration."

"But you are able to have dinner with me!"

Esin paused and didn't say more. She put her hand under her chin and a serious expression came over her face. She was sitting across a table, eating with a girl whose head was covered. And they had lots to talk about. There were so many things she wanted to talk about and share with her. She was not ill at ease; on the contrary, she was enjoying this.

For a while, they said nothing and went on nibbling their food. Neither of them ate much.

Kübra watched Esin fixedly from time to time. She was in awe of the elegance with which she handled her fork and knife. Esin had small hands and a French manicure. People thought Kübra had beautiful hands too. Her long, thin fingers were lovely. She didn't use nail polish but her nails were always clean and well groomed.

"I'm going to try fasting too," Esin said to her suddenly. "Should I wait for the Night of Power again? But that's a long way off."

This sudden assertion pleased Kübra.

"There are twenty days till the Night of Power. Try it out before that. You can do it; it's not that hard."

"I have problems with my blood sugar. I can't leave the house in the morning without having breakfast."

"You'll have breakfast a bit early, before dawn. You can do it."

"Done, I'm going to try it. My husband will be very surprised."

They laughed...

Dinner was over and it was time for dessert. They ate *güllaç*, a traditional Ramazan sweet pudding with rose water. They both scraped the bottom of their bowls.

Kübra asked for the check. Esin offered to share but Kübra wouldn't have it, "I invited you," she said. When Esin replied, "Well then, I owe you a dinner now," it was decided that they would meet again.

When they went outside, they each got a taxi and went home.

# Esin's Days (Will Power)

It had been two days since Esin had the Iftar dinner with Kübra. She'd been too busy to dare try fasting and had put it off.

She and Alp were sitting in the salon in the evening, watching a DVD. As always, Alp wanted to watch an action film and Esin insisted on a romantic comedy. They had the same sweet argument every time. Usually, Alp would have his way and they'd watch an action or adventure film, or something with lots of fighting in it. Alp could not stand nonsensical romances or dramas as Esin herself put it.

They'd both fall asleep while watching TV or reading magazines on the big couch in the salon. While furnishing the apartment, they'd looked around for a long time to find the right L-shaped couch. There were lots of choices but it hadn't been easy to find one big and comfortable enough for them.

Alp loved to munch on snacks while watching DVDs but "Ms Will Power" Esin refused to eat things bad for her health like potato chips and popcorn. Their bodies were always touching while they watched films. Their hands, their arms, their feet, their legs... They no longer stayed in embrace like a ball of hugs as they used to but the touch of skin still felt good.

Esin was not knocked out by the film's plot and fell asleep with her head on Alp's shoulder while watching the film. When it was over, he turned off all the electric appliances with the remote. He woke her up gently, whispering, "Come on, darling, let's go to bed." Esin got on her feet, half-asleep. She went into the bathroom, brushed her teeth and put on her face cream. She got into bed and set the alarm clock on the bedside table for 4:30am. She turned to Alp and said, "Just so you know, I'm going to fast tomorrow, I'm getting up early for the before-dawn meal."

"What! What brought this on?"

"Darling, I'm going to try it. I'll do what everybody else does…"

"You'll never get up at the crack of dawn, you'll see…"

"I *will* get up, Alp. Oh, and by the way, I can't cook dinner tomorrow. Please take me somewhere for Iftar. You'll be doing a good deed."

Alp turned away. "What next!" he whined. His wife was always surprising him. He'd never get bored as long as he had Esin.

Near dawn, Esin woke to the bitter buzz of the clock alarm. She stretched in bed and looked at Alp. He didn't stir.

She washed her face and shuffled off to the kitchen. She took olives, cheese, and milk out of the refrigerator. She took a couple of slices of bread from the bread basket and put them in the toaster. She put water in the kettle that Alp's adman mate, Volkan, had got them as a housewarming present and plugged it in. She picked out a herbal tea from the variety of tea packets in the upper cupboard. She put the tea bag in her mug with the picture of a cute dog on it. The toast was ready. She put the strawberry jam on the kitchen counter and sat on one of the high bar stools. The counter was cold as ice. She began eating her before-dawn meal. Thinking she'd definitely get hungry during the day, she ate a bowl of cornflakes too after her toast and jam. She wasn't very hungry but she ate it anyway. She drank a glass of water, and brushed her teeth. While she was getting back into bed, the call to prayer began. She got under the light bedcover, recited the phrase for the intention to fast she'd memorized from the internet and drifted off to sleep with a smile of contentment on her face.

In the morning, the alarm rang for Alp alone. Esin was going to get up whenever she felt like it. She had no work to do early in the day. She'd chosen that day to fast because she had nothing to do. How did people who worked in offices from morning till evening fast for a whole month?

Alp took his shower. He got a clean, pressed shirt from the closet. He put on his suit. He planted a kiss on Esin's forehead and left quietly. He planned to pick out a nice place for Iftar when he got to the office.

It was almost eleven o'clock when Esin woke up. Getting up before dawn and going back to sleep had left her muddle-headed. She sat up in bed. She locked her fingers together and lifted her arms over her head, giving them a good stretch and yawned and yawned. She went into the salon with the newspapers Alp had brought inside from the bag by the front door. She put her feet up on the ottoman and began to read. She found all this a bit strange – reading the papers without tea or anything to eat.

She didn't feel hungry but her mouth was a bit dry. She realized the hardest thing about fasting was not drinking any water.

When she finished reading the papers, she felt sleepy. She dozed a while on the couch. She put a CD in the music set and turned it on loud to try to get herself to wake up. Then the loud sound made her uncomfortable and she turned it down.

She spent almost the whole day dozing on the couch. It seemed having an empty stomach made a person yawn a lot. She made a few phone calls, checked her email and answered the urgent ones.

Alp got home an hour before Iftar. When he saw Esin in her jogging suit half asleep, he joked, "Didn't I tell you it would be hard? What do you care about fasting, my beauty?"

They sat down facing one another in the salon. Alp was smiling slyly. He held up a piece of paper.

"Esin, I was worried about you today. I went online and looked up how to fast. Look here, I wrote it all down; I'll read it to you. 'To fast is to abandon food, drink, and sexual union with the intention of worship from just before dawn until sunset. A person ends the fast by doing one of the prohibited things after the sun has set.' That means you can end your fast by having sex with me. Pretty good, huh?" He ended his speech, laughing out loud.

Esin leapt to her feet.

"Boo to you, Alp. What a weirdo you are. What next? You've really twisted things your way, haven't you. What a joke! Come on, get dressed, we're going to be late for Iftar. I'm starving to death!"

# Kübra's Days
## (The Old Fez Factory)

They all piled into Merve's car. The lines of her face were coarser than those of her friends. Kübra sat next to her in the front and put on her seat belt. The other girls lined up in the back seat. Since none of them was very fat, all four could squeeze in.

When you looked at Merve's face, your attention was caught by her huge nose. Her lips were thick. She didn't pluck her eyebrows, even though her friends insisted she should. She had the harshest personality of them all too but under that coarse appearance, she had a heart good as gold, a spotless soul. She shared everything she had with her close friends.

Merve had just got her driver's license and her father had given her a small car. She was very happy about it but afraid to drive alone. She always wanted to have someone with her. This evening, she and her girlfriends were going to the old Fez Factory, which had been redesigned as one of the best places to have fun during Ramazan.

When they got close to Eyüp and saw the crowds, they were a bit dismayed. They had to pass by the Fez Factory to get to the parking lot but they could barely inch forward. Hundreds of people were walking along, mostly families with children. The festivities here during Ramazan were very popular. The number of people who visited The Fez Factory in the month of Ramazan was in the tens of thousands.

They broke their fast in the "Ramazan Delights" section. They soon left the table without stuffing themselves. They wanted to look around right away.

All the activities were free, and there were programs for every age group. There were comedy skits and a shadow puppet theater, canto singers and magicians. Children were gaily running up and down. A mini-sized amusement park had been set up as well.

Kübra, Merve and the others didn't want to eat sweets right after the meal and so, took a tour around the whole site. There was corn of every variety being sold: popcorn, boiled or roasted corn, on the cob or shaved off. Roasted chestnuts, various pastes, and cotton candy were all available.

They left the outdoor fair and went into the building where there was an exhibition of calligraphy. Then they came to a large open area where all sorts of gift merchandise were sold. In this part of the Fez Factory building, there were no partitions and you could view the structure in all its simplicity. Each of the girls found something she wanted to buy.

Kübra stopped at a stand where she saw prayer rugs of the kind her aunt had given her. There were scented prayer rugs too. She wondered if the artificial scent would make her sneeze when she went into prostration during prayer. Did the scent last, or was it just a trick? She wasn't sure and didn't buy one. But she bought a rosary scented with rosewater, a pink one. She kept opening the box and smelling it. She stopped at another stand selling rose-scented merchandise and bought rosewater face tonic and hand cream.

Merve was interested in some scarves designed with *ebru* marbling patterns. She chose one of the highest-quality silks for her mother. She didn't want to spend too much money and bought herself one of the less expensive satin scarves.

They went into another large hall and found veiled outfits sold there at outlet prices. Tunics, topcoats, light coats, two-piece suits and long skirts were on display. One of the girls bought a denim topcoat because it was inexpensive and was showing it off. But Kübra didn't like anything, she turned up her nose at it all. Even if she was veiled, she took great care with her clothes. She chose the most high-quality fabrics and bought imported silk scarves in the rarest designs.

They looked at each other, shopping bags in hand; they were all tired. They went outside to drink some tea and rest on stools set out on the grass. They sipped their tea in pleasure. At the next table, a group of men were smoking water pipes. There was a couple with children at another table.

The girls talked about the Ramazan vacations they would take with their families. This year, the Ramazan holiday would start on the same day as the Jewish Rosh Hashanah.

# Esin and Kübra
## (Breath)

Oxygen spread throughout Esin's body and her hands and feet fell asleep. She was lying down but had no awareness of the position of her body. It was as if she were unconscious, passing over into another dimension. Her breathing was even and full. When her breathing coach said, "Come on, shout out loud!" she slapped her feet on the floor and shouted "Aaaa," as hard as she could. Then she went back to breathing quietly.

After about an hour, her breathing coach pulled the plastic mouthpiece from between her lips. Esin closed her dry mouth. Her eyes were still shut. She gradually became drowsy and drifted into sleep. In her dream, she saw ethereal waves moving like clouds. A light at the center of her forehead seemed to calm her... a smile spread over her face. She was happy. After another ten minutes of lying there with a white sheet spread over her, in a trance unaware of the world, she woke to light prodding by the person next to her.

She slowly opened her eyes. She sat up. The silence in the room remained unbroken for a while.

Everyone felt light and happy. When their eyes met, they greeted each other silently with filial love.

Another breathing session was over. With this one-hour spiritual journey, the cells of the body were refreshed and the mind rested. You felt transformed, overcome with physical and spiritual goodness, strengthened. A higher consciousness came into play, giving you the courage to live life as you yourself imagined it, not as it was imposed upon you.

This system of breathing allowed you to shed bad breathing habits, clean out the body with the oxygen flowing in your veins and purify yourself of traumas carried around since childhood. And that opened up space for joy, happiness, health and plenitude.

Just being able to breathe correctly was enough to make a person happy. Esin had been attending breath therapy for a few weeks and was very satisfied with it. She had been self-confident and happy before she began this method but she now looked at life differently. A positive life energy had come into her and the value of spiritual pleasures had increased for her. She was experiencing an enlightenment of her own. She was more content, more aware…

She felt as if no one could question her. And she shouldn't question anyone else. Love had to be unconditional. Some things were the way they were because they had to be, and she had to find inner happiness independent of other people and the events happening around her. To hold on to what happened outside you was to live on slippery ground, and it was dangerous. She was the most valuable thing in her life. She had a sublime power within her. She had to find it and sense it deep within and reach its essence. The rest was empty: clothes, cars, jewelry, possessions, lovers, relationships; dependence on material things was an illusion. Most people forgot about spirituality in the rush of daily life and focused entirely on material things. So many of the things we obsessed about and thought we couldn't do without were so meaningless.

Esin was only now beginning to grasp these things. As a woman just entering her thirties, she was experiencing the higher pleasure of being able to make this distinction.

From now on, she was going to do what she wanted. Whatever she felt like doing… Who decided what was right and wrong anyway? She wanted to leave relative concepts behind. She was gaining a feeling of self-confidence. And she was filled with curiosity. She learned new things. Every new thing she learned brought her new questions. The more she learned, the better she understood what she did not know. Thus, a road of development without limits opened up before her. She was just beginning to discover herself.

All the while she was going back and forth to those sessions, she thought of her mother. Her mother had overcome cancer with the support of alternative as well as regular medical treatment. She'd get up with the sun and meditate. She'd become a more serene woman. If a glass fell on the floor, she'd say nothing; she'd just clear away the broken glass. In the past, she'd have raised hell.

Esin left the center with a smile of contentment on her face. Today, she was going to meet up with Kübra. She was a little late; Kübra must have already arrived. Esin was taking her out to dinner as she'd promised.

It excited her to be leaving her journey through the breath to meet someone she saw as belonging to another world.

When Kübra saw Esin come through the door smiling from ear to ear, she smiled too. Full of energy, Esin kissed Kübra on the cheeks and sat down across from her.

"My, my, Madam Esin, why so happy?" Kübra began. "If you have any left over, give it to me!"

"I'm feeling so good because I'm coming from those breathing classes. There's nothing like it! I swear, I feel born anew."

Kübra narrowed her eyes. "What do you do there?" she asked.

The two young women had talked on the phone a few times since their meeting during Ramazan and had finally gotten together for dinner. They had plenty of time to talk. With great pleasure, Esin described every phase of her breath therapy.

"So that's what it's like," said Esin. "In the end, you feel relaxed and filled with inner peace," she said, stretching out her hands behind her chair.

Kübra smiled and looked Esin in the eye.

"Look, Esin, I have that feeling you describe every day since I was eleven years old."

She knew she'd said something mysterious, and that it would arouse Esin's curiosity. She was enjoying it.

Esin collected herself.

"What? What do you mean?"

Kübra lifted her eyebrows and a knowing look came over her face.

"I feel a sense of calm, of lightness and infinite peace every time I perform the *namaz* prayer," she said, and now she leaned back in her chair too.

Surprise and confusion spread over Esin's face and stayed there for a while. How could it be that she was just now discovering the spiritual peace Kübra had found when she was only a child? She herself was born into Islam and yet, found that peace in Eastern philosophical doctrine.

Kübra saw she wasn't going to get a coherent response from Esin and went on: "I can experience in five or ten minutes what it takes you an hour to do."

Esin had recovered her sense of humor and leapt in: "Yes, but you have to do it five times a day, my darling."

"If God commands it so, five times, my darling."

"So the effect doesn't last long. Clearly, you have to keep reminding yourself."

"Aw, that's enough, Esin. I don't believe one questions religious regulations that way. You have to believe in religion unquestioningly according to the requirements of faith. I thought you weren't going to question anything anymore, remember?"

"So you look at me like that with your eyebrows arched. I don't like this know-it-all air of yours. Weren't you an understanding religious person?"

Kübra didn't answer.

Esin took a more mature tone.

"Look, Kübra, as long as a person has a mind there will be new questions. And it's possible to find new answers to old questions. Since God gave intelligence to us all, it's our right to ask questions. I get it, there are some things in religion that are not to be changed but there can be a variety, different forms, changing according to changing conditions. If you broaden the field where religious doctrine rules, you cut off the mind."

Kübra listened to what Esin said but it was impossible for her to bring this way of thinking into her own life and view of things. She remained silent. Esin began explaining again about the benefits of breathing and how it had to be done, taking care not to ramble.

"They say that our habits of thought and blockages in memory we carry around from the past can cause us to lose our physical, mental, and spiritual health. You change your way of thinking, and everything becomes easier. It's that simple."

The philosophy of life she'd just discovered made Esin as happy as a child with a new toy. Kübra could see very well the excited happiness she felt and could understand it.

Esin was excited all over again by everything she could think of about breathing therapy.

"We have talks about transformal breathing, and we turn within. The other day, we did something I found very interesting – a kind of chanting. We all chanted "Ruahelohim" out loud continuously. Then we learned that this invites the higher frequency into us. Just as in Islamic *zikir*, when you chant "There is no god but God..." It really surprised me how similar it was."

"The teachings of our own religion are really beautiful and beneficial, aren't they?"

Esin pouted like a spoiled child.

"Yes but my questions aren't finished yet. Especially now, because of the breathing, I'm really interested in these subjects. Do you find it hard to perform *namaz*? I mean, how did you memorize the prayers?"

Although Kübra was younger than Esin, she sometimes took on the role of older sister because of her knowledge about religious things.

"I started doing *namaz* when I was very young. First, I imitated my mother as she bent over and straightened up, and just like you did when you were small, I moved my lips as if I were praying. Then I read a picture book about *namaz* my mother gave me, and I memorized the prayers. I kept praying, and after a while, I got used to it. It's as if I always knew how, as if I've always prayed. Now it's not hard for me at all."

Kübra was just about to ask if Esin would do *namaz* with her one day but Esin didn't give her a chance: "Kübra, what about if I do *namaz* with you sometime?"

They smiled contentedly at having had the same thought at the same time. When two people breathed freely, it was easy to meet on the same frequency. For both of them, the answer was yes.

"Please don't misunderstand, Esin. I don't want to influence you. No one should interfere with anyone else. But believe me, I really like it that you are interested in these things and that you put aside prejudices you have clung to for years in order to ask me these questions. The more time we spend together, the closer I feel to you."

"It's so interesting... I never would have thought I'd be having a conversation with a veiled woman. Until I met you, it bothered me when I saw women who looked like you. I was even angry to see veiled women in the protocol section at the awards ceremony where we ran into each other. I thought you were all angry and cross, closed in on yourselves, and boring. I like it too that we can be like this together. Let's continue to meet. Don't tell anyone but I get a lot out of it."

As Esin always used to say, "The energy at the table was fine."

# Esin and Kübra
## (Cream)

Esin was an Istanbulphile and when she went to Ankara, she'd usually take the first plane back as soon as she'd finished what she had to do. So she didn't know Ankara well. She just couldn't warm to it. She thought of Ankara as a land-locked city where state business was carried out in official grey buildings. It was only the fact that the tomb of the great leader Ataturk was there which lent the city importance, in her opinion.

Esin and Kübra were going to Ankara for the wedding of a mutual friend from college – Burcu.

Burcu was finally marrying Erdem, whom she'd met in America and been together with for years. She'd invited a lot of her friends from college. Kübra was not as close to her as Esin but still, she had not wanted to refuse and accepted with pleasure the invitation to the party in Ankara on the eve of the wedding. Alp did not know the bride or groom, so he hadn't warmed to the idea of going to the wedding.

Both Kübra and Esin had made reservations at the Sheraton where the wedding was to be held. Burcu had given them the phone number of a couple that was coming to Ankara for the wedding, saying they could all travel together. The young couple had been married for five years and drove a deluxe SUV which carried them all to Ankara in comfort.

Kübra had not told her parents there would be a male in the car. They'd make a fuss over nothing and she knew they would not permit it. They would even have her use a chauffeured car from her father's company. She did not want to be denied permission for such a childish reason and be embarrassed before Esin.

They got together around noon. They would change their clothes and go to the wedding as soon as they arrived in Ankara. The husband was driving, and his wife sat next to him in the front. Esin and Kübra spent the four hours' journey in the back seat. It was a bit crowded because they'd put some of their things on part of the back seat as well, and their legs touched now and then. At one point, Kübra accidentally brushed her hand against Esin's leg and said, "You work out a lot Esin; what muscles you have." Her slight touch did not bother Esin, and what Kübra said pleased her.

Along the way, they listened to music or talked. They reached Ankara late in the afternoon. They gave their small suitcases to the doorman in front of the hotel. They picked up their room keys at reception. Esin and Kübra had rooms on different floors. They only had a short time left to get ready.

Esin took a shower and lay down on the bed in her bathrobe to rest a bit. Her eyes were just about to close when the phone rang. It was Kübra.

"What? You're ready? I haven't even started getting dressed. Come to my room if you like. You can help me zip up my dress. I'd forgotten I can't do it by myself."

A short while later, Kübra was in Esin's room. Esin was still in her bathrobe, and when she opened the door and saw Kübra, she couldn't believe her eyes. Kübra looked so beautiful, despite the fact that she was wearing a veiled outfit. "The girl really has taste," Esin thought to herself. Kübra did not look like she was wrapped up in pieces of brightly colored cloth like most veiled women did. She was wearing an elegantly simple long black evening gown with sequins here and there. The black eyeliner on her green eyes looked so good with her skin. Esin could not get enough of looking at her.

"You look great, my girl. More so than I expected, wow! You have the face of an angel. If you didn't wear those kinds of outfits, you'd look great in photographs; you could be an incredible model."

"Not the job for me." Kübra smiled and tossed the idea aside. She was embarrassed but didn't let it show.

Esin pushed it further. "But why do you hide your beauty? Why should a woman, especially if she's very beautiful, cover herself up?"

"It's best if you get ready right now but I'll explain briefly. I cover myself because of my religious belief. No one has forced me. I have read the Gracious Koran and I fulfill the commands of my religion as a Muslim woman. Some parents *do* force their daughters but that's a different discussion. As for hiding one's beauty, beauty is valuable and should be hidden. Veiling gives women value and a position of honor, like a jewel or a priceless work of art. Who would want to openly display something rare? One should keep it hidden away."

"Why? Because something could happen to her? Look at it another way: being attractive is what is forbidden."

"You're very close, yes. In order to protect her, keep her chaste and safe from the prying eyes of men."

"That's a ridiculous way to see things. So I'm impure?"

Kübra wanted to calm Esin down. "No, you're not. But to veil is to be faithful and honorable, to be a good Muslim. And it is good for the well-being of the family."

"Look, Kübra, Turkish society is beginning more and more to see the turban as a symbol of opposition to secularism. This comes of politicians signing their names to mistaken views about it. The percentage of women who veil decreases as more women are educated. Considering that a rise in education does not lessen religious belief, don't talk to me this way about what it is to be a good Muslim."

"Look, dear Esin," Kübra said, "Let's perform an experiment this evening. Observe how the men at the wedding look at you. Where do their eyes come to rest on your body? Do they pay attention to what you say? Or are they falling all over themselves to gaze at your body? Do we have a deal?"

"It's a deal, little lady," Esin said and looked around the room vaguely as if she could not decide what to do in it. Then she said, "I'm going to get ready right now. First, let me put on my cream. My evening gown shows a lot of skin, so my skin has to shine," and she went into the bathroom, took off her robe and began applying cream to her body starting with her legs. She called out to Kübra through the bathroom door: "Kübra dear, forgive me, but I took out some clean underwear and left it on top of my suitcase. Could you bring it to me? I'm not coming out naked because you're there."

Kübra got up and found Esin's thong panties on top of her leather suitcase. First, she felt them with the tips of her fingers. Then she went to the bathroom door and held them out for Esin, keeping her face turned toward the room. But she couldn't help herself and asked: "How can you be comfortable in those things? I mean, don't they ride up between ..."

She was also thinking of her older sister who spent all her time in Agent Provocateur, a shop selling the latest in fantasy lingerie. The dressing rooms in that shop had red velvet wallpaper and leopard-skin chairs, and since she got married, she was always buying seductive fantasy lingerie she tried on in those dressing rooms.

Esin put on her panties and walked out into the room, wearing nothing else, with her breasts bare, as she'd got used to doing in the locker room of the high-class gym she went to.

"If it embarrasses you, turn away but I'm in a rush to get ready. As for your question, no, thongs don't make me uncomfortable. It's not like I wear them every day. I wear them on nights like this because I have to. If I don't, this flimsy material will show the lines of my panties," she said, pointing to her long dress hanging in the closet.

She was just about to put on the midnight blue dress when she remembered she hadn't put cream on her back. "Damn, I didn't cream up my back. I'm flexible but I can't reach everywhere."

Before she could ask outright, Kübra came to the rescue: "I can put cream on your back if you like," she said.

Esin said nothing and brought the jar from the bathroom, handed it to Kübra and turned her back.

Kübra was speechless before her magnificent body. Esin's shoulders were broad for a woman, her arms slightly muscled and her back well developed. Kübra was standing centimeters away from this well developed back, on display in all its vitality and seductiveness. The natural scent of Esin's moist skin fresh from the shower, mingled with an expensive perfume, spread a head-spinning fragrance through the room.

Kübra could not take her eyes off Esin's neck, her back, her waist but she collected herself and began spreading cream slowly over her body.

Esin suddenly shivered from the cold of the cream.

"Don't put it on so slowly. I'm getting cold. Please spread it all over, so I can warm up ..."

Two or three moments earlier, Kübra could never have guessed she would be having such an electrifying experience. This touch was something she'd never imagined. She was merely spreading cream on a girlfriend's back and it was hardly different from what women did on the beach in their bathing suits. When they put cream on each other, it was quite a normal thing, there was nothing immoral about it. And clearly, Esin found it very ordinary; she did not react in any unusual way. But to touch a naked woman's body in a hotel room aroused very different feelings in Kübra and her cheeks had turned bright red. She could not speak. Her creamy hand was still wandering over Esin's body. She sensed blood rushing to the tips of her fingers. She went numb.

These passing moments seemed ritual-like, and in the end, she felt like kissing Esin's shoulder. If she hadn't held herself back, she would have.

Esin suddenly turned to face Kübra. For a few seconds, their eyes were locked in an indescribable gaze. Then Kübra bowed her head bashfully and looked away. Esin said, "Oh, excuse me, sorry," and covered her breasts with her hands.

She started to put on her dress, pulling it over her head but got stuck, hands up in the air, head inside her dress. "Help!" she cried in English, "Help me, Kübra!" and laughed.

Kübra helped her friend get the low-backed dress on and pulled up the side zipper.

Quickly, Esin put on her stiletto-heeled, open-toed shoes and checked the contents of her evening bag once more. They left the room.

They took the elevator to the ballroom on the ground floor of the hotel where the wedding was being held.

Kübra and Esin had been assigned to different tables. It was only when they got their place numbers from the hostess girl that they realized it, and at this point, they were not about to go find the bride Burcu and ask how the mistake could have been made. They went and took their seats. As they sat down, they politely wished the other guests at their round tables a good evening. Although they'd been raised in very different families and different sorts of neighborhoods, their polite manners were quite similar. In fact, Burcu's seating plan was not far from the mark. Kübra's table was made up entirely of women; there were no men and that would certainly make her more comfortable. There was another veiled young woman at her table. But most of the guests were unveiled women.

Esin shared a table with the couple that had driven them from Istanbul. The seating at her round table was arranged man-woman-man-woman, western style. Conversation began with small talk. While this was going on, Esin looked around her intently. There were only a few familiar faces; this was not a group requiring she go to each table and say hello, as would be the case at a wedding in Istanbul.

The bet she'd made with Kübra for the evening came into her mind. She began chatting with a man at her table in his forties about Ankara. It really was just as Kübra had said: the man was listening to her, grinning from ear to ear, pleased as could be. He wasn't from Ankara and neither was his conversation all that entertaining. But he was very pleased with himself simply because a beautiful and attractive woman in a low-cut dress was talking to him. While she talked, his eyes fixed on her face and slid down her neck to her shoulders and breasts. Esin felt sure the test was complete and cut off the conversation. The man was surprised. She looked over to where Kübra was sitting.

Kübra was sitting a few tables away and stole a glance at Esin now and then too. She was scrutinizing her in every way and taking great pleasure in it. Esin was fascinating and she could not get enough of looking at her. She couldn't put a name to this feeling but it gave her a sense of excitement mixed with humiliation.

Esin wanted Kübra to be wrong and decided to perform another experiment. She got up from her seat. She walked slowly among the tables, swinging her hips, pretending she wanted to say hello to someone she knew, sitting way in the back of the room. It didn't take long before she sensed people at each table, especially the men, turning to look her up and down, openly or covertly. Normally, it would have pleased her. But this evening, the stares of men hit her like arrows in the back. She wanted to return to her seat as soon as possible. Tonight, here at this gathering, she did not like it that she was attracting so much attention.

When Kübra got to her room, she realized it was almost midnight. She took off her clothes and removed her make-up. She did her ablutions and performed the nighttime prayer. She did not want even the slightest shadow to fall over her spirit.

She couldn't sleep. She was lying in bed on her back, staring at the ceiling. How could a young women believer who did her five daily prayers have weird feelings about someone of her own sex? She could not find the source of her feelings for Esin, and as she thought about it, she was ashamed of herself. She felt like what was going through her mind was spreading out through her room and would pass under her door to wander down the hall, descend to the room where Esin lay sleeping and enter her mind. She shivered. She was afraid. After struggling with herself for hours, she fell asleep exhausted, listening to the howling of the wind outside.

# Esin and Kübra
## (Gauze)

"Come over to our house if you like. My husband's at work during the day."

Kübra laughed. "As if I were not. You seem to forget, I go to work every day with my father. But don't worry, I'll arrange for a day to come and teach you *namaz* with pleasure," she said.

"I'll tell you right now, Kübra, it's going to be hard work. If it were just *namaz,* that would be fine but you have to remind me how to do the ablutions too. I swear I'll get the order mixed up."

Kübra felt like she was Esin's big sister, not five years younger than her. They made a date to meet in two days.

As soon as Esin put down the phone, her friend Sevim called.

"Hello ... my curly-haired friend. Are you feeling any better? How are you?"

Sevim's voice sounded full and rich. Clearly, she was feeling good.

"Of course, sweetie, that's all over. It's always painful at first but that passes. I couldn't have cried my eyes out anymore, especially for a guy who wasn't worth it."

"So it seems we'll have to find someone else for you."

"God forbid. I'm going to stay away from the nation of men for a while. It's going to be hard for me to trust anyone. If a man comes near me, I can't help wondering if he's gay."

"What a disaster! There really are no men left," said Esin. "I should give my husband more credit. "I'm glad you called. Want to get together on Thursday? Let's have lunch."

Esin was just about to accept when she remembered she was having Kübra over in two days.

"I can't do it Thursday, a friend is coming over."

Sevim was interested. "Who? Which friend?"

Esin didn't know how to explain. Alp was still the only one who knew of her friendship with Kübra. It wasn't that she was hiding it but she hadn't felt like talking about it. It wasn't a friendship everyone would find easy to understand. The women she knew were all unveiled and modern, even too European. They would think it strange that she went out to dinner with a veiled girl. And that's what happened when she told Sevim that a veiled girl she knew from college was coming over.

"What? What is a girl in a turban going to do at your house? I mean, what will you talk about?"

Esin didn't want to explain further.

"We'll find something. I'm happy about it," she said without letting her displeasure show.

"Wow, Esin, you certainly are an interesting girl."

Two days had passed.

Kübra was at Esin's apartment in Etiler. Esin had opened the door like an excited student anticipating the arrival of a private tutor. They hugged.

She took Kübra's light coat and hung it on the hall coat stand. Kübra began taking off her shoes right there in the hall as she did at home.

"Don't, don't take off your shoes. Make yourself at home. We wear shoes in the house."

"No, I can't wear shoes in a home. Give me some slippers."

Esin led her friend into the salon. Kübra glanced around, busy taking off her head covering. Her silk scarf fell to her shoulders the instant she took out the straight pin under her chin. She took off the black bonnet beneath it by pulling it from the back. Esin was standing at the door to the salon watching her in amazement. She could not believe her eyes. She was seeing Kübra with her head uncovered for the first time. She had not been able to think of her without her turban. She was completely at sea.

Kübra's wavy brown hair fell to her shoulders and she looked at Esin. Seeing her gaping expression, she straightened her blouse and looked at her pants, asking, "Is there something weird about my clothes? What's wrong?"

Esin stammered and came up beside her.

"I was just surprised to see your hair."

Kübra touched her hair, then understood why Esin was confused and smiled.

"Oh, yes, of course, my hair. I'm inside the house now. There's no one here but you. So I can uncover my head."

Esin was still dumbfounded.

"What can I say? I wasn't expecting this. Suddenly it seemed like you were someone else."

Kübra smiled. Esin pointed to the couch and said, "Pardon me, I didn't offer you a seat. Come, sit over here."

Esin was studying her as if she were from outer space, looking at the color of her hair, its shape, and texture.

"Kübra, you are so beautiful. I can't believe you cover up that thick hair of yours. Mine is as stringy as leeks."

Kübra took her scarf from her shoulders and folded it. "That's the way it is with us. Bare-headed at home, covered up outside."

"Who is allowed to see you like this? Your mother, your father, your sisters, and other women, I guess."

"Yes, they can see me like this. Women have to cover up in front of all men except their fathers, husbands, brothers, and uncles."

"So, inside is for insiders, and outside for outsiders. Oh, it sounds like a jingle," Esin said, then made as if to bite her hand and smiled saucily.

Esin got a plate of biscuits and cookies from the kitchen and put it on the large coffee table in the middle of the salon.

"What will you have to drink, my dear Kübra? I'm drinking herbal tea."

Esin was clearly not much of a housewife and Kübra did not want to make things difficult for her. "I'll have the same," she said.

They sat and chatted for half an hour. Then Esin said, "Come on, teacher. Teach me ablutions and prayer, and we'll see," and got up energetically.

They went into the bathroom. "Do you have a head covering of gauze or something like that?" Kübra asked. No, Esin didn't. She had only a jersey knit black scarf with flowers on it and embroidered edges which she used for special occasions like funerals or going to the mosque on holy nights. Kübra went back into the salon. She took out of her purse the two white prayer head-coverings she'd brought with her, just in case.

In the bathroom, she taught Esin how to perform the ablutions before prayer. First, she rolled up her sleeves as far as her elbows. She said, "You declared your intention by saying, 'I have made the intention to perform ablution for God's acceptance'."

While she was showing Esin how to wash her hands and arms up to the elbows three times, she saw the wedding ring on Esin's ring finger and told her to move it up and down so that water could get under it.

Esin performed the ablutions according to her instructions and then tried to make a joke: "It would be better to wash all over than struggle with so many details."

Kübra kept up her big-sister role.

"That's called *gusul* – full ablution but since you can't always take a shower ..." she said and winked.

"So when do we do the *gusul* ablution? I've heard it's done after sex."

Kübra would have blushed but she had to teach the young woman well. Kübra was still a virgin. She'd never had a sexual relationship with a man in her life. Even with her fiancé, she'd gone no further than holding hands. Among the very religious, it was wrong to hold hands before marriage, or even touch a member of the opposite sex.

"Full ablution is performed after sexual relations and the end of the menstrual period," Kübra said, briefly to the point like an encyclopedia and told Esin not to ask more about that subject.

Esin laughed out loud. "Ooo, in that case Alp and I will have to perform the full ablution once a minute." Now that she thought about it, she always did take a shower after sex. But she did it more for cleanliness and hygiene.

"Ok, here's another question for you but don't laugh at me. Does a person who has sex in a dream, or wakes up in the morning and finds the bed wet, have to perform the full ablution?"

"Um-hmm," Kübra nodded, "of course."

Esin was astonished.

"But who can control dreams? And maybe you don't remember when you wake up in the morning, it's usually like that; you remember later."

Kübra did not answer. "Come on," she said, pointing to the salon.

As she'd thought, there was no prayer rug in Esin's house. True, *namaz* could be performed in any clean place; a prayer rug wasn't absolutely necessary. It was possible to do *namaz* on the ground, on straw matting, on wood, on any floor that did not appear to be dirty.

Since street shoes were worn in the salon, they went into one of the back rooms for prayer. Esin didn't find it as hard to learn the *namaz* as she'd thought she would, because once she got started, she began to remember the movements she had learned, watching her mother as a child.

Kübra was right next to Esin and they were both facing the direction of Mecca. Esin followed Kübra and did whatever she did. Of course, she could not recite the prayers from memory. She moved her lips as if she were reciting a prayer, as she'd done as a child. With one difference: this time she wasn't laughing.

After *namaz,* they went back to the salon. Esin kept thanking Kübra. It had been a beautiful experience but she didn't think she could do it all the time. She had merely satisfied her curiosity.

"Look, I want to be completely open and sincere with you, Kübra. This way of life and dressing is not my sort of thing. It doesn't go along with the modern way of life either.

Some religious duties are rarely fulfilled in our country anyway. People just believe in God. It strikes me as peculiar to live according to centuries-old religious forms in a civilized age. But I'm not criticizing you. I'm just trying to understand you. That's all I'm trying to do. You seem different to me, and what you say is interesting."

"You are reluctant to give up your colorful life, that's why you think this way. These are the same excuses all unveiled women make. Whatever, my dear, live and let live. No one should pressurize anyone else."

"I agree with you there, live and let live. At this point in my life, I'm not about to get up early in the morning and pray, I was just curious. I am a Muslim and I should know what the rules are, but I believe I don't have to fulfill them."

"Is this a new religion? The religion of Esin! According to what Esin believes... Esin's rules... If you're a Muslim, my girl, be like a Muslim. Anyway, we weren't going to interfere with one another. All right, I'm going to hold my tongue."

Kübra stayed a while longer and then said her goodbyes. She was so happy that she had pleased her friend and taught her something good. Kübra now doted on Esin. She liked her, she found her beautiful, she appreciated her, and lately, she had begun to think of her a lot. But Esin was in her own world. She was friendly to Kübra too but the happiness she felt came more out of curiosity. Kübra was an interesting new friend who had helped her understand things she hadn't understood before. But now...

# Esin's Days
## (Pursuit)

Mehtap turned the key to her apartment and came in quietly. She locked the door behind her in the same way. Her heart was beating loudly. The back of her neck was sweating with the strain. She put her expensive snakeskin purse in the bottom of the wardrobe, taking out only her cell phone.

She did not turn on the lights. She went into the salon, where almost the entire Bosphorus was visible from the large windows. She headed for the big couch in the salon. She hid in the tiny space between the window and the back of the long leather couch. She found "my husband" in her cell phonebook and pressed the button. "Ahmet, my sweet, I'll be home a bit late. I'm at the hairdresser's. I'm calling so you won't worry if I'm not home."

Her spirit was as cramped as her body in the small space. She kept on sweating, and her dress stuck to her skin. She wanted to cry already at the pitiful state she had come to but she needed to get the proof first. She had to see for herself if the rumors were true or not.

Minutes seemed like hours. Suddenly, she heard the sound of the key in the lock. Mehtap held her breath. Ahmet came in.

He came into the salon and turned on the lights. He lit a cigarette. He put one of his favorite jazz albums on the CD player. He took his cell phone out of his pocket and called a number.

Mehtap was holding her breath, wondering who her husband was calling and what kind of tone he would take. She pressed the record button on her own cell phone, taking care not to make a sound.

"Hello ... My beauty. How are you? My wife's not home. I left work and came here to relax a bit. I called you the first minute I had free. I can't do without hearing your voice anymore. I miss you. My love."

Mehtap could not believe her ears. What she had not wanted to know but now could not avoid, had happened: the *other* woman was now in her life too. Yes, her husband was cheating on her. And he missed his lover, he called her "my love." She was going to lose her mind. No woman ever thinks such a thing will happen to her. Her heart was beating very fast. She wanted to leap out from behind the couch and attack her husband. But she controlled herself and did not move. She checked her cell phone; yes, it was all being recorded.

Ahmet walked toward the couch where his wife Mehtap was hiding. He had a cigarette in one hand and continued to talk with his lover, Irem, on the cell phone he held in the other. He talked about how much he missed her, how he longed to kiss her and sit and talk with her. This passionately romantic phone call went on for twenty minutes.

It was very hard for Mehtap to keep still behind the couch. She was listening to her husband speak words of love to another woman. It took a supreme effort for her not to cry and shout.

When Ahmet was finished on the phone, he headed for the bathroom to take a shower and throw off the fatigue of the day.

He had no idea there was anyone else in the house as he stood under the wide showerhead in the stall in his luxurious bathroom, letting the water fall down on him like rain.

By the time Mehtap heard the sound of the shower, her whole body had fallen asleep, cramped behind the couch and she got up with difficulty. Her legs were trembling. She headed quickly for the front door. She got her purse from the wardrobe. In the corridor outside, she straightened her hair and clothes.

Then she went back into the house using her key as if this were the first time she was entering it that evening.

Right at that moment, Ahmet was walking down the long corridor toward the salon, having got out of the shower and wrapped a towel around his waist. He heard the sound of footsteps. "Mehtap darling, are you home?" he called out. Mehtap answered in a false voice, "Yes darling, it's me."

The pain inside her was snowballing but she did not let on. She erased the jealousy, hurt, resentment and rage on her face and said, "I got out of the hairdresser's early."

How could the man she'd shared her life with, the man who slept next to her every night in bed and fathered her child, cheat on her? Still, she did not confront her husband about it that evening.

Mehtap would get her revenge on her husband. She would gather more evidence and then hire the best lawyer there was, sue for divorce and get a record settlement. He'd see.

For now, she would collect his credit card and cell phone bills, check the presents he'd bought and the toll payment records of his trips across the Bosphorus.

# Kübra's Days (Weeping)

Hikmet Bey left Nermin's house distraught. His head was in a muddle. He did not know what to do. He no longer wanted to hide the way he was living but was not sure if he should do anything about it. Things had gone on a certain way for some time but now, Nermin was saying she wanted her child to have his name.

Hikmet Bey had known very well that this would happen someday but had tried not to think about it and kept avoiding the issue. In two years, the boy would start primary school, and he had to have an identity card. But if Hikmet Bey gave his surname to his son, it would confer an official status on his marriage with Nermin, sanctioned only by an imam; the situation would become known and he would be thrust into an intolerable dilemma.

While these thoughts were eating away at his brain, he decided to talk it over with someone close to him. He couldn't keep it to himself any longer.

His son-in-law, Bilal, who worked with him at the company, loved and respected him. They spent time together. Hikmet Bey didn't have any son he could talk to, and he felt close to his son-in-law. He'd supported his daughter Müberra's decision from the start. She'd married a young man with a good head on his shoulders.

He was going to talk it over with his son-in-law.

First thing at the office the next morning, he called his son-in-law and said he wanted to see him in his office. Bilal was outside the building. As soon as he got back in the afternoon, he went straight to his father-in-law's office.

When Bilal came out, his head was in a whirl. He could not believe what Hikmet Bey had told him. He'd been surprised but received the news calmly. He'd heard of men who had relationships with women other than their wives. It was not rare. The matter of the young son had upset him a great deal. The only advice he could give Hikmet Bey was to first tell his daughter Müberra and then Kübra. It would be better if the smallest daughter did not know about it for now.

That evening, when they left the office, they went to Bilal's house in Florya. Hikmet Bey had called Kübra and told her to come to her big sister's home that evening. A separate company car could take her there, rather than their going together. He was in no state to sit in the car and breathe the same air as his daughter today.

Müberra opened the door. She had just put her son and three-month-old baby down to sleep. They all went into the salon. Bilal had called on the way to say her father was with him. Müberra had put the tea on.

As they were finishing their first glass of tea, making small talk, the doorbell rang. It was Kübra. She came in and sat with the others right away.

Müberra and Kübra were giving each other calm but inquiring looks. Neither of them knew the reason for their father's sudden visit.

Hikmet Bey took a deep breath. He faced his girls and began to speak.

"My darling girls, you know that I have a heavy work load. And I take trips, to Ankara, other cities, and abroad... I feel lonely when I travel a lot. I want to have a woman with me. Your mother can't keep up with me. I need a woman in my life."

After these opening sentences, Müberra and Kübra still didn't know what awaited them but a strange feeling of disquiet had already begun to invade their hearts. Their faces became serious; they were listening to their father intently.

Hikmet Bey went on. "You will not like hearing this. Believe me, it is also very difficult for me to say. I love your mother, she is the mother of my children. And she will be my wife till my life comes to an end."

The girls could not understand the direction his speech had taken. The discomfort they felt was now coupled with fear.

"Your mother is on one side, and the world on the other, understand this. But..." He paused. He had not been able to pick up any momentum, and when he got to the point where he should say what he'd really come to say, he suddenly lost his nerve.

Bilal, Müberra, Kübra ... The three of them sat holding their breath, waiting for Hikmet Bey to spit it out.

And Hikmet Bey let it rip: "There's a woman in my life. You'd hear about it from someone else soon anyway. I wanted you to hear it from me first. We've been together for five years ..."

"What?" Kübra shrieked. Müberra could not speak; she had gone stiff as a board.

Hikmet Bey could not look his daughters in the face but he kept talking. He began to justify himself by talking about other people's lives.

"There are many examples of this around me. I'm not the only one in this situation. Businessmen take a lot of trips and new worlds open up to them. Unfortunately, after a while, our wives at home are no longer enough for us. Believe me, there are many people living like this around me."

Kübra's eyes were stuck on her father's mustache, which trembled as he talked. It was she who broke the silence.

"You were looking for someone to accompany you on your travels, Father? I don't get it."

Hikmet Bey was not about to explain to his own daughters that the real reason was sex and excitement. The excuse of travelling had just come into his mind but his daughter was not easily fooled. He tried to add more realism to the question by adding layers to his excuse: "Since I couldn't be with just any woman on my long trips – I didn't think that suited me – I wanted someone steady. Nermin is polite, she has a good character, she is an intelligent woman…"

Kübra saw that her father was sinking faster the more he struggled. She couldn't take it anymore.

"So her name is Nermin. You've really accepted her into your life, Father. You talk about this with us as if it were something normal. I can't believe it."

She was now upset and couldn't control herself; she'd begun to cry. Müberra couldn't stand it either. She was wiping away the tears rolling down her cheeks.

Hikmet Bey fell silent. He was weeping now. Yes, great big Hikmet Akansan was weeping. Not like his daughters but he couldn't hide his tears.

Bilal brought three glasses of water from the kitchen and passed them around. The girls drank listlessly, while Hikmet Bey did not touch his glass. He took a deep breath and turned toward his daughters.

"Don't weep, girls. Look, I'm telling you about it, and I'm telling you why. There's another problem, listen to me carefully now."

Kübra and Müberra braced themselves.

Hikmet Bey and his son-in-law Bilal exchanged glances. Bilal nodded for him to go on, and gave him an encouraging look full of kindness. Hikmet Bey let the bomb fall: "I have a son with this woman."

Kübra began crying again. Müberra seemed to have stopped breathing; she was like someone punched in the chest. She hurt inside. She was sweating and her palms were soaking wet.

Müberra turned to her father: "So you made a mistake but why did you have a child as well?" She could not believe it. Her father was a man with two grandchildren.

"I don't know, I didn't want it to happen but it did. We had a falling out for a while because I was angry about the child. The boy is now four years old and he does not know who his father is, the poor thing. I have to give him my surname. It is because things have come to this pass that I decided it was best to share this with you. I am afraid to tell your mother."

"If you are afraid, why did you do such a thing, Father?" Kübra railed. "My mother takes good care of you; she waits on you hand and foot. Where did the idea of another woman come from? I'm in shock, I don't know what to do or say!" She got up and began pacing around the room. She was so upset, so grieved, so confused, she did not know what she was doing.

"I did not want to put you through this but that's what happened," Hikmet Bey said regretfully.

"I am not getting divorced!"

Despite her tears, Nadide Hanım's voice was very firm.

She had suffered a horrific disappointment. "I will not let your father into this house. Don't you dare tell me to open the door!"

Their mother had cried for hours after she found out but then a resolute mood took the place of her sorrow and shock. Her mood had changed swiftly from one state to another. After her shock, disbelief, rage, and despair she had wept uncontrollably, become timid and feeble, then calm and silent, then began to think logically and become decisive … A boulder had settled on her chest and she could not move it. She was in terrible pain. But the pain that doesn't hurt you makes you stronger …

She was eating her heart out. "If I live inside the home, unaware of the world, of course, my husband, who knows everything about the world, will have experiences like this," she told herself. Hikmet Bey was better off than before. He got along very well with his other wife, who waited for him to come to her and never interfered with what he did.

The girls were never to see their father's illegitimate son. They did not want to see the boy. They were angry with their father and hadn't spoken to him for days.

Kübra didn't go to work; she was protesting against everything. She did not feel at all like going to work with her father, not at all. And since she was the boss's daughter, no one at the company was about to say anything about her not turning up for work.

The girls did not leave the house. They were trying to be a support to their mother. Müberra took her son and baby girl and went to stay with her mother. She could leave Bilal alone for a few days in such a family emergency. But something else awful happened. Müberra's milk stopped flowing. One day, shortly after she'd learned of her father's situation, her baby cried after sucking on her breast. Clearly, there was little milk and the baby could not get enough. Müberra was still recovering from the birth, and the tension in the family affected her psychologically so that her milk dried up completely.

The smallest daughter, Büşra, got suspicious when fits of crying took hold of the house like a new fashion, and eventually found out the truth. An expression of rage came over her face when she heard about her father's secret little family, and she'd sulked for hours. She pouted like a child whose toy has been taken away, folded her arms across her chest and sat in a chair, swinging her feet for hours.

The mother, her three daughters and two grandchildren were now living in the two-storey villa. In time, friends of the family heard about the gloomy situation and began laying siege to the house. Maternal and paternal aunts, cousins, Müberra's mother-in-law ... Everyone had something to say. Everyone gave Nadide Hanım the best advice they could, while she suffered unbearable heartbreak. The whole family wanted them to make up. Nadide Hanım did not intend to get a divorce anyway but she couldn't figure out exactly what to do either.

One evening, Hikmet Bey came to the house. Their maid, Auntie Kadriye, opened the door without thinking and he came inside. Nadide was in the sitting room, stretched out on the couch she had not been able to get herself to throw out and had brought from the old house. She sat up when he came in. For a while, they said nothing.

Then, Hikmet Bey broached the subject ...

"Forgive me, Nadide. I did not want to hurt you. That's why I hid it for years and lied. Please say you have forgiven me."

Although Nadide Hanım's eyes were red from crying, she turned coolly to Hikmet Bey as he tried to talk himself out of his guilt, and put an end to his floundering between resistance and submission: "You know, it's no good to come here and ask forgiveness from me, God's creature, for doing something God has forbidden. You have been defeated by your own soul. You should first of all repent to God. Beg God to forgive you," she said, striking Hikmet Bey where he was most vulnerable: his faith.

# Esin's Days (Counterattack)

Ahmet was unable to take secret vacations abroad these days because he had too much work and he missed his lover. He had met Irem at a lovely hotel in Istanbul. Mehtap called the office and learning he was not there, became suspicious. Her feminine intuition sent her straight to her cell phone. At that moment, Ahmet was secretly with Irem, the beans were in the oven and they were going from position to position in bed. His cell phone was lying on the bedside table and when it rang, their bodies separated.

It was his wife. Ahmet hesitated before picking it up. He was thinking of what he could say to Mehtap to put her off.

"Mehtap?"

"Where are you? Don't you dare say you're at the office; I already called there."

Ahmet sat up. "I'm talking business with some friends from Ankara, my love, I'm out of the office."

Mehtap didn't fall for it. For an instant, she pictured her husband naked in bed making love to that woman called Irem she didn't know, in a room in one of those five-star luxury hotels with wall-to-wall carpeting. And immediately, she said: "Stamp your feet on the floor, Ahmet."

Ahmet was taken aback. Irem was cowering in a corner of the bed, holding her breath.

"Don't be ridiculous, Mehtap. I'm in a meeting."

Mehtap was determined. "Stamp your feet on the floor, I said. Let's see what kind of meeting you're in."

Ahmet understood what Mehtap was getting at. If he stamped his bare feet on the carpet, it wouldn't make any sound. There was nothing to do but dodge. "Mehtap, my sweet, I'm hanging up. The other guys have arrived now. I kiss you, my darling," he said and hung up. His face was as white as a sheet.

At the other end of the phone, Mehtap's face was even whiter, she was as white as whitewash. She had long ago learned that in situations like this, a good liar doesn't tell an outright lie, but rather one very close to the truth.

For a while, she wept. Then she pulled herself together and began to get ready for the detective work she had to do.

Mehtap had covered her eyes swollen from crying and eyebrows eternally arched from Botox injections with a pair of sunglasses which were not too dark.

She was in no state to drive. She had their chauffeur, Mustafa Bey, drive her to the shopping mall where the shop they bought almost all their jewelry was located.

She found herself in front of the luxury jewelry shop. She usually came here in a happy mood, excited by the prospect of buying a new piece of expensive jewelry but this time, she was forced into a timid mood. She pressed the tiny buzzer to the side of the shop entrance. One of the shop clerks inside saw her through the glass and let her in right away.

She answered the greeting, "Welcome, Mehtap Hanım," with a curt "Thank you."

She'd begun to feel like a detective and it made her uncomfortable. It surprised the clerks a bit that she did not take off her sunglasses but they were used to famous customers who did not want to be recognized.

Ahmet always bought gifts from this shop for his wife Mehtap and his girlfriends. Mehtap Hanım went up to the shop clerk who always waited on her and asked, "What have we bought from you? May I have a look at our records?"

The clerk was shrewd and experienced enough to know what this question meant coming from a married woman and without letting on, counter-attacked with another question: "What pieces do you have, Mehtap Hanım?"

The shop clerk knew what Ahmet Bey was like. A playboy who bought gifts to pamper his lovers. He could not give his wife that information.

Mehtap had sensed the man would not be helpful. He only mentioned a few pieces she had. Poor Mehtap realized she would learn nothing from a luxury sector based on secrecy.

She returned empty-handed from the expedition but she had enough evidence already. The conversation she'd recorded of her husband talking with his lover in their home, his frequent calls and text messages to the same number… It turned out to belong to a woman named Irem.

Now, the most important thing was to find a divorce lawyer. She called Ergin's wife, Seçil, right away. She asked her to keep quiet about it for now, and explained everything. Seçil said she could recommend two lawyers on the bar. Mehtap should meet with them. And when the court case ended the way she wanted it to, she would be a free and wealthy woman. Nothing else could satisfy her. She did not want to remain married to Ahmet. However much her social status might suffer, with so much evidence in hand, she could not squander it.

And she did settle on a good divorce lawyer. She received heavy damages from her husband, monthly alimony, a summer home, and a car. She did not want to work at a job anymore. For now, she would swallow her sorrow and make the most of her money. Those around her were much surprised to see a woman like Mehtap, who appeared to be all about wearing nice clothes and going to nice places with her husband and son, make such a daring move. Mehtap turned out to have teeth. She was not a career woman, she did not work. Her social status could have dropped instantly when she divorced. But she paid no mind and got rid of her rich husband, carrying off the loot.

# Esin and Kübra
## (Breeze)

Esin's blonde hair was flying in the gently blowing breeze. She could feel the burning rays of the sun on her eyes despite the dark glasses she was wearing. She had on Bermuda shorts and a sleeveless T-shirt but the heat still would not let her alone. If she weren't by the Bosphorus, breathing in the cool Bosphorus air, the heat really would be unbearable. Kübra had her head covered as usual and was dressed so that only her hands and feet were showing. She had on blue jeans and a loose, long-sleeved tunic made of a thin material.

The boat trip was good for both Esin and Kübra. They kept giggling like children. Despite her childish pleasure, Esin was distressed that Kübra should be all covered up in such hot weather. She touched the sleeve of Kübra's tunic as if she were curious about the material and said sympathetically, "The weather is so hot. Don't you find it unbearable in that outfit? How can you put up with it?"

The expression on Kübra's face did not change. She looked at her tunic and then at Esin.

The material of the tunic is very thin but you get used to all kinds of veiled outfits anyway. When you believe, you don't think critically about it and you don't wish it were otherwise."

"Um-hmm," Esin responded. But she could not understand it. Kübra was young and her veiled dress relatively modern but what about the others? They wore layers and layers of clothing; they looked like piles of fabric. And on top of it all, always a long raincoat... Esin thought how women and girls must perspire, covered up under all those layers of clothing, especially in hot weather, and suddenly, she caught the smell of sweat. But no, that bad smell could not be coming from Kübra. Kübra always smelled sweet. Yet, she couldn't stop herself and asked Kübra, ashamed as she did so: "Kübra dear, you don't have any problem but wouldn't any normal person wearing so many layers of clothing sweat? Sometimes I see a couple on the street; the man is free, wearing a very thin summer shirt but the woman next to him is swathed in veils. It seems like the man is walking with a woman soaked in sweat. Don't so many clothes make a person sweat? Am I wrong?"

Kübra had gotten used to these sorts of questions from Esin. She knew her head was crowded with question marks. But like other people her age and the people around her, Esin did not completely understand Islam. Most had not even read the Gracious Koran.

Kübra didn't want to go into the subject of religious requirements again but she had to answer: "If we can, we perform ablutions five times a day for the five prayers. So, even if you sweat all day, you wash yourself clean."

"Darling, I take a shower every morning too but I don't know ... in this heat ... You have it rough, I swear," Esin said. However much Kübra said she dressed that way in order to be a good Muslim, it cut Esin to the quick that she had no choice. She couldn't help but smile.

Kübra felt the need to explain the matter of dress a bit further: "Basically you're right. We *do* have it rough when it comes to dress. You can put on whatever you want when you go out. We have one outfit for home and another for outside. A normal person can put together an outfit with two pieces. We have to take the trouble to put at least seven pieces together and on top of one another. Home, the street, scarves ..."

Esin laughed. "So you agree that you are abnormal; look, you said so yourself."

Kübra gave her a look like, "Enough!" but she smiled too.

"All right, I agree, veiling in hot weather is sometimes suffocating. The minute you cover your head, your outfit becomes something else entirely. You have to mostly wear skirts, for example, not pants. But you all wear miniskirts too. All right, I can't say it makes me very uncomfortable but it does seem weird to me."

Esin arched her brows.

"You too, Kübra? Veiled women always attack unveiled women on that score. As if all unveiled women wore miniskirts. Or you ridicule rich and famous people with the 'society type' label. You have clichés like that in your minds too."

"But some *do* wear them... Some women even go out on the street in outfits made of so little material, it's like they're wearing nothing at all."

Esin waved her away, saying, "Oh come on, Kübra. Let everyone wear what they like. I won't ask you about anything anymore, all right."

To head for the ferry, token in hand and cross the Bosphorus was one of the easiest ways to enjoy Istanbul. Esin, in particular, felt like doing something different today; she wanted to breathe different air. Kübra had traveled over from the Anatolian side and when they met up in Etiler, Esin was glad to see her friend was in the same mood. They jumped into a taxi and went to Beşiktaş, where they got a ferry to Üsküdar.

Right where they got off on the other shore, there was a run-down tea garden. The uneven legs of the wobbly wooden tables and chairs like spindle-legged girls, all matched with the magnificent view of the Bosphorus lined with seaside mansions. The whirling waters of the Bosphorus played host to both city ferries and gigantic tankers. The simplicity and down-at-the-heel air of the place delighted both of them. They sat and drank their well-steeped tea while gazing at the far shore.

"Isn't it beautiful?" said Kubra. "Can you imagine such a miraculous creation?"

Esin answered Kübra without taking her eyes off the view: "And how... It's enchanting... I feel like I'm in a wonderful fairy tale."

Kübra took a sip of her tea. Esin could not take her eyes off the dreamy deep blue playing with the rays of the sun like a lover.

Kübra looked in the same direction.

"How easy it is for a person to feel happy, actually. Everything depends on thanking God for His creations and realizing the grace they bestow," she said.

For a moment, Esin thought about what she had said. She took her eyes away from the blue waters and turned to look straight into Kübra's face.

"Do your kind know the value of earthly blessings?"

Kübra was surprised, and shook her head with a pained expression as if she hadn't understood.

Esin felt she'd found an opening and smiled, pleased with herself. When she was with Kübra, she was always raining down questions on her and looking for cracks in the Islamic life.

"But I thought this world had no importance for you; the only really important thing is the other world, the afterlife, I mean, that's why I said that. You abstain from worldly pleasures as far as I know. You've come to this world only to be tested, in order to go to Paradise in the afterlife ..."

Kübra knew where Esin was trying to go and was not ruffled at all. She smiled. However much Esin might try to catch her unprepared, she had an answer for everything.

"The greatest goal for the believer is to earn the acceptance of God and experience the delight of being His creature. Worldly pleasures are just benefits which come from God. God bestows them if He wishes, and holds them back if He wishes. It is not right for a person to be unhappy over them, to be stressed about them. Do you know what it means to have a pure heart? A person with a pure heart is eager to know God; he does not run after worldly adventures and petty pleasures. Stop making fun of me and let me give you a concrete example. As it says in the An'am chapter of the Koran, the life of this world is but play and a diversion. Do not forget that one day each person will give an account to God."

Esin was taken aback, put off by this pedantic explanation but at the same time, awed that Kübra could quote from the Gracious Koran on every issue like a walking encyclopedia.

But she still didn't find her answer logical and restated her own thesis, adding one question after another: "Does trying to earn God's acceptance mean ignoring the good things of this world? And didn't God create the world?"

Kübra was about to answer when Esin charged on, unable to stop: "We all earn money, we all buy nice homes and cars. Shouldn't we care about the place where we live? Don't you decorate your home? Don't you buy expensive furniture? Accept it or not, your kind are becoming worldly."

Kübra answered patiently in an even tone: "Of course, it is not a blameworthy thing for a person to take care of their home. But it is wrong for a person's entire world to be limited by these four walls and her ideals, habits and problems to be confined by these four walls. If you think of people only in terms of their houses and cars, they live in a tiny little material world, having tiny little goals, aims, and calculations."

Esin was about to object but Kübra grabbed her hand and stopped her.

"You're starting again, Esin. We are going to look at the beautiful view here and drink a couple of glasses of tea and you're talking your head off, tearing things apart. A little peace and quiet, please," she said, smiling. As always, Esin played the excited young girl and Kübra the mature woman.

Esin leaned against the back of her chair like an obedient child. Although she was always questioning Kübra half-jokingly, she respected her.

Kübra pointed to the far shore.

"Look, Esin, you live over there in Europe. I live on this side in Asia. We are that near to one another and that far apart."

Esin thought near and far were dangerous concepts. The two opposing concepts were generally used to describe an almost non-existent relationship between two things, two different cultures or two lovers. We seem to be close but we are far apart… Or on the contrary, we appear to be distant but we are close…Yes, two different continents, yet so near. You could pass over from one continent to another by crossing the bridge or taking a ferry. So what exactly was Kübra trying to say?

On the boat on the way back, they sat downstairs with their feet propped up on the iron bars and gazed at the sea. Esin had once again understood today that you could get pleasure out of life without spending a lot of money.

A Jewish businessman she much respected used to say, "Money has two sides. First, it is a means of exchange. With money you can buy food, clothing, a home, and even health. Second, it allows you to conquer your fear of the future. But there are things beyond money, above money, things money can't buy: pleasure and joy. You can take pleasure in paintings at free exhibitions. Concerts are not expensive either. Going to the theater is the price of a hamburger. Love and affection are anyway free. If you can enjoy the setting of the sun, the whispering of the sea, or playing a game of chess, it costs nothing to checkmate a king with a rook. How much does it cost to make the sun go down? What is the price of the sound of the sea? These pleasures and joys are as important as the rainy day money you save for your old age and maybe more so."

He was so right. She was sorry Kübra did not think the same as she did on that score. But she couldn't be completely sure. At this moment, Kübra was with her, enjoying the pleasure of the Bosphorus, the sea and the fresh air of the trip for the price of a ferry token. They seemed to be very distant from one another in how they thought but in the end, it all came out the same gate.

When they got to the Beşiktaş pier, the inner child in both of them was feeling good. The weather was very fine and they felt like going someplace else. As if reading Esin's mind, Kübra said, "Let me propose something this time. Come on, let's go to Sultanahmet."

Esin clapped her hands in delight.

"Super! I've always loved old Istanbul. Come on..."

They got into one of the yellow taxis waiting by the pier.

They moved forward, following the shore to Sultanahmet. It was hot and the taxi did not have air-conditioning. There was a sports channel on the radio and the driver was listening to the results of the pick six. Now and then he looked into the rearview mirror to sneak a peek at the two young women sitting in the back seat. The windows were open all the way but the traffic jam in Karaköy prevented them from picking up speed and getting a breeze. Esin couldn't keep herself from saying: "If only we'd taken my car. Why didn't I think of it? We could listen to my CD player, and we'd be cool and clean with air-conditioning."

Kübra would also have preferred to go in a comfortable car but she felt the need to say something to comfort Esin: "But then, we'd have the problem of parking. Look, we got to Beşiktaş and from there to Sultanahmet... it's easier with a taxi; don't worry about it."

She'd almost made it her job to comfort Esin.

At that point, Esin's cell phone rang. It was Alp.

"I'm with a friend, my love, on the way to Sultanahmet in a taxi. We're going to stroll around, just us girls."

"Who?" Alp asked, in a normal tone of voice. "Which friend?"

"Kübra."

Did Esin have a friend named Kübra? Suddenly, he remembered. "Ah, are you out with that turban girl, my love? May it go easy for you," he said and hung up. The name "Kübra" was so widespread in the conservative sector that it was enough to make Alp realize right away that she was Esin's mysterious turbaned girlfriend.

Finally, they got to Sultanahmet Square. As Esin held the money out to the driver, he tried to touch her hand. His beard was filthy, and he had an insinuating smile on his face. Esin ignored him but the way she pulled back her hand made it clear that she was annoyed. When they got out, Esin was glad to get free of the man's harassment which Kübra hadn't noticed, and Kübra was glad to be free of the oppressive air in the taxi.

They were like clueless tourists at first and couldn't decide which way to go. Then Kübra took Esin's arm and headed toward Sultanahmet Mosque. They walked that way through the park which was filled with tourists in shorts carrying maps, middle-aged women sitting on the benches munching on sunflower seeds they extracted from their shells, and mothers calling to their children racing to and fro.

They came up to Sultanahmet Mosque, one of the most famous monuments of the Islamic world, known to tourists as the "Blue Mosque." The site of the peerless mosque with six minarets is ringed by other earlier important works of Istanbul architecture. They walked through the broad outer courtyard into the inner courtyard. From the gate where you entered, you could see the symbolic ablution fountain at the center and the domes rising one upon another over the galleries encircling the courtyard. As Esin looked at the courtyard, Kübra was studying the rich, colorful designs on the tiles and stained glass which completed the exterior.

Kübra poked Esin and showed her the walls of the balconies which circled three sides of the mosque interior.

"Look, we're going to use similar Iznik tiles for the bathrooms at our new construction project," she said.

Esin began to look more carefully at the designs. They really were spellbinding. They left without going into the mosque. Esin was beginning to feel like a tourist who'd come to see Istanbul.

Esin very much liked Kübra's suggestion that they go to the Covered Bazaar but she was hungry. Suddenly, she thought of the famous Sultanahmet Meatballs, where she used to go with her family when she was little. She took Kübra by the arm and said, "You're hungry too, aren't you? Come, I'm going to take you someplace really terrific."

The more Esin and Kübra spent time together, the more they got used to each other and the closer they became. After a few times together, they had gotten over their shyness and were beginning to behave like close friends.

Esin chose the classic fare of meatballs, white beans, and raw onions with parsley, and semolina halva. She wanted a yogurt drink first but gave up on that because she thought it would make her drowsy. They were going to the Covered Bazaar afterwards.

After they'd filled their bellies, they walked from the tram stop through Nuruosmaniye and entered the bazaar at Çemberlitaş.

Everything was shiny and full of life. The first street they came to was one of the places the ladies liked most – a street of jewelry shops lined with shop windows displaying gold and gems.

They looked at a few windows and continued on to the rug sellers, from there past leather, antique, and copper sellers until they got to the area where gifts were sold. They went on enjoying their walk through the labyrinthine bazaar.

They took one of the side streets to the innermost part of the bazaar where the most valuable goods were kept. They saw stools outside and sat down at one of the coffeehouse's tiny tables. Once they sat down, they realized how tired they were. It had a peaceful atmosphere. Kübra asked for Turkish coffee. Esin ordered apple tea.

While Kübra was drinking her sugary Turkish coffee, she thought of that awful day when Samet's family came to ask for her hand. She felt the need to share this with Esin, even if just a little. Without showing how bad she felt, she smiled and said, "I made coffee for them when they came to ask for my hand. Whenever I see coffee, I think of that day. Ugh, what a shame ..."

Esin was surprised. "Why a shame? It's a good thing you found someone you might want to marry. There are no decent fellows left these days, my sweet. Know his value."

When she saw Kübra staring unhappily into the distance, she became a bit more serious.

"You don't love your fiancé? Is there a problem?"

"It's as if I don't have the right in my family to wonder if I love him or not. I'd have wanted to be in love when I got married but unfortunately, I have no strong feelings for Samet."

"Is there someone else?"

"No, it's not like that. No man interests me. It seems I'll leave this world without ever getting married."

Esin's eyes were roving over her surroundings while she listened to Kübra. "Coffeehouse of the East" was written over the entrance but to the side of the door was a sign advertising a "western" coffee company. She pointed out the sign to Kübra and making a gesture like counting money, said, "Money talks." Kübra paid for the coffee and tea this time. They left the bazaar by a different gate and hailed two separate taxis. They kissed and said goodbye. Kübra smiled and said, "Spouses to their homes, villagers to their villages."

# Esin and Kübra
## (Changing Places)

Esin looked at her face for a long time in the mirror, at the shape of her hair, its color, its length ... She was looking at herself like a child afraid of what was about to happen. Her pupils were dilated. Pupils contract in negative states of mind but Esin was neither happy nor distressed, just excited.

She shivered when Kübra suddenly appeared like a shadow at her side. At that moment, for some reason, she perceived Kübra not as Kübra but as a shadow. The shadow had touched her shoulder as if to say: "Don't be afraid!"

Esin threw her friend a look, meaning: "What are we doing?"

"Do you want me to help you? Or do you want to be alone?" Kübra asked in a soothingly delicate tone.

"Let me try by myself, I'll call you in a minute, all right?"

Kübra headed for the salon. But she'd wanted to stay, to be with Esin in front of the mirror, to be seen together, and caress her cheek.

She glanced into the bedroom as she passed by. It looked like a real love nest, mostly red and covered with mirrors. A small leopard-skin rug on the floor ... red scones at each head of the bed ... So that was where Esin played with her husband. A strange feeling of jealously ran through her. Who, what was she jealous of ... she herself didn't know.

Alone again before the mirror, Esin was telling herself she was only doing this for fun. But it was not that simple. Even if it was only symbolic, the turban she was about to put on was going to change her psychological state. It was just a piece of cloth but this piece of cloth displayed a person's religion, their political position like a badge, while it concealed other characteristics.

She looked at the silk scarf in her hand. She was in no hurry to put it on. She combed her hair back as Kübra had just told her to do and put on the black jersey bonnet so that it did not cover her ears. Even like this, without the scarf, she had suddenly taken a big step toward becoming someone else. Not even one strand of her hair was showing. Her face was completely bare, like a gourd. It seemed weird to be merely a face without your hair showing. She could not take her eyes off her image in the mirror.

She looked at herself from different angles, thinking it was a good thing she had a beautiful face. She was sure that if she hadn't, she would look very ugly once her hair was covered.

She took the scarf and folded it diagonally in two. She slowly tried to place it on top of the bonnet but it would not sit straight. It slipped to the side, or was crooked on one side; she could not get it even. She tried and tried, then got up from her make-up table and went to find Kübra.

Kübra was sitting in an armchair, going through the magazines lined up under the coffee table. Neither she nor Esin could keep from laughing when Esin appeared, wearing just the black bonnet.

"Getting this thing on is hard, girl. I'm pissed off. Maybe music will help. I'll put it on loud so I can hear it in the back. If not, I'll get so annoyed, I'll never be able to do it."

She put on a CD by a Turkish pop star from the section next to Alp's collection of U2s, the Rolling Stones and Bon Jovis. The classic and jazz music they both liked was in a different section. The night before they had watched a film at home and the DVDs were spread out on the floor. A half-full dish of nuts and next to it a bowl full of plum pits were still sitting on the coffee table. The place was a mess but Esin hadn't had the time or inclination to do anything about it.

Back in the bedroom, she folded the scarf again and tried to get it on her head straight the way she wanted it. The Turkish song was playing in the background. She thought about the concepts of sin and redemption in the words of the song; her head was all mixed up. She had no good answer for why she had wanted to try wearing a turban. What was the feeling she wanted to know and taste?

In the end, she got the scarf on and secured it with a straight pin under her chin. She didn't put acetate inside the scarf and frame her face like Kübra did. No need to go so far; she was going to try it once, then take it off.

When she walked into the salon as a veiled young woman, Kübra looked at her scarf with admiration and quietly applauded.

"Congratulations! You did a good job of putting it on."

She found one thing lacking when she took a closer look. She got a pin out of her handbag and secured Esin's scarf to her bonnet.

Esin turned up the sound on the music set and began to dance. She danced to the song as if she hadn't a care in the world.

Then she suddenly thought of something and turned off the music.

"It's enough if I only wear a long tunic, isn't it? I can't wear a raincoat in this heat."

"Wear whatever you like. It just has to be discreet and cover you as it should."

Over a singlet, Esin put on a deep purple, long-sleeved tunic with tiny stones around the collar. It was made of a delicate material and came down to her knees. Underneath, she wore black woven pants and plain black shoes.

"Ah, what handbag should I take with me?"

"What do you mean, what handbag? Take whatever handbag you have. Don't worry, there are no veiling rules for handbags!"

She took her black leather Louis Vuitton in the shape of a sack. She threw her wallet, her cell phone, lip-gloss and house, and car keys into the bag.

Where had curiosity led her! Soon, she would be out on the street in veiled dress, walking around like a veiled woman.

There were two things she wanted to do today. Firstly she wanted to walk around in luxury spaces like Nişantaşı or Kanyon, frequented by unveiled modern women and secondly, to walk around a conservative district like Fatih.

Esin felt quite strange as she got into the car in this outfit. She sat in the driver's seat and as she adjusted the rear-view mirror, her eye was caught by the line of her scarf on the side of her head. The turban wasn't just something you wore, you had to steer the car in it too.

They pulled out into the traffic. Esin kept looking right and left instead of straight ahead at the road. Kübra noticed her anxious state of mind and warned her: "Esin dear, you keep looking around. Be careful, let's not have an accident."

They got to Nişantaşı, spent ten minutes looking for a parking space and finally found an empty one. Kübra got out of the car but Esin just couldn't bring herself to. She felt like all Nişantaşı would recognize her the minute she stepped out.

There was a cafe directly across from where they parked. Esin felt like all the customers were looking at her.

They walked for a while, Esin trying to appear calm. She felt herself blushing. She was already uncomfortably hot. What would people say if they recognized her? She didn't want anyone to recognize her that day; she just wanted to experience what it felt like to be a veiled woman on the street.

They walked into Abdi İpekçi Boulevard where she always went when she came to Nişantaşı, passing by the shops and cafes. No one was paying them any attention at the moment. She'd thought everyone would turn to look at them but no one did. She even felt that she was being ignored.

A woman at one of the tables outside a luxury cafe turned to a friend sitting next to her and pointed to Esin and Kübra, giving them an ugly look. Esin had now satisfied her curiosity about how turbaned women felt outside "their own zone." Only a few people stared at them.

"Kübra dear, I saw that woman sitting there give us an ugly look. But if I went bareheaded to a place where women were veiled, I'd get stared at there too. These ugly looks are mutual. We shouldn't accuse just one side. The *other* is excluded wherever she doesn't fit in. Of course, I think everyone should dress as they like on the street, go wherever they like but you know what the problem is? The turban now appears in public spaces … that's what doesn't work. That's what is creating tension."

A teenage boy with his head shaved, wearing an earring and leather pants passed them by. Kübra smiled and turned to Esin: "You don't like that either, do you? So why do you care what other people wear?"

"I have to have an opinion. And I'm not talking about what people wear on the street, or about women this turban I'm wearing now is making me so hot. It's when they stick it in our faces as a political symbol that I lose it. I can't put up with that."

"It's as if you think I invented the rules of veiling. Those in power do something and Esin Hanım thinks the turban is my fault."

Esin studied the cool-looking young people walking down the other side of the street. They all had on branded coats, shoes, and sunglasses. The teenage boys with their slicked-down hair, the girls with blow-dried coifs – all wore clothes of the same style, had the same gestures and the same expressions on their faces. Arrogance seemed to drip off them like rain. But they were young…

Esin reminded Kübra of what she'd said about "youth raised without spirituality." But it wasn't only the spirituality Kübra meant that was lacking. Esin added, "You know, the trend for young people to be apolitical has recently reversed quite dramatically. I mean, who would have thought that there would be tens of thousands rioting in the streets for freedom of speech and equal rights. Ten years ago, this would have been inconceivable!"

They walked the streets of Nişantaşı for a while longer until they came back to where they'd parked and got into the car to go to Fatih.

Now they were on the streets of Fatih.

Esin's experiment in wearing the turban was becoming a tour of old Istanbul as well. The two veiled women blended into the conservative crowd and walked along without being noticed. Of course, Fatih was different from Nişantaşı and Etiler; here no one glanced at veiled women. But if an unveiled, casually dressed female came here, everyone would stare at her.

Lately, Esin had begun to engage in selective perception. She counted the number of veiled women on the street and studied them from head to toe at every opportunity. Most of them had a round protuberance at the back of their turbans. Their necks and half of their foreheads were covered. A full-length coat was worn, with padded shoulders, and some were made of denim. Some of the younger women wore a loose dress over a tight undergarment with long arms and a turtleneck. That was the general look. There was a different style which Esin couldn't figure out. The hair was completely covered by a turban as usual but the torso accentuated by a tight jacket, tight pants, and loud accessories... Some had too much make-up on. Esin couldn't understand how loud, tasteless dress went with veiling. It was not that she thought tight clothes or loud colors were incompatible with a religious way of thinking but there had always been this kind of contradiction in the way people like Esin regarded veiled women. Everyone had their own idea of Islam. There was no single point of view or rule.

But still, not all women on the streets of Fatih were veiled; it was not as Esin expected. Wasn't this one of the ancient places where three religions had abided side by side? Once upon a time, Romans, Jews, and Turks had lived here together.

They passed by an Imam and Preacher Lycée, and browsed shops in Çarşamba selling light overcoats, shalvar pants and raincoats used in veiled dress.

Veiled dress shops projecting an Islamic way of life were lined up side by side with bridal gown stores. Esin remembered how a foreigner friend of hers had said some parts of Fatih were like a miniature Tehran. In Iran, jet-black chadors covering women from head to foot, formed a contrast with scarves worn casually without bonnets which did not cover the hair completely.

Modern types never came to this part of town and had a Fatih-phobia. It was described as a frightening place of alien traditions where Hizbullah kept death houses. But as Esin walked the streets, she saw how religion fit with daily life. It was not terrifying at all, this place where some people feared to set foot. As long as this way of life stayed here, of course! These people had formed their own Islamic ghetto, with everyone dressed the same: men with long beards and clothes from the time of the Prophet Muhammed.

On the other hand, there was no lack of lingerie stores either.

"I've heard the turbaned set wear sexier lingerie than we do; is that true?"

"It might be. Who cares what women wear underneath their clothes… My sister bought herself a pair of red tanga panties the other day, for example. Married women can very well buy sexy lingerie, from lacy to satin."

"You're one thing on the inside, another on the outside. You're like pomegranates. One thing at market and completely different at home!"

They walked past churches and mosques; one historical treasure after another. The most important monuments in the area – İskenderpaşa Mosque and Hırka-i Şerif Mosque, were quite close together. They walked past them also. Kübra was calm but did not know at the time that she would soon be coming often to the magnificent İskenderpaşa Mosque.

In the square, they passed by the coffeehouses crowded with men and went to fill their bellies at Old School, "the Lucca of Fatih."

Later, they went to a tiny cafe with only three tables to have Turkish coffee. It was quiet inside. There was no one there but a man sitting alone reading a newspaper and the owner, a woman, waiting on the tables. While Esin was sipping her coffee, she asked the woman if she would read her fortune in the coffee grounds. Esin seemed to have put her finger on a sore spot; the woman began to relate her sad tale: There was a young woman from the neighborhood who was very good at reading fortunes. She'd also worked cafes in Beyoğlu. The woman wanted her to work here now but her neighbors had found the girl's dress too modern and created problems.

They drank their coffee and left. Suddenly, Kübra thought: "It's not where you go, it's who you go with." Walking down the side streets, Esin, under the influence of her veiled outfit, had taken on a lady-like style. After spending a day under layers of clothing, the unrestrained display of the female body would have seemed offensive to her. Could clothes change a person's psychological state so much?

The scarf was just a piece of cloth but what great debates it caused in Turkey and all over the world!

# Kübra and Esin
## (Fire)

"No, girl; enough," Kubra's mother told her. "Don't stay mad at your father. Don't neglect your work. If you do not take charge of your father's business and assets, someone else will move in. I can swallow my sorrow. You should hold on to life, my dear."

Kübra embraced her mother. Nadide Hanım let her tears fall drop by drop within her; she did not let anyone know. Even if she were torn up inside, her heart weeping blood in indescribable pain, she was steady as a rock. Kübra's eyes welled up. Her mother was right. She should not be distancing herself from her father and her work. She would go with him to the ceremony in Kars. It was to be the opening of an international railroad and three heads of state would be there.

She went up to her room and phoned Esin.

"Hello, Esin. I'm feeling bad and I wanted to talk to you. I have been angry with my father for some time – not only me, my whole family. And you know, I've been neglecting work. But my mother says I should stand by my father. Do you think so? When I'm so angry at him ..."

Esin did not much like getting involved in other people's family problems, even as a sympathetic ear. But Kübra's voice was heart wrenching. And she liked it that Kübra had sought her help in such a private matter.

Kübra told her a bit more and when she asked, "Do you think I should go to Kars with my father?" Esin stood up from her chair.

"Kübra! I'm hosting that ceremony. What a nice coincidence; think of it. Of course, do come, it will be great; we'll explore Kars together. I'll be bored with all those men anyway. We can hang out."

Kübra was very pleased to hear this. It was decided. They were going to Kars.

They took the direct flight to the city at the easternmost end of the country. Esin left for the hotel with the organization team and Kübra with her father.

Esin had chosen to stay at a newly opened boutique hotel, and Kübra and her father were staying there as well. Because it was small and had limited space, the others were staying elsewhere.

They drove down broad avenues and winding streets till they arrived at the fine stone landing at the hotel entrance. It was an old Russian mansion and had a unique décor with modern lines and eastern motifs.

In the lobby, Kübra noticed an old-fashioned tile stove set into the wall, of the type called *gömme peç*. Esin was more interested in the clean lines of the space. Soon, they went up to their rooms.

Each room was named after a region of Kars province: Sarıkamış, Akyaka, Aras, Arpaçay, Digor, Susuz... Kübra's was a larger room on the ground floor named after the Aras River. Her father also had one of the larger rooms – Sarıkamış on the top floor. Esin got a room called Susuz.

Esin needed to leave immediately and dropped off her small suitcase in her room. She had to go to the ceremony site for rehearsal.

Huge carpets were being spread out over the dusty open square. There was another long red carpet for important personages. Esin was used to rehearsing in cool environments for events held in air-conditioned hotels and conference halls, and here she would work in the open air. Luckily, this was not one of the cold months when Kars was blanketed in white snow.

Ragged children swarmed around the square, besieging the Istanbul guests like moths around a flame. Some of them noticed Esin and started following her. She took on a big-sisterly air and asked them what they wanted to be when they grew up. She was amazed when one of the little boys said he wanted to be Polat, a Mafioso character in a TV series.

Banners with the logos of the construction firms undertaking the project were being raised up along with the flags of the three countries involved. Esin's eyes searched the banners for the name of Kübra's father's firm. She found the logo of Hikmet Akansan's company on one of the large cloth posters hanging from a huge road grader.

Esin noticed an important omission amidst all the logos, flags, and portraits of leaders of state. The portrait of Ataturk that one saw at every ceremony, in every official building, every school, was nowhere to be found. Anxiously and somewhat angrily, Esin asked the officials there about it right away; someone had forgotten to have one hung. A portrait of Ataturk was found immediately and hung in the most prominent spot.

She went up to the podium to do a sound check and made sure the platform was properly placed. The ceremony was to be broadcast on several television channels and cameramen were making changes in the disposition of the stage.

At last, the heads of state arrived and the ceremony began. The President of Turkey, as host of the occasion, was the first to set foot in the square. He moved into position to greet the other two presidents. Shortly afterwards, the presidents of Azerbaijan and Georgia drove up in limousines with tinted windows and polished hubcaps.

The three heads of state shook hands, posed for the press and took their positions. At this point, Esin was onstage at the microphone, introducing them with their official titles. She was happy and proud to be serving at an occasion marking the building of a railroad to cross three countries located on the ancient Silk Road. To be presenting at this groundbreaking ceremony attended by three heads of state made her feel she was a part of history.

She saw Hikmet Bey and Kübra sitting in the front row, directly across from the cordoned-off protocol area. Kübra was trying to maintain a blank expression but Esin noticed her glancing around with timid curiosity. Her shy looks made her seem all the more delicate and innocent. They were getting to know each other better day by day and had begun to gauge each other's state of mind at a glance. There was a positive charge running between them.

The heads of state left after the ceremony. Esin had performed flawlessly once more, and now she could relax. She ordered two glasses of tea. Kübra came up and sat next to her. Hikmet Bey was chatting with some businessmen a little way off. Kübra praised Esin enthusiastically as they sipped their tea.

"This is the second time I've seen you onstage, Esin. You were fantastic today. Congratulations."

The beautifully designed Kars Hotel was clean and tasteful with simple lines and an atmosphere at once modern and mystical. One did not expect to find such a hotel in a remote place like Kars. As they sat in the courtyard sipping their drinks that evening, Esin was having so much fun, she felt like she was on the Aegean in Bodrum. Western trends had caught on in the east of the country as well.

Esin and Kübra were surprised that the cuisine was not regional. Their dinner at the chic restaurant was made up primarily of Italian dishes. Hikmet Bey was still having business meetings. This suited Kübra, who still did not know what to talk about with her father, or how she was going to re-establish a dialogue with him.

Esin went up to her room, decorated primarily in white. She kicked off her shoes and stretched out on the big bed. She was tired but not yet sleepy and phoned Kübra. They were staying on the same floor and agreed Esin should come to Kübra's room so they could talk some more.

Kübra was still wearing her turban when Esin got there. She was sitting on her double bed, propped up on the pillows. Esin perched on a chair. They talked for a while about what had happened that day, and then Esin asked her how things were going with her father.

"Are you still able to talk with him?"

Kübra pursed her lips and looked down.

When she did not answer, Esin tried to comfort her by talking about her own life.

"The relationship between a father and a daughter is so strange, isn't it? So delicate. My father never let me do anything; he was very authoritarian. He was a military man anyway. He lived his life by the rules. Frowning and serious ... creating tension about nothing. When I got to be a teenager, I had to be home before dark. My friends could go out; I was the only one not allowed. I used to cry in my room. It really hurt me. Then I got married. It turns out my husband is not like my father. It would have killed me if he'd tried to restrict me too."

"My father is also hard but he's softened up as he's gotten older, thank God. Not all fathers are like that, are they?"

Esin asked about her mother.

Kübra looked up and began talking about her mother. She'd cried all the time when she first found out but gradually calmed down. Divorce was not even mentioned among people like them. They'd find their way but how?

"My father never used to leave the house in the morning without getting my mother's blessing," Kubra said. "And she never asked where he'd been or who he'd been with. She never asked what time he'd be home. It seems nothing is guaranteed in this life."

Kübra had reacted violently to her parents' situation at first but grew accustomed to the pain and had even begun to delude herself.

"As far as I know, most men cheat. They keep both things going. If a man is going to be with someone other than his wife one day and move on to another the next, it's better that he choose one and marry her in a religious ceremony, though it's illegal. Since cheating is inevitable, it's better for the health of all concerned. At least, that way the wife will not get AIDS or syphilis."

"You say the woman is protected and the man satisfies his animal impulses that way. You're so Pollyannaish, Kübra!"

Kübra spread her hands in a helpless gesture. Esin wanted to give her friend a little lesson in life.

"Look, here's some big sister's advice for you. Put aside these excuses. You're well educated, you went to college in the States. You work for your father, you have a good job. Soon you will be married. Please do not give up your job when you marry. Girls who veil usually stay at home. If you do that, what has happened to your mother will happen to you."

"Thank you for your advice, dear Esin. What you say is right. Most young girls do not think the way I do. Most of them want to find rich husbands and be housewives. I'm not like that. But on the other hand, don't generalize and say it's only housewives who get cheated on. Even successful businesswomen can be deceived by men. Wearing sexy clothes and going around in a miniskirt is no answer."

"Many women get cheated on and so we call men animals. But don't be silly, Kübra, with that generalization about women who wear miniskirts. What a cliché!"

"And your kind are not clichéd? We veil our heads, not our brains. Don't assume all veiled women have the brains of a spider."

"So you educate yourselves and then what, girl? You are all married off and become housewives. Then at least three children, five prayers, and your lives are set."

"And women like you, bravo, one man after another. There's no honor, no shame."

"I'm bringing it up again but your mother behaved herself and what happened to her? You father found another woman. Do I behave that way? If we stayed at home after we got married, if we never saw other men, maybe we'd always find our husbands attractive."

"What's this? Are you looking elsewhere? What about Alp?"

"I'm in love with my husband. I like Alp, I find him attractive, I love him but I'm in love with him and faithful to him even though I see what's around me."

"I still don't know what love is. Maybe ..."

"Veiled girls don't talk with men outside their families; they don't spend time with them unless they have to. But men are living out in the world. Especially, men like your father, too much so. That is what patriarchal society depends on. If you ask me, you can't trust it."

"Yes, that may be so; it makes sense."

"You know what I'm thinking... You know how some men suddenly up and leave the kind of women you're talking about, beautiful, intelligent women. In fact, a man like that is afraid a woman with such good qualities will fall in love with someone else and leave him. Men are very egotistical. Even a man who won't let his wife wear a low-cut dress does that because of what people will say about him, not about his wife."

Kübra noticed that Esin was sitting perched on her chair as if she might get up at any moment.

"You're not comfortable there. Why don't you come sit by me," she said, pointing to the bed.

Esin stood up. "Oh, my back," she said, pressing her hands into the small of her back and stretching. She perched on the other end of the bed. She sat up at first but as the conversation went on, she gradually leaned over and stretched out on the bed.

"You know, Orhan Pamuk called Kars a far-off, lonely, desolate metropole in his novel *Snow*. It is far off but it's not desolate. I really like it here," Esin said.

"It's because we're having a good time, that's why," Kübra encouraged her friend.

They were lying side by side, thinking out loud.

Kübra began to feel warm inside. There was that strange feeling again. Esin looked much more beautiful to her than ever before, and she wanted to snuggle up to her and hold her tight. She wanted to gaze on her cheeks, her lips, her eyelashes and brows, that little nose of hers. She was burning to caress

Esin's face. And so she did. Very lightly. She couldn't believe she was doing it.

Esin was confused for moment, and then she laughed.

"What's up, Kübra, dear? Where did that tender touch come from?"

Kübra was ashamed and looked away. Luckily, it didn't bother Esin. She thought the sudden impulse to touch her was tenderness. But Kübra knew it was not just tenderness. She wanted much, much more; she wanted to touch Esin in a straightforward way. This brief, slight contact was not enough; it had not driven away the hunger inside her. She still didn't know what to say to Esin but her tongue started to move: "I don't know. I just felt like it. I find you beautiful. I guess I wanted to touch that beautiful face, to feel you were close to me. If only I knew ..."

Esin did not react negatively. But when she thought about what Kübra had said, she realized it could mean something else. She had never thought about two women being physically close before.

Esin was interested in men. She'd had many lovers before she married Alp. She took pleasure in kissing men, inhaling their scent, making love uninhibitedly. She and her husband had a happy sex life. Even if there were times when she did not want to make love, she was generally a passionate woman. But it had never occurred to her to touch a woman in anything other than friendship, and she had never thought about being desired by a woman. She'd held hands with her girlfriends like all young girls, and hugged them and even lay down next to them but in her culture, these were innocent things. She felt extraordinarily excited and curious. But she could not share that with a woman, especially not with Kübra. Yet, still, she couldn't keep from asking: "Have you ever kissed a woman?"

Kübra was startled. This was a question she had not expected. She was used to Esin's curiosity about the religious life and the turban, but she wasn't ready to have such a subject spoken of out loud.

"N ... no," she managed to say.

Esin averted her gaze shyly, slightly flirtatiously, and looked up at the ceiling. She gently tossed back her blonde hair.

"Hmm. I've never tried it either. I wonder what it's like to kiss someone of the same sex."

What was Esin trying to say?

Kübra felt uncomfortably hot. Her own emotions frightened her, probably for the first time in her life. She felt guilty and ashamed. She longed to sense Esin's skin, feel her breath, lie beside her.

She wanted her.

Now she understood what it was, she used to sense was missing when she looked in the mirror. She was seeking a spiritual connection with someone, either man or woman.

Kübra tried to picture in her mind the scenario Esin's question suggested. She realized she was trembling. The wrong sort of person could easily misinterpret an open-ended question like that. For a moment, she forgot where she was. She felt she was floating, hemmed in by terrifying emotions. It seemed as if a horrific storm were raging outside. But instead of frightening her, the storm was drawing her in, summoning her into the unknown. She wanted to be buffeted by those winds but what would happen when the storm died down? What if she fell and crashed to the ground?

She gathered her courage and looked at Esin. Their eyes met in a gaze promising danger. Did they know then that in the language of the body, the dilation of pupils signifies consent? The conflict they felt was reflected in their eyes. There was at most, ten inches distance between them. If one of them moved the slightest bit closer, she would be at the other's feet. And then, perhaps ...

Esin stretched out her hand and caressed Kübra's cheek. They gazed at each other with tender warmth. Esin seemed to dig into her soul, trying to bring the feelings hidden there out into the light.

They knew what they were doing made no sense but they couldn't help themselves. They felt they had passed the point of no return. They had grasped hold of a thrill not easy to find, and they kept going. The unknown was charged with attraction.

They were alone. No one would ever know what happened in that room. This moment belonged to them alone.

Esin's touch on her face calmed Kübra and her anxiety left her. There was no point in seeking the reasons for her feelings. She was plunged in sweet emotions she'd never experienced before. She had sensed these feelings ever since she ran into Esin after all those years but she couldn't be sure. Each time she had seen Esin, she'd trembled inwardly and quietly buried those feelings deep inside.

Esin was of two minds. She felt like she was standing beside a swiftly flowing river. Either she could let the current sweep her off into the unknown, or remain on the shore, never to know the pleasures she might have tasted. For the moment, she just watched. Pleased, enjoying it, aroused, sad, drunk on it, innocently, secretly, naturally... one feeling flowed into another.

Her hand roved over Kübra's face for a long time. Kübra's eyes were closed. She brimmed over with incoherent emotion, helpless as a little girl. She looked so innocent, so beautiful. Esin was still as a statue, unable to tell what she should do, how far she should go.

Could Kübra somehow be the key for her? The more she'd known her, the more she'd warmed to her and loved her, discovering qualities that made Kübra different from everyone else she knew. It was as if Kübra had opened up Esin's own life to her. Kübra was also aware of how rare the friendship she had with Esin was. The relationship had been good for both of them. They had gained new experience of life by seeing things from each other's point of view.

To reveal the secret she had kept inside for so long, even to the one it concerned, seemed to Kübra a betrayal of her own self. Somehow, no one had found out but the heroine of her secret was now before her, looking deep into her eyes. An invisible trembling spread all throughout Kübra's body. A drop of sweat rolled down her back and made her shiver. She had lost all sense of time and space. She no longer even heard the sound of the wind blowing outside.

They were on the brink of realizing the inevitable. It seemed one of them might enter that forbidden realm at any moment.

Tension was growing inside both of them, threatening to spill out in an avalanche. The silence echoed against the walls. Their eyes told it all.

It was Esin who first got a hold of herself, telling herself that when she thought about something too long, she never could make a decision. She wanted to go back and erase that bold question which had slipped out of her mouth just a moment before. It was that question which had brought them to this pass, lying there on the bed. She couldn't get her body to move. She withdrew her hand from Kübra's face and just lay where she was.

Kübra was in a daze, sorry and frightened. She had been on the point of discovering who she was, and at the last minute, each of them had silently given up. They held back because the thrill of the moment could endanger their friendship, and they realized they valued one another more than they'd thought. That's how much they loved each other.

For whatever reason – a desire to experiment, to seek out new experience, curiosity – they had warmed to one another at the moment when each of them had almost everything she wanted and was idealized by those around her. Their intimacy was beyond sexual; it was a curiosity about the other's experience.

Although they appeared to live in completely different worlds, they shared the same country's suffering, searching, pain, and joy. The two women now understood each other. Both had learned much from spending time with someone beyond their niche in life. They had seen that everyone has weaknesses, that it didn't matter where you were from, everyone could make mistakes.

It was best that it remain an innocent moment left unrealized.

Neither of them got up from the bed; they stayed there. It was as if they were wrapped in white lace. They lay under a gauzy white veil imbuing them with infinite peace. Their eyes were fixed on one another in a gaze so beautiful, neither of them had ever looked that way at anyone else.

Kübra leaned over on the bed and sat up on her knees. She moved closer to her. There was only the sound of their breathing in the silent room.

Kübra's arms wound around her neck and Esin leaned her head slightly to the side. She brushed her cheek against Kübra's hand, caressing it. They looked at each other. Now Kübra's hands were caressing Esin's shoulders. Her hands slid down gently to her breasts. She hesitated to touch them but then she did. A delicious body ... magnificent, firm breasts ... She saw the nipples harden. Then she felt that hardness with her fingertips. Esin's body was opening like a flower. They gazed at each other again. It was very brief but her curiosity had overcome her shame and was now feeding her desire to touch.

Kübra began squeezing Esin's breasts in her hands. It was like she was discovering a new world. She moved over Esin's body carefully and gently; she knew what she was doing. When she squeezed Esin's breast slightly, a deep sigh escaped her lips, emboldening Kübra. That sigh conquered Kübra's brain, her body, her whole self, echoing and echoing through her.

She lowered her lips to Esin's breast and ran her tongue over the nipple. She sucked, beating it softly with her wet tongue. Again and again, she squeezed, kissed squeezed. Her mouth, her lips, and tongue seemed a part of Esin's breasts. Esin threw her head back. Now they had both lost control and surrendered to sweet intoxication.

Kübra's hand was moving down Esin's belly. She did not know where she was going but the silken skin she caressed made her feel good and happy.

Esin trembled when she felt the hand on her breast move over her belly and further down. Her legs opened slightly, involuntarily. Half-consciously, she was showing the way ... The hand roving over her waist, her belly, her legs, her calves, her ankles, and feet, knew it would find her panties in the end and grew impatient. Then it was there. Each touch meant Kübra had lost a little more of her fear. Esin's entire body had become taut as a bow. Just as Kübra was about to slip her hand inside Esin's panties, she stopped and looked at her. Her friend gazed back.

Esin drew Kübra to her and they began to kiss. Sweet, soft caresses led to the embrace of lips, the embrace of tongues, and every part of their bodies.

Kübra was living a dream from which she never wanted to wake.

Kubra did not know how much time had passed. When she woke to the morning call to prayer with her clothes on and her headscarf fallen to her neck, she realized she had drifted off to sleep that way. Esin was sleeping deeply beside her. They'd fallen asleep talking. In each other's arms. Without realizing; innocently.

Kübra watched Esin for a while. It was the first time she'd seen her asleep. She caressed her blonde hair, careful not to wake her up. She didn't dare touch her face, lest she wake her, and she wanted to keep that promise they'd made without words.

She lay her head back on the pillow. Peaceful sleep drew Kübra into its embrace once more.

# Esin's Days
## (What Happened Next)

Their lovemaking was weird. Esin wasn't able to really get into it and let herself go. Only her body was there in bed; her soul was elsewhere. She felt like a poor housewife having sex as a duty with a weariness built up over years. Alp sensed his wife's cold and distant mood. Esin usually loved long kisses, yet her mouth evaded his. The wife who made love passionately and drove him wild had left and in her place there was a frigid woman whose mind was elsewhere.

Alp was tired of it all and lost interest. Like Esin, he too was now just going through the motions. He gave up trying new positions and took up the missionary, reaching climax quickly. Esin immediately got up and went to the bathroom, scrubbed herself and did a full ablution.

Alp was sitting in bed smoking a cigarette irritably. It annoyed him even more that Esin took so long washing up. She usually had a quick shower and came right back to bed, curling up in his arms like a cat.

Finally, Esin came out of the bathroom, wrapped in a terrycloth robe. She was just about to take a nightgown out of the closet and put it on when she let out a cry.

"Alp! You're smoking and in the bedroom!"

"Yes, madam, thanks to you, I've started smoking. I never see your face. I didn't know you noticed if I was smoking or not."

Esin came into the room angrily and opened the window.

"Put that cigarette out right now, Alp. The stink of it will get everywhere. Don't you know I hate it?"

Alp put out his cigarette in the ashtray on the bedside table.

"Why did you stay so long in the bathroom? Can a shower take so long? Or were you trying to wash all trace of me off you?"

Esin sat on the edge of the bed, tired of his reproaches.

"No, my dear Alp, I did a full ablution."

"What? What ablution? Have you started doing ablutions now? What are these new habits?"

"A full ablution is necessary after sex. Kübra taught that to me."

"Ah, turban girl. What is your friendship with that girl about? Are you going to start veiling now too? Have you found the true religion? What's going on, baby?"

Esin thought of what had happened in the hotel room in Kars. Although she felt strangely guilty, she was confident that nothing physical had really occurred. She had to begin cleaning her conscience, empty it out as if she were cleaning a house. She knew that lately, she'd been under the influence of feelings difficult to define. She gave Alp no answer; she said nothing.

For a long time, Alp had been wanting to talk with Esin but like a man he held it in, acting cool and hadn't let on. When they'd got married, they had promised each other that whatever problems they might have, they would sit down and talk it over. But Alp had chosen to stay quiet for a while. A nagging woman was bad but a nagging man was an unmitigated disaster. Alp kept his mouth shut because he knew that.

But now he was irritable and unhappy. He was full of doubt. He hadn't smoked since his wild oats days in college. Now he'd concocted various scenarios in his mind. For a moment, he'd even suspected Esin might be cheating on him. He felt weak, like a person who could not confront things he did not want to see, surrendering himself to them instead.

"I cannot understand why you feel close to her."

Now Esin knew she had to speak.

"She's a girlfriend, that's all. The only thing different is she has a turban on her head. I don't feel all that close to her." She blushed as she said this and her cheeks turned bright red.

Alp took a deep breath and moved closer to Esin. He took hold of her chin lightly and gently pulled her head back. He looked into his wife's pretty eyes and said what had been on the tip of his tongue for days: "This is not a good thing." Esin felt sad. She was in love with her husband. The man sitting next to her, looking into her eyes at this hour of the night, seemed to her very handsome and attractive. But lately, she felt that she'd moved on to other dimensions. Her new goal in life lay in spiritual satisfaction. And her difficult-to-define intimacy with someone of her own sex had really confused things. But she felt good, quite comfortable, in fact, about what had happened with Kübra. At the time, it seemed natural to her. She was a young, sexually awakened woman. This was recreational and should not affect her life. Kind of like taking tango lessons.

But suddenly, Esin was afraid. Was she losing her husband? What came after "This is not a good thing"? She held her husband's hand tightly, as if to say, "Don't leave me, don't go away."

Esin had been quite experienced by the time she got married. She'd learned never to tell a man how he should behave. She knew well that you could never change anyone, only change your own point of view. It was not easy to get men to be more understanding than they were. You had to force a man to be romantic. They were not willing to take responsibility or put themselves to trouble. Esin had already understood that when she began to go out with Alp. She'd accepted his proposal of marriage because she knew she would not have to change him much. She loved her husband and did not want to lose him.

Alp embraced her and her eyes filled with tears. She wanted to cry, she had to weep for some reason deep down that she didn't know. But she controlled herself so as not to worry Alp even more.

Alp began speaking in a serious tone of voice, his hands still in Esin's.

"Look, Esin, you don't know this but a few weeks ago, I caught you in the bathroom in a very strange state. I'm telling you about it now because the time has come to say it. You'd left the door partly open. I was about to go in and shave when I saw you standing in front of the mirror. What I saw when I came in, shocked me. My beautiful wife, my charming, sexy, modern, self-confident Esin was standing in front of the mirror trying to arrange a colored scarf on her head. I was about to cry out, "Esin, what are you doing!" but I was so shocked I couldn't speak and I went out."

"Yes, it's true, I did something one day that I kept from you and I was experimenting. It isn't anything for you to worry about. I was curious what it would be like to walk in the street veiled like Kübra. I even tried it myself for a few hours one day. It was an experience, that's all."

Alp tried to smile a little.

"You'd think you had a very boring life, the way you love to dramatize things like scenes from a film. Why do you always want to try things, I don't know. So much curiosity will get you into trouble one day. If you only knew what I felt when I saw you at the mirror that day. I was frightened ... I ate my heart out worrying you were planning to take the veil."

Now Esin really laughed. She knew that the things that add color to life are not logical choices. She stroked Alp's hair and lay down and kissed him on the neck. She realized she longed to cuddle up in her husband's arms. Alp began laughing too.

"Esin, you know, a guy finds his wife in the bathroom with a vibrator; well, I found mine with a headscarf. It was like a nightmare ..."

They laughed together. Esin wanted to get her husband to relax a bit: "My darling love, it's the unknown that is frightening. And you can't love what you fear. That is probably why you were anxious. I'm trying to learn about the way of life and thinking of the *others.* I want to learn so I can make up my own mind whether to be frightened or not."

"All right, fine ... I'm not about to interfere with your thinking. As you've said, we haven't bought each other's brains just because we got married. Do you know what I think you're like sometimes? You're like a rebellious woman trapped in a harem. You haven't lost your identity, you haven't been cowed but you understand intrigue very well."

"My love, I'm trying to understand what is going on in this country best I can. Apparently, it's not good to generalize. Can you call everyone who veils a "turban girl"? They're all different. They all have different reasons for veiling. Some, because of their father, some, because they themselves want to; some are pushed into it by those around them; some because the traditional lifestyle requires it. And people like me veil just for a day because we are curious."

Alp pulled Esin to him and she put her head on his shoulder. They cuddled. Alp took a sassy tone and called her "my goofy wife." She called him her "idiot." They laughed together.

"Tell me about the wildest thing you ever did," Esin said.

Alp was a bit confused.

"Tell me about something you experienced but hid, something you're embarrassed to talk about, something you can't forget."

In fact, Alp did not like this question but when Esin insisted, he admitted that he'd had group sex once at a bachelor party for one of his friends just after he graduated from college.

"What! Did my husband do such a disgusting thing?"

"You asked, you insisted, so I told you. All right then, that's enough; no more details for you. And what brought on that weird question?"

"No reason ... But look, it's good I asked, or I never would have known my husband had done such a kinky thing."

"Men are easier. Most men have done something like that. But you can relax. I never had sex with whips and handcuffs, don't worry."

Esin realized she shouldn't press further. Alp had begun to rise to the top like olive oil.

They kissed tenderly and lay down. Alp embraced her as she liked, spooning her. And they fell asleep.

# Kübra's Days
## (Chanting)

Guests were coming to the home of Kubra's brother-in-law and older sister, Müberra, this evening. Kübra was going to spend the evening there as well, because Beyza was also coming and she loved talking with her.

Kübra was the first to arrive at Müberra's house in Florya where she lived with her two children. She and her husband had the place done by an interior decorator noted for striking designs. The dining and sitting sets in the salon were not of the overly showy, carved and inlaid kind her parents had in their home. This house was dominated by more modern lines; what had not changed was the calligraphic tableau on one wall reading, "Allah."

Kübra did not take off her headscarf because her brother-in-law was sitting in the salon.

She hugged her nephews before they went to sleep. She helped her sister to give them their bath and put them to bed.

She went into the salon to chat with her brother-in-law, Bilal, before the guests arrived. She knew he was a member of the Nakshibendi religious order, and she had always wondered about it.

Once she had watched the chanting ceremony at the Cerrahi Tekke after the nighttime prayer. Women on the top floor and men in the salon below led by a hoca chanted "La ilaha illallah" and "Hu" until they went into a trance.

She asked her brother-in-law a few questions and he spoke about Nakshibendi philosophy in a veiled manner. He said the *tariqat* was a path leading to God, and the goal was for a person to perfect himself spiritually and physically and reach God.

The more Kübra saw of Esin, the more she too had begun to want to discover other sides of life. Esin's descriptions of her breathing sessions so impressed her that she now wanted to achieve nirvana.

Somehow, delicately, she managed to ask her brother-in-law to take her to the order and introduce her to the disciples. Bilal was not sure at first but after he thought it over for a bit, he was pleased that his sister-in-law was taking such an interest. They agreed to go to Fatih together the following week. Just then, the doorbell rang.

Müberra's schoolmate from lycée Beyza and her husband arrived with a young couple from the neighborhood. The men and women did not shake hands but rather greeted one another from afar. The men went into the salon and the women into the sitting room, creating an old-fashioned division of the sexes. Men and women usually sat in separate rooms when guests were visiting. Kübra went into the kitchen to help her sister prepare tea and coffee. Müberra brought a large tray with three glasses of steeped tea and small slices of cheese *börek* as far as the entrance of the salon. She tapped on the door with her hand, and Bilal came to take the tray and serve the men himself. This was the custom in most religious homes.

Kübra joined the conversation in the sitting room with the three young married women.

They talked of their homes and children. Beyza and her husband had liked a newly built villa in Florya they'd seen while passing by on the street and met with the architectural firm listed on the advertising poster. They told the architect that they'd seen his work, thought it was marvelous and wanted him to build a house for them too. The architect said he'd also built homes at a gated community in Silivri and Beyza asked excitedly if he could show them the project on a computer, which he did. Four days later, they stopped by his office without an appointment and told him they'd gone to the gated community and bought twin villas still under construction. They gave him the keys and asked him to make up a budget to finish them as soon as possible. Each villa cost a million dollars. The new social segment to which Beyza belonged was unstoppable.

The guests rose to leave before the hour was late but Kübra didn't want to cross the Bosphorus and spent the night at her sister's.

Kübra was very excited about going to visit the order with her brother-in-law. She'd tried long and hard to convince her sister Müberra to come too but she'd refused, saying, "With two children, I don't have the time to even raise my head. Don't involve me in new things."

They arrived at the cloister in Fatih. Kübra remembered that this was attached to the mosque she'd passed with Esin when they strolled around Fatih. Bilal had left word that Kübra was coming, and an elderly woman took her inside.

Like everyone else who wanted to join the order, Kübra had first to perform eight written conditions. She took the small piece of notepaper with the heading, "Courtesy." She was to perform the eight conditions at home.

In order to join the order, one had to be presently carrying out certain conditions of Islam. Training in the order began with chanting and moral perfection. Members of the order had to train themselves constantly.

Kübra shut the door to her bedroom. She had asked her mother not to disturb her for a while. She put her cell phone into silent mode.

She sat on the carpet in the courtesy position, on her knees with her feet bent to the left side. She had a rosary in each hand. She put on a long covering over her head.

Kübra began her first chanting session with five thousand *lafsatullahs*. She was going to chant "Allah" five thousand times but she was supposed to do it with her heart, not her tongue.

She began saying "Allah" inwardly. Her lips did not move; yes, she had begun to chant with her heart. This was a private kind of chanting to be done at home. It was recommended that one begin in this way.

When the Shaykh in his robe and white beard asked the company at the cloister: "Who among my children has outdone the donkey in the matter of chanting today?" Kübra at first had not understood but soon the reason one must begin with five thousand times was explained.

According to doctrine, everything in the universe was constantly recalling God. Each kind of animal had its own kind of chanting. The animal that least recalled God was the donkey but even the donkey recalled God's name five thousand times a day.

This was what was meant by "outdoing the donkey" and that was how the way was opened for disciples to recall God more frequently. The bellowing of the camel, the roaring of the lion, the buzzing of bees were all considered a form of chanting. The donkey only brayed when it was hungry or wanted to mate and so was considered a slave to hunger and lust. Believers who had the love of God in their hearts and thought neither of food nor sex should recall God more often than the donkey.

Today, Kübra was beginning with five thousand times. Later, she could go on like the others to numbers beginning with an odd numeral – seven thousand, nine thousand, eleven thousand, as far as one hundred and one thousand. Some could go beyond these numbers too within six months, others, not in twenty years. Kübra could not yet know where her place would be in the world of Sufism she was trying to enter.

She brought the middle finger and thumb of her right hand together and put her hand under her left breast over her heart. Because the nerves of the middle finger were connected to the lower half of the body, they were to be kept fixed, something like the "chakra opening" in eastern meditation. In Sufism, it was called *letayif* instead of "chakra," and the lower half of the body was called *sufli* and considered unclean, so there was no reason to open the points there.

Every time she chanted "Allah," she turned over one of the hundred beads on the rosary she held over the index finger of her right hand. The rosary was held over the index finger because the nerves in that finger went straight to the heart.

She was unaware of the passage of time. After she'd done the first thousand, she seemed to gradually leave the room. She was becoming detached from the actual world. Slowly, she began to approach another dimension. By the time she was close to five thousand, she was somewhere between sleep and the waking state. This was her first chanting session. Things would change as she increased the number, her spirit would travel, and the eye of her heart would be opened.

The next day, she finished her day's work and went to the Fatih cloister. She was in a room with women of every age and spiritual state. Some had been beaten by their husbands. Some had husbands who were drunks or gamblers. They found solace by coming here to feel at peace.

The group chanting was like a kind of therapy. Today, Kübra was going to join the group chanting. Someone advanced on the path led the group chanting. Some of the women did not cover their heads. Everyone had their eyes closed. The mystical atmosphere gave Kübra goose bumps. She went into an ecstatic trance like the others. At the point when the chanting sped up to a climax, Kübra's delicate waist tingled. No one opened their eyes until the chanting was finished. The energy in the room was at a height. This was what made group chanting so beautiful. They were together in sisterhood.

# Esin and Kübra
## (Help)

Esin and Kubra ate at a cafe by the shore in Ortaköy. They preferred to eat outside even though the weather was cool. A few punks walking by, stared long and hard at Esin. One of them even fixed his gaze on her as if he would eat her. That wasn't enough for him. He called out, "What a pretty thing you are! You know what you've got, give it to me..."

Esin was very annoyed.

"I feel like yelling, 'What do you think you're looking at?' and slapping him, No, a slap isn't enough; best thing, I'd punch him right in the middle of that goon face of his, and kick him where it would do some good."

Kübra laughed pleasantly.

"That will keep you busy. See, I've won the bet we made in Ankara. When a woman is unveiled, she becomes an object of desire. Is there anyone staring at me, making comments? You see that the 'turban' makes a woman free."

"How can you say that? You seem to think the turban equals protection from harassment. Can't a woman defend her own honor? Anyway, don't brag about the turban. And since the Gracious Koran says to dress moderately and not attract attention, why is it that most of you wear veiled outfits so colorful and covered with flowers? You look like Phosphorus Cevriye of the pop song."

"Not everyone is the same. I can't take you as the basis of comparison for all unveiled women, so don't ask me to account for all the veiled. Some are religious, some belong to cults, and others veil just to fit into a socio-economic group. But you're right. I think it's a mistake to dress so strikingly. It's against the philosophy of religion. Veiling is an inward thing which completes a daily life planned around the five prayers; you're more conscientious about relationships with people and more careful about attention to morality. And maybe, it's something to hold on to ... But I think total veiling is too extreme. I don't approve of that. It is not a requirement of our religion. It is beautiful when everything is in balance."

"The black face veil and sheet-like covering are virtually torture for women who wear them. The color black doubles the heat of the sun's rays. You could even miscarry if you are pregnant, I swear. If they really can't give it up, at least they could wear white."

"Look, years ago, that sort of veiling gave way to wearing a raincoat. There's a revolution in that too. Women coming to Istanbul from the Black Sea or the East used to wear a face veil but we don't see that anymore. A girl with her head covered can wear Converse sneakers with her jeans. Don't be so surprised. Don't blame them so for having their homes done by interior decorators and their wedding gowns by designers. Don't be angry when you see a veiled woman in a four wheel-drive luxury jeep. It's not conservatism that's on the rise in Turkey, it's modernity. Turbaned women don't want to stay home anymore. They want to go to university, they are seeking equality. Anatolia has begun to come to the center. If the gross income of the country has risen, it has come about through the work of every segment of the people. But the *other* type of people, the people you don't like, have entered into social life with their own religious ways. I think the issue is partly one of class."

"But covering hair ... I don't think hair is something arousing. Maybe a hair style can be."

Kübra smiled. "If you wrap it around yourself like in the Blendax commercial, it's arousing."

"But, for example, you cover your head, while your feet are showing. I've seen women with their heads wrapped up tight but wearing open-toed shoes or sandals. Their toes are showing... If they're not trying to avoid showing off their beauty, why do they cover up? There are lots of men aroused by the sight of women's feet..."

Kübra smiled shyly.

"I don't know what arouses men but one should veil in such a way that the parts of the body you wash in ablutions, the hands as far as the wrists, the feet up to the ankles, and the face are not covered. It is not objectionable for the toes to show."

"Is the command so detailed? I'd heard 'you should veil in such a way that the limbs of your body do not show.' Very interesting... What lovely perspectives and defense mechanisms you all have developed."

"Esin dear, let me say this so that both of us can be comfortable. No one's religion or nationality can be harmed by the words of another; words do not change that. Everyone's criticism, everyone's faith is their own. And the 'turban' ruckus in this country is created by the politicians. There's no great turmoil about the subject within families. The turmoil begins when the politicians get involved. And don't forget, the only book that does not change is the Gracious Koran."

"That's why some behavior is always contemporary, I see. All right, it's clear the Koran was not written by a human being; it's a book of rules but everything in this life is updated, Kübra."

"May God forgive... Islam brings new order to the relationship between humans and religion. It offers solutions. The tensions between the traditional and modern segments apparent in the questions you're always asking me arise because religion is resituating itself in daily life, along with the changing society. What you call modernism is really a project to change the structure of religion."

"Not its structure but rather its function ... We don't interfere with anyone's belief. We can look at it like this: human beings, like birds, need two wings. One wing is religion and the other is the worldly wing of knowledge and technology ... Religious communities keep only the religious wing and use only that. Many intellectuals pay no attention to religion and use only the technological wing. No one can do without belief. Even an atheist believes in something. You can't excommunicate people like me because they don't confront others with religion in daily life. There is such a thing as public space. Public space is the reflection of modern society. That's why, religious behavior should be kept out of it. Religion should remain private. This is what we are saying."

"Public space is a symbolic expression."

"I mean, that for modern social life, religious symbolic behavior belongs to its *other*."

"To be other is in the end not just a matter of covering one's head or not. Two veiled women, or two unveiled women, can become alien to each other. The problem is not in a difference of point of view. The solution lies in bringing a bit more clarity to these perspectives."

You couldn't expect everyone to perceive and think about things in the same way. Those who saw people unlike themselves as belonging to a different world were mistaken. Nobody wanted a fight. Alienation would decrease as they came to know each other. Esin and Kübra had felt strange to each other at first but as time went on, their friendship had gathered momentum.

Kübra didn't want to go on. "Esin, my head is beginning to hurt. We've gotten into deep subjects again."

"Yeah, it starts with a tiny little thing and grows the more it grows. You're here, and I want us to understand each other. If only everyone were as open to dialogue as we are. And look, once prejudices are broken down, what is left is humanity. Isn't it better to talk about these things? When we stay silent, we both get into strange states of mind. Remember Kars."

Esin had let slip a subject she should never have touched. What had happened in the hotel room in Kars was to be forgotten and never spoken of.

Kübra was very embarrassed and averted her eyes. Esin turned away and waited for these few seconds to pass.

They got up and began to walk. They were near Esin's car.

"Let me drop you at home before it gets late."

"There's no need. Don't go all the way across the Bosphorus now. I'll take a taxi."

"It's not like I'm going to carry you in my arms, girl. We've got a car. Come on, get in."

They took the shore road toward Beşiktaş. There wasn't much traffic. When they got to Barbaros Boulevard, they were going at a normal speed.

Esin had just sped up a bit when she realized that a little way ahead, a car had suddenly pulled out where it shouldn't have. When she turned the wheel to avoid a crash, the car started to skid. They were spinning like a top. They both screamed out the formula of witness to the faith.

The car spun three or four times, hit a post and fell on its side. Esin was crushed on the bottom in the driver's seat and Kübra was on top. Esin had never let go of the steering wheel as they skidded, and when the car hit the post, her ribs were broken. Her face was covered with cuts and bruises, she'd broken some teeth, and her mouth was bleeding. She was conscious but the air bag was making it impossible for her to breathe.

In spite of the horrendous pain in her head, she turned to look up and saw Kübra in the passenger seat with her eyes shut and her head leaning to the side. She was not moving. Suddenly, Esin panicked. Was Kübra dead? The air bag prevented her from seeing clearly but she could tell her friend's face was bruised. And one end of her turban was caught somewhere she couldn't see, so that it pulled like a noose around Kübra's neck. They both had their seat belts on. Esin's head began to spin. Then Kübra stirred slightly but she was being strangled by her scarf. Esin made one last effort and despite the terrible pain in her ribs, managed to unbuckle her seat belt and reach up. But she could not get a hold of Kübra. With all her strength, she pushed a bit further into the narrow space and succeeded in undoing the scarf around Kübra's neck. She had taken off Kübra's turban and saved her life.

Lightning Source UK Ltd.
Milton Keynes UK
UKOW01f0919280616

277233UK00001B/8/P